A DARK SIN

HIDDEN NORFOLK - BOOK 8

J M DALGLIESH

First published by Hamilton Press in 2021

ISBN (Trade Paperback) 978-1-80080-998-7
ISBN (Hardback) 978-1-80080-580-4
ISBN (Large Print) 978-1-80080-828-7

EXCLUSIVE OFFER

Look out for the link at the end of this book or visit my website at **www.jmdalgliesh.com** to sign up to my no-spam VIP Club and receive a FREE Hidden Norfolk novella plus news and previews of forthcoming works.

Never miss a new release.

———

No spam, ever, guaranteed. You can unsubscribe at any time.

A DARK SIN

PROLOGUE

PASSING the larger of the two car parks, preferring the shelter from the surrounding copse, he drove the car further down the hill, slowing to make the turn. The excited snuffling from behind the cargo net meant Bodie knew they'd arrived. He glanced in the rear-view mirror.

"That's right, boy, we're nearly there."

There were no other cars present. In the summer there would be several. He wasn't the only local to get out for an early-morning walk before the rest of the county came out to go about their daily business. The cold was keeping them home now, he was certain. The larger car park he'd just driven by had a solitary vehicle in it; not one he recognised but it was still dark, still early. Switching off the engine triggered the interior lights to burst into life, the signal for his dog to make himself ready to leap from the car. Bodie let out an excited bark.

"All right, all right. I'm coming."

Cracking open the door let in a blast of freezing air and the warmth of the heated seat and steering wheel would, no doubt, soon become a distant memory. The protection from the wind offered by the trees, even though not in leaf, was still of benefit. Perhaps the path around the woods would be more pleasant than braving the open ground of the common up to the high point overlooking Grimston Warren Reserve. Zipping up his coat, he waggled a foot beneath the rear bumper and the electrically operated tail lift raised the boot lid. Bodie immediately made to leap from the car but his owner was ready, as always, grasping the dog's collar firmly and reaching up to clip the lead in place.

The dog hustled past and jumped to the ground, nosing the earth and taking in the fresh smells that accompanied a heavy frost. The mud of the car park was churned up by visiting vehicles but had subsequently frozen. The winters here could be harsh and none more so in living memory than this one. Several crows cawed to one another from the nearby trees as the inky darkness of the night sky slowly shifted towards a slate grey as dawn approached.

They set off through the gate and on into the woods beyond, Bodie pulling as they went; keen to get moving. Once in the sanctuary of the woods and within the fenced reserve, safely away from the road, he pulled the dog back, making him sit down before releasing the lead. Dogs were supposed to be kept under control but he often chose to ignore that rule if there was hardly anyone else around. One of the car parks here was well known as a location for some rather salacious night-time activities that the police didn't seem to bother trying to stamp out, so why shouldn't Bodie be allowed to run free?

The dog took off along the path ahead, tail in the air and nose to the ground. He wouldn't go too far. The trees were thinning as he approached the access to the open ground of the common, the bracing freshness of the crisp breeze gathering pace against his cheeks. They felt numb and his head was cold.

Only now did he realise he wasn't wearing his woolly hat. Glancing back through the trees towards the car park, he considered nipping back for it, envisaging it on the passenger seat where he'd left it to be warmed by the heated seat. It never worked but he still tried it most days. Maybe there needed to be weight applied on top. There's a thought. He'd try that tomorrow.

"Bodie!"

He waited. The dog didn't appear. He whistled. Still there was no reply. Muttering under his breath he carried on, quickening his pace. Who knew what the dog would be up to if he left him to his own devices and went back to the car? He was irritated to find the gate out of the woods was unlatched.

"Bodie! Here, boy!"

An excited bark carried to him from a distance. He recognised it. Bodie must be halfway across the common. Hopefully, he hadn't come across anyone of a nervous sensibility. Most dog owners, the only people daft enough to be out here at this time in sub-zero temperatures, would be okay with Bodie; but there were others who turned their noses up at a large golden retriever charging across the field towards them, particularly if they had one of those miniature dogs who were often a little skittish in the presence of a larger cousin.

Clearing the woods, a gentle hum of early-morning traffic from the distant Queen Elizabeth Way broke the silence and he scanned the gently undulating common for an overexcited hound, seeing him a few hundred metres away bounding back and forth, barking at something. With no one else in sight, the second car park sky-lined off to his right was now visible and looked empty from this distance but, admittedly, his eyes weren't what they used to be. Bodie must have chased down a rabbit or forced a squirrel back into one of the two trees standing proudly and isolated in the centre of the reserve.

"Bodie!"

His shout was one born of a forlorn hope. If the animal hadn't returned after the first round of calls, he wouldn't do so now. In fact, the dog didn't even look back at him which he would usually do, just before ignoring the call once again. Instead, the barking continued. He hurried across the field, taking care to avoid the cow pats deposited in random places among the wild grass. A sheen of frost disguised them from the human eye in the diffused early-morning light, and the cold masked the smell, but the contents beneath the surface were just as unpleasant. It was okay if wearing wellies, as he was, but it was still a pain to deal with before getting back into the car.

Bodie must have sensed him getting nearer because the barking was growing in intensity, almost continuous now, as he approached, carefully picking his route across the uneven surface. Upon reaching the dog, panting heavily with its tongue lolling to one side as a result of his noisy efforts, he quickly reattached the lead before the dog saw fit to take off again. The dog nuzzled his hand and barked once more. He ruffled the top of the dog's head with his free hand. Bodie whimpered.

"What is it, boy? What's all the fuss?"

Looking to his left, his mouth fell open. Shielded from view on his approach, he hadn't seen it. He hadn't seen him. The breeze felt colder now, biting. A nearby collection of saplings were fenced off to protect their growth, and he decided to tie Bodie to one of the posts, almost tripping over the creature as he stepped forward. Cursing, he gathered himself, hurrying the two of them over to the nearest post, securing the dog in place and returning to the trees.

The body swayed gently in the breeze, the ageing branch it was hanging from occasionally creaking under the strain. The teenager's facial expression could easily be judged as one befitting that of a deep sleep if not for the tinge of black to his lips and the noose around his neck, forcing his head to rest offset at an awkward angle. The discolouration of the boy's skin disturbed him as he came to stand beneath the child. Not only was he understandably very pale, but his skin was blotchy with a green or bluish hue to it; in this light he wasn't sure which. Tentatively removing his glove, he reached up, slowly placing the palm of his hand on the boy's right leg. The body felt frozen, the skin stiff and rubbery to the touch. He had been dead for hours. The dog whimpered again but he didn't react. He couldn't take his eyes off the boy; what was he, fourteen, fifteen at a push, maybe?

Easing his hand away, he slowly backed off whilst rummaging in his coat pocket for his mobile phone.

What a waste of a young life.

CHAPTER ONE

"THE TRICK IS," Tom Janssen said, leaning forward and carefully guiding the skewer to roughly a hand span above the flame curling up from the nearest log, "to make sure you keep the marshmallow close enough to toast but not so close that it catches fire."

Saffy, the eight-year-old daughter of his partner, Alice, focussed hard on the task in hand. Tom gently released his grip, giving her full control and watched on as Saffy's eyes darted briefly to her mother, a smile forming at the corners of her mouth as she slowly turned the skewer in her gloved hands. Their little terrier, Russell, sat patiently next to Saffy, his eyes fixed on the marshmallow, tracking its path with an unblinking stare. The evening was still, crystal clear and despite the orange glow of the fire, the heavens were glittering above them. Tamara Greave's house was some distance from the nearest town, surrounded by a small, but established, woodland and very private.

Alice reached a hand out to Tom, smiling and slipping it through his arm and leaning into him. Saffy had talked about little else for three days now, such was her excitement at the

gathering. The scene was as exciting as it got for an enthusiastic, outgoing child such as her. Not only was she attending an
adult party, outdoors under the stars, but she also got a fire pit
and the opportunity to toast marshmallows – an activity that
seemed to be a childhood rite of passage in much of her social
media and coming of age children's television films. Up until
tonight, Tom was certain Saffy had never seen a toasted marshmallow, let alone eaten one.

"Am I doing it right?" Saffy asked without shifting her
gaze.

"You're doing it perfectly," Alice said. Saffy grinned.
Dressed in a thick coat and her favoured artificial fur-lined
wellington boots, with unicorn adornments, and a woolly hat
knitted by her grandmother; a red, yellow and green offering
with two tassels that hung from the front and back, Saffy
didn't flinch at the cold. Tom saw Becca, DC Eric Collet's
fiancée, wasn't faring as well. Tamara noticed Becca's discomfort as well, tapping Eric on the forearm and gesturing back to
the house.

"There's a throw on the sofa in the front room that could
double up as a blanket."

Becca smiled warmly and Eric set off back to the house just
as one of the logs in the cast-iron pit crackled and spat as an air
pocket ignited. It didn't bother Saffy, still slowly turning her
charge.

"When Eric gets back, we should raise a glass to him,"
Tamara said, looking around at those present. "Everyone have
drinks? I'm empty, so I'm going to get another bottle anyway."

Cassie Knight, the detective sergeant of the group, checked
the bottle of beer in her hand with the light from the fire. It
was half full. Her partner, Lauren, did the same, indicating she
was okay. Alice's glass was empty.

"I'll go," Tom said, unhooking himself from Alice's arm and

first of all gently easing Saffy's arm up a little and moving the marshmallow away from the flame, before heaving himself out of his camping chair.

"Just inside the kitchen on the left," Tamara told him.

As soon as he stepped away from the fire, he felt the true chill of the winter evening. Even by Norfolk's usual standards, where winters could be brutal affairs, this year was proving worse than normal. The geography of the north Norfolk coast with the lack of any mountainous terrain to unsettle the weather ensured they seldom experienced dramatic snowfall, but the expanse of low-lying open land in proximity to the North Sea made sure the nights were exceptionally cold. They were fortunate there was only a gentle westerly breeze tonight. It was the perfect conditions for their celebration.

The hinges of the back door creaked as Tom entered the kitchen meeting Eric returning with the fleece blanket for Becca. Tom saw several bottles exactly where Tamara told him they would be and he set about choosing one.

"How are you feeling about tomorrow?"

"I'm looking forward to it," Eric said, folding the blanket over his forearm again to make it less likely to catch on anything as he moved through the house. "It'll be nice to get back to normal, you know?"

Tom smiled and nodded, then selected a bottle and looked around for the corkscrew. "And what about Becca?" In the corner of his eye, he saw Eric shrug. "That good, huh?"

Eric sighed, leaning his back against the worktop and frowning. "She knows it's what I do ... but ..."

"She's worried?"

Eric nodded.

"You can't blame her," Tom said. Eric shook his head emphatically agreeing with the sentiment. "We all thought we were going to lose you for a while."

"Yeah, I know," Eric said glumly. "I think she's got used to me being home when she finishes work and, when all is said and done, I think she'd prefer it if I worked in a book shop or something."

Tom laughed. "Repeatedly the number one answer given when surveyed as to your perfect choice of profession."

"Is it?"

"Apparently so, yes. I don't think there are enough shops to go around though."

"There're certainly enough criminals to keep us busy though, aren't there?" Eric said with a wry grin.

"Not at the moment," Tom said. "You've picked a good time to come back, ease you in gently."

A knock at the door interrupted the conversation. Tom indicated he'd get it and Eric manoeuvred his way through the kitchen and back outside, careful not to swipe anything off the work surfaces as he passed. Tom sympathised with Becca's plight. It was four months since Eric was last on duty, and it'd been a long road back to fitness, both physically and mentally, for someone who had been in incredible shape. What the long-term impact of the ordeal would mean to Eric, and the couple, remained to be seen.

Opening the front door, Tom was met by a woman with a broad grin on her face which quickly subsided as she looked him up and down; an excited smile switching to apparent shock in an instant.

"Well don't tell me she's moved someone in already without bothering to mention it."

Tom was at a loss, standing open mouthed. He quickly cast an eye over the woman, wondering whether she'd called at the right house. He was certain they'd never met but at the same time she looked familiar in some way. She appeared to be in her seventies, well presented with fastidiously applied make-

up and sculpted hair, not over the top but stylish with attention to care and detail. She had two matching suitcases at her
feet and looking past her towards the end of the drive, Tom
saw a taxi pulling out on to the main road.

"Are you going to invite me in?" the woman asked.

"I–I guess... sorry, who are you?"

"Francesca Greave," she said and the penny dropped for
Tom just as he was forced to step aside to make room for her to
pass. "Bring my cases in would you, young man? There's a nice
chap."

Tom did as he was asked, hefting both into the hall.
Francesca had already removed her coat and was looking for a
spare hook to hang it on.

"You might want to keep that on," Tom said. She met his
eye with a quizzical look. "The coat. We're outside in the back
garden."

She looked around, slipping her right arm through the first
sleeve. "And you are?"

"Tom. Tom Janssen," he said, turning to close the front door.

"Well, Tom Tom Janssen. Is my daughter anywhere around
here?"

He smiled and gestured with an open hand and a warm
smile towards the kitchen. She followed him to the back of the
house and the small group were visible through the kitchen
window, illuminated by the glow of the fire.

"Who has a party on a Sunday night?" Francesca asked but
Tom was confident it was a rhetorical question.

He hurriedly uncorked the wine bottle and picked up
another glass. "It's not exactly a party."

"Shame. I could do with letting my hair down after the
journey I've had. If you're not going to have train stations in
Norfolk, why on earth don't you build some motorways?"

Tom raised an eyebrow, rapidly reaching the conclusion

that any answer he gave would probably be wrong, so he smiled instead and opened the door to the garden. Holding it open for her to walk through first, he silently contemplated how this was going to go down. He'd got to know Tamara fairly well since she took up her role, and he liked her. More than that, he cared for her deeply, but she'd never been forthcoming about her background. He wasn't the type to pry, believing she had her reasons, perhaps keeping a boundary of sorts in place between her and her colleagues. Her mother had certainly never come up in conversation and he didn't need to be a detective to know this visit was unannounced.

As the two of them approached the group sitting around the fire pit, several eyes turned to them. Before Tom could speak, Saffy ran up to him holding her skewer aloft for him. He dropped to his haunches and inspected the offering. It was charred black on one side and the other was still pink but the partially eaten marshmallow was gooey on the undercooked side.

"You can have it," Saffy said, pushing it towards Tom's free hand.

He smiled. "Thank you, but it's yours. I can get my own."

Saffy stubbornly shook her head. "No. You can have it."

"But it's yours ..." he glanced over to Alice and she shook her head, a half-smile on her face. "You don't really like it, do you?"

Saffy shook her head again and thrust the skewer into his hand before hurrying back to take Tom's seat next to her mother, wellies dangling over the edge of the chair, her feet swinging gently back and forth. Francesca had been observing the exchange without speaking and, aside from Tamara, everyone else was looking at the newcomer. Tamara had her back to them but spoke over her shoulder.

"I was beginning to wonder who'd kept you chatting at the

door."

"You can wonder no more!" Francesca said.

Tamara started, spinning in her chair and failing to mask the surprise in both her tone and her expression. "Mum!"

"Surprise!" Francesca curtseyed. "Hello, Tammy darling."

Tamara was barely on her feet before she was enveloped in an embrace, her body compressed and her head resting on her mother's shoulder and staring at Tom.

"W–What are you doing here?"

"Can't a mother pay her daughter a visit?" she said, holding Tamara at arm's length by her upper arms. "Have you lost weight?" She cast an eye up and down, assessing Tamara's figure with a critical eye. "You're looking tired. Are you getting enough sleep?"

Tamara frowned, shaking off the questions. "But you could have phoned—"

"I did, darling, but you never answer or return my messages," she said, releasing her hold on her daughter and looking around the group. Tom came alongside, placing the open bottle of wine and spare glass on the table to the right of Tamara's chair. Francesca slipped her arm through Tom's and pulled him close to her, smiling. He was off balance and awkward, seeing as she was much shorter than he was, and a similar height and build to Tamara. "Of course, if you'd told me the men in Norfolk were all this handsome, I'd have come across much, much sooner."

"Mum ..." She looked beyond her, back to the house. "Is Dad with you?"

Francesca waved the question away. "I'll tell you all about it later. So how long has young Tom been living with you?"

"We're not an ... I mean, he's not—" Tamara said before breaking off and sighing.

Tom eased his arm free and crossed to stand behind Alice,

resting his hands on her shoulders. Saffy glanced up at him and smiled. Tamara, although doing her best to mask it, was embarrassed. Tom caught sight of a wicked twinkle in Cassie's eyes. Of all those present, she was the one who arguably knew Tamara best, seeing as the two of them went back the furthest. She was viewing this exchange with some amusement.

"So, what are we celebrating? Tom says—"

"It's just to welcome Eric back to work tomorrow," Tamara said, seemingly resigned to losing control of the conversation.

"Have you been away?" Francesca asked, fixing Eric with her gaze.

Eric looked uncomfortable, his eyes furtively glancing to Becca sitting alongside him.

"I've been off for a few months," he said. "I–I had … an accident at work."

"Oh dear. That's a shame. A strapping young man like you couldn't be kept down for long though, I should imagine." She looked at Becca, despite her sitting under an extra blanket, she must have realised she was pregnant. "I can see you've been keeping yourself busy, though."

"Mother!" Tamara said, shooting her a withering look. Eric flushed and Becca stifled a smile. Cassie was the only one to laugh out loud, a response cut short by Lauren jabbing her elbow into her ribs.

"How far along are you, my dear?" Francesca asked, unabated.

"Seven months," Becca said proudly, placing her hands on her stomach.

"Getting a little uncomfortable now, I expect?"

Becca shook her head, smiling at Eric. "No, not really. We're doing fine, aren't we?"

Eric nodded and then he checked his watch. "Listen, this has been lovely, but I really think it's time we shot off. I wouldn't mind getting an early night ahead of tomorrow. And Becca will be tired—"

"I'm not tired," Becca said.

"That's right, dear." Francesca smiled, tilting her head to one side and raising a pointed finger. "You're pregnant, not disabled."

Clearly unsure of how to respond, Becca smiled politely. "But Eric's right. We should probably make a move."

"Us too," Alice said. Saffy immediately protested.

"But I'm not tired," she whined. "And I need to toast another marshmallow."

"That you won't eat," Alice said gently. The reason and logic of the argument made no impact on her daughter who looked to Tom for support.

"Sorry, young lady. I'm with your mum on this one – and it is a school night."

"I don't want to go to school!"

"Vegetarian meatballs on the menu for lunch tomorrow, though."

This information resonated with Saffy and her stern expression lightened, not that she'd concede. She'd never concede. Tom silently wondered where she got the stubborn streak from – a question he would never have the courage to voice aloud.

"Everything's vegetarian these days, isn't it?" Francesca said. "If not, then it's vegans telling you what you can and can't eat."

"Mum, you were the one who inspired me to minimise my impact on the world, eating sustainably… what happened to you?"

Francesca looked over at her daughter, her brow furrowing as she considered her response.

"Well… I came of age in the sixties, didn't I? It was a different world back then." Her expression clouded. "We were so full of hope... full of idealism. It's all so different now. My values are still there, Tammy. It's just... I don't know... maybe it's not all quite as pressing as I once thought it was."

Tom saw Tamara tense and roll her eyes, arms crossed defiantly against her chest. The reply was evidently lacking as far as Tamara was concerned. He sensed this was a comment she'd heard in the past. Cassie and Lauren rose from their chairs as well, taking everyone else's lead. Tamara seemed relieved the gathering was breaking up. Francesca grasped Tom's forearm.

"Be a good chap and put my suitcases in the guest bedroom, would you?"

Tom exchanged a look with Tamara.

"So, you're staying here... with me?" Tamara asked. Her mum looked shocked that it was even in question.

"Do you want a hand clearing up?" Tom asked, looking around them.

Tamara shook her head. "I'll take care of the bags, Tom. You get yourself off home and I'll see you in the morning." She turned to Eric. "It'll be great to have the team back together."

Eric beamed.

They all thanked Tamara and said goodnight before gathering their belongings and setting off to their cars parked at the front of the house. Francesca called after them.

"Don't forget, *keep 'em peeled!*" Francesca said, drawing a withering look from her daughter. "What? Shaw Taylor, *Police Five*... it was his catchphrase. "

Tom looked back over his shoulder and smiled. The comment was lost on the others, who exchanged confused looks but carried on walking. Tom could hear the frustration in Tamara's voice as they walked away.

"As if they are going to have watched *Police Five* back in the seventies, Mum ... most of us weren't even born ..."

CHAPTER TWO

Tom was pleased to find Eric already at his desk when he walked into the ops room. The detective constable had disconnected his keyboard and moved it to the next desk along with his paperwork trays so that he could set about wiping down his desk. It brought a smile to Tom's face; it was Eric's monthly routine. He would do it on the first day of every month, sometimes offering to tackle Cassie's as well. Not that she ever accepted. DS Knight was a bit more laissez-faire when it came to her workspace. Often he thought they wouldn't find two detectives less similar: one very focussed, methodical and a stickler for operating within the rules and the other, unpredictable and instinctive. However, the balance they brought to the team garnered results and Tom wouldn't have it any other way.

Eric only realised Tom was there almost as he was upon him, his approach masked by the canister of compressed air Eric was blasting the keys of his keyboard with to clear the grime that collected out of sight. He smiled warmly.

"Morning, Eric. How does it feel to be back?"

Eric shrugged, doing his best to appear casual but he was

anything but. Tom placed a supportive hand on the young DC's shoulder and winked.

"Good to have you back. We've missed you around here."

"Not missed the air horn, though," Cassie said from the corner of her mouth. Eric aimed the straw connected to the can at her and fired a blast of air in her direction, parting her long hair at the base of her neck. She looked around at him, grinning. Eric returned it. "The DCI is in your office. She wants a word but I'd tread carefully if I were you."

Tom looked at her quizzically.

"I don't think Tammy had a good night," Cassie said with a wry grin.

Tom nodded and walked into his office. Tamara was sitting behind his desk poring over some paperwork in front of her. There was something different about her this morning but he couldn't put his finger on what.

"Morning," he said. She looked up and then he realised what it was. "New glasses?"

"What? Oh, yes, they are." She sat back in the seat, raising her eyebrows and taking on a thoughtful expression. "Those headaches I kept having?"

"Yes. You said you were going to see the doctor, I recall."

She nodded. "It turns out there's nothing wrong with me; just that I'm getting older like everyone else." She took off her glasses and held them up to him. "Sorry I borrowed your office."

Tom smiled, waving away the apology and perching himself on the end of his desk. "So, how did it go last night, after we all left?"

Tamara shook her head, rolling her eyes. "Nothing to tell. Mum took herself off to bed pretty soon after you left; it's a long trip from Bristol using public transport, to be fair. And she wasn't up when I left for the office this morning."

Tom eyed the two empty cups of coffee on the desk in front of her. Glancing at the clock, it was only half past seven, so Tamara had made an early start. Perhaps he was cynical but ducking out at the crack of dawn made it easier to avoid a conversation if that was your intention.

"So can you do it?" she asked.

Tom realised he'd zoned out for a moment and hadn't heard her. He shook himself awake. "Sorry, what did you say?"

"The chief super wants one of us to attend a suicide; potentially a suspicious death and they want CID to give it the once over."

"Sure, no one mentioned it," he said, glancing through the window to Cassie and Eric.

Tamara shook her head. "No, it's a little off our patch."

"Where?"

"Royston Common, I think he said—"

"Roydon."

"That's it."

"King's Lynn should handle that, surely?"

Tamara shrugged, slipping her glasses back on. "Busy, no one available ... restructuring ... whatever. They just want a favour and let's face it," she pointed at Eric, now wiping down his monitor with an antibacterial screen wipe, "I think we can spare a body."

"I'll leave Eric here today, let him settle in," Tom said. "I'll take a run down there with Cassie. It'd be nice to get out."

"Fair enough."

"Thanks for last night. The three of us enjoyed it. Saffy loves coming over to yours. I think the size of our back garden is more like a prison to her in comparison with the open expanse you call a garden."

"She can come and cut the grass any time she likes," Tamara said without looking up. Tom made to leave the office, turning back and leaning on the door frame. Tamara looked up. "What is it?"

"Would you prefer it if I called you Tammy?"

He could barely contain the smile that threatened to sweep across his face as Tamara searched for something she could throw at him. He skipped away, back into ops, before she found something that fitted the bill.

"Cassie, get your coat."

"Where are we going?"

"A suspicious death."

ROYDON COMMON STRETCHED from the village that bore its name through several miles of rolling countryside encompassing two nature reserves, woodland and rough heathland. The common covered a large area to the east of King's Lynn and was popular with locals for dog walking or as an escape from the nearby town. Just minutes away from the hustle and bustle of residences or trading estates you found yourself in open fields, shared with ponies, grazing cattle or as was often the case, no one else at all.

Much of the visitors' car park located next to the nature reserve was cordoned off by a couple of liveried police cars and they were allowed beyond the cordon when Tom brandished his warrant card. By the look of it, a number of locals were displeased at having their morning routine interrupted; several people were standing around and observing goings-on, their animals excitedly barking at one another and obviously keen to get on with their daily exercise. Getting out of the car, they were buffeted by a stiff breeze. The wind direction had changed since the previous night, now coming in at pace off the North Sea and where they stood was very exposed. They were directed towards the left beyond the gate and the centre of the reserve. Once over a small crest they could see down into the nature reserve and up the other side to where the commuter traffic bypassed the main town, a continuous hum despite the wind carrying sound away from them.

There were two trees standing at the centre with open heathland all around them. Several people were milling around. One of them would be Dr Fiona Williams, the on-call Forensic Medical Examiner. She saw them approach and rose from her haunches, where she'd been examining a body. They exchanged muted pleasantries under the circumstances.

"It would be nice to talk to you one day, Tom – whilst not standing over a deceased body."

"Yes, wouldn't it?" Tom said, half smiling. "What do you have for us?"

Fiona Williams looked down at the body, Tom and Cassie edging closer. "Deceased male, mid to late fifties—" she lowered herself back onto her haunches. Tom did likewise. "No sign of any intrusive wounds or injuries nor any scuffs or scrapes to suggest he put up much of a fight."

"Then why assume he was involved in a fight?" Tom asked with a raised eyebrow.

"Here," she indicated the bridge of his nose with the tip of her pen, "his nose is broken and I think it's recent judging by the damage to the skin tissue. And the trickle of blood that's run from the nasal cavity and dropped straight to the ground. You can see it better from this side." She beckoned him to join her on the opposite side of the body. The body was lying face down, almost in the recovery position, with the man's head facing away from Tom and towards the trees.

Tom moved and saw what she was pointing at. He looked at the ground around where they were. It was uneven and despite it being late November the wild grass was still present, concealing the surface beneath,

"He could have stumbled and fallen. Maybe he landed face first? It happens."

Fiona shrugged. "Yes, but … he's not geared up for walking around here."

Tom cast an eye over the deceased. She was right. He was wearing a pair of polished brown loafers and beneath his over-coat he wore a shirt and what he guessed was a cashmere jumper.

"You've got a dog, Tom. Would you be out walking around here last night dressed like this?" Tom had to admit he wouldn't be. "He hasn't even got any gloves on."

Tom met her eye, pursing his lips. "Curious. Time of death?"

"Since death, I'd usually take an hour off for every degree of temperature lost, but it was cold last night, so I'd suggest time of death was around one in the morning, give or take."

Tom's brow furrowed. "That only leaves more questions as to what he was doing out here last night."

"Not half as much as this," Cassie said, calling to Tom. She'd stepped away to speak to the uniformed officers already at the scene.

He rose and looked over to where she was standing, under-neath one of the trees, looking up.

"Yes, and that's the other thing that'll have you scratching your head," Fiona Williams said, raising both eyebrows inquis-itively.

The two of them crossed the short distance to join Cassie and Tom saw what they were talking about. A hangman's noose hung from a branch above them, swaying slowly back and forth in the breeze. It didn't look right to him. Fiona seemed to notice and shared his view.

"It's not like any noose I've ever seen," she said.

"An enthusiastic DIYer?" Cassie asked.

Tom thought she might be right. The person who tied it couldn't have known how to do it properly. The rope was thick and coarse by the look of it, certainly up to the job but the tying of the noose looked amateurish. He glanced back at the body.

"It begs the question; was the noose for him or for someone else?"

Cassie nodded. "Maybe he intervened and stopped someone else from topping themselves and they took issue with him?"

"Not exactly a hero's gratitude if that's the case. No sign of a struggle, though," Tom said, turning to Fiona. "You're sure about that?"

"There are no outward signs, no cuts, grazes, or abrasions to the skin. Perhaps there will be some trace evidence under the fingernails but if there is a violent struggle then skin tends to build up under the nails as you rake someone's hand or arm and is clearly visible. The deceased's fingernails are long – for a man anyway, so I would expect to see it. Aside from the facial injury, there is nothing to indicate he was brought here under duress or was involved in an altercation."

Tom looked back at the car park. The number of onlookers seemed to have increased.

"Any chance he was planning to hang himself and fell from the tree, landing face first?" Tom asked, although the suggestion seemed daft to him the moment it left his mouth. It didn't look like an easy tree to climb; the branches were evergreen and densely packed.

"There's a stepladder propped up behind the second tree," Cassie said, pointing it out to Tom. That confused things even more. Had it been under the noose then his theory might work, but for it to be leaning against the next tree was impossible unless ...

"Someone else must have been here," Tom concluded.

"My thoughts, too," Fiona agreed. "As to what role that person—"

"Or persons," Cassie said.

"Or persons played, I'll leave with the two of you, Tom," Fiona said with a smile.

"Thanks very much," Tom said quietly, glancing between the noose and the body. He looked at Cassie. "Better have forensics get down here," he made a circular motion with his hand, "have them try to make sense of all of this." Looking back up to the car park, he added, "And when the photographers are here, make sure they take some pictures of all those people over there paying attention. There might be one who's keener than the others."

"Got yer," Cassie said, looking at the members of the public now lining the police cordon, her mobile already pressed against her ear.

"Do we have an identification for the victim?" Tom asked.

Cassie passed him a plastic bag containing a black leather wallet. Donning a pair of gloves, Tom opened the seal and took it out. The button clasp looked like it had ceased working a long time ago and the wallet fell open in his hands. He took out the driving licence. The picture was a few years old but it was easily identifiable as their victim.

"Gavin Felgate," Tom said quietly. "I recognise that name."

"Where from?" Cassie asked, angling the mouthpiece away from her lips. She was on hold.

"Not sure, but I recognise the name." His brow furrowed. "I don't think I've nicked him before." Tucking the licence away again, he examined the rest of the contents. He counted forty pounds in cash and there were several credit cards still in their slots. He looked back at the body. "Does he have any valuables on him, watch, mobile phone?"

"Both," Fiona said. "But no car keys."

"We can probably rule out robbery as a motive, unless he has a nice car. How did he get here, anyone know?" The question was asked of anyone in earshot and one of the uniformed constables stepped forward.

"There were no cars in the car park when we arrived, other than that belonging to the local man who found the body and called us." Tom encouraged him to continue. "Local, lives nearby in *King's Reach*," he gestured towards a housing estate that was beyond their view, "walks his dog here every morning. Stumbled on this."

"Right, we'll need to speak to him," Tom said, nodding to Cassie who agreed. "Has anyone run Gavin Felgate through the system?"

"Lives in Heacham," the constable said. "No criminal record. Married, but we've not been able to reach any next of kin yet."

"Okay, thanks. We'll take care of it."

The officer seemed relieved, which was understandable. Passing on such news wasn't the most enjoyable part of the job, and sometimes, from a detective's viewpoint, it paid to be present when the relatives learnt of the death, especially if they were suspects. Eyeing the noose again, Tom couldn't help but think that there was a lot more going on here than they yet understood. He stepped away from the others and called Tamara Greave, she picked up on the third ring.

"This suspicious death you had me visit …"

"Straightforward?"

He glanced back at the body. "Far from it. Can you ask Eric to find out everything he can regarding a man called Gavin Felgate? He's our victim, if I can call him that."

"Felgate. Right. That sounds very cryptic. What do you think we are dealing with?"

"To be honest, it's all a little odd and I haven't got my head around it yet. You may come to regret agreeing to do this favour. I already have his address in Heacham, so Cassie and I will drop by there before coming back in."

"Okay. We'll see what we can find out this end."

CHAPTER THREE

THE HOUSE LOOKED UNOCCUPIED. The curtains were drawn across every window and despite repeatedly ringing the doorbell, there was no response from inside. Tom stepped back from the porch and scanned the windows for any flicker of movement; a twitch of a curtain or an interior light but there was nothing to see. There was a car in the driveway, a blue Mazda saloon. Tom tried the handle but it was locked. Cassie turned and looked around the surrounding area.

"Are people afraid of heights around here or something?"

Tom followed her eye line, unsure of what she meant. "Say again?"

She nodded towards the properties opposite. "The bungalows. There are rows and rows of them in this place."

Tom smiled. Heacham was a coastal village occupied since the Iron Age, but one that had grown over the years off the back of becoming a popular seaside resort following the advent of the age of steam. There wasn't a lot of substance to the old village; a few rows of terraced properties and larger Victorian semi-detached houses but the main construction in recent times had been the building of single-storey residences and the expansion of the holiday parks.

"Well, it is Norfolk. We're not known for high points around here," Tom said.

Cassie shrugged. "Not a lot going on, is there? The place is dead."

"It's rammed during the summer though. Haven't you been this way yet? You can walk or cycle the coastal path from Hunstanton. It doesn't take long."

She frowned. "Lauren's been on at me but ..."

"But?"

"I prefer the gym."

"Excuse me." They both turned to see who was addressing them. A short, rotund man with red cheeks and a receding hair line leaned on the boundary fence between Gavin Felgate's house and his own. "Can I help you with something?" He was eyeing them warily. Tom approached, taking out his warrant card and introducing himself and Cassie. "I'm Terry Sherman," he said, nodding his head back towards the house behind him, "and I live next door."

"We were hoping to speak to Mrs Felgate."

Sherman shook his head. "I never see her these days. I don't think they're together anymore. At least, if she's ever here I don't come across her. He does have a lady friend who calls round a couple of times a week. Never spoken to her, mind you."

"Right. How about Gavin Felgate? Have you seen him recently?"

The man's brow creased as he thought about it. "Yesterday morning ... maybe. Otherwise, the day before I reckon. Why? What's he done?"

Tom figured the question was asked out of voyeuristic curiosity rather than concern. He ignored it.

"How did he seem?"

"Normal. He's not the chattiest of fellows. Sometimes he'll stop to talk about whatever he's up to but, other times, I'm lucky to get more than the briefest hello. A man who likes a chat when he hasn't got anything better to do would be an apt description."

"And what it is you do, Mr Sherman?" Tom asked.

"Ah ... I used to do a bit of this and that, you know."

"And now?" Cassie asked. He hesitated momentarily before scratching absently at the back of his head.

"I'm afraid I'm on the sick." Cassie bobbed her head in understanding, Sherman pointing down to his right leg. "I have a cartilage problem with my knees." He sighed. "I'm on the list ... but who knows when the appointment will come through?"

"Operation?" Tom asked. Sherman nodded. "Do you know what Gavin did for a living?"

"Journalist," Sherman said. "Nothing highbrow, local stuff, I think. I don't know if he was freelance or salaried somewhere. He once told me he used to work down in London but the lifestyle didn't suit him."

"Lifestyle?" Tom asked.

"Yeah, he said it was fun during the eighties when he was starting out but he didn't care much for the way things went after that."

"Meaning?"

Sherman shrugged. "Don't know. He didn't say, not to me anyway. What's he done anyway?"

"Who says he's done anything?" Cassie asked.

The neighbour didn't answer. Looking back at Felgate's house, Sherman casually pointed to it. "Listen, I have a key to the house if you want to go in." Tom and Cassie exchanged a glance. "I mean, he gave it to me for emergencies. Does this count as an emergency?"

Tom smiled. "Yes, I believe it does."

TOM HAMMERED his fist on the frame of the back door but there was still no response from inside. He turned the key in the lock and the hinges creaked as he opened the door. Terry Sherman was standing behind Cassie, trying to see past her into the interior, and judging by Cassie's expression she thought he was invading her personal space. She turned to him and held up a hand.

"What are you expecting to find?" Sherman asked eagerly.

"What do *you* think we might find?" Cassie countered.

He was confused for a moment, then raised his eyebrows. "I don't know. Say, you don't think he's done himself in or something, do you?"

Tom was curious. "Why would you ask that?"

"Just … I–I don't know really. Gavin was an up and down kinda guy, you know? Like I said, some days he would talk and others he'd brush you off without looking at you. I did wonder if he was depressed."

"Was he depressed?" Cassie asked.

He shrugged, shaking his head. "If anything, I'd say he had a spring in his step recently. I thought it was his new lady friend but…"

"But? Go on," Cassie said.

"Well, he'd been going out more at all times. Usually, he was a creature of habit but recently he'd been keeping odd hours. As I said, at first I figured he was out with his new love interest, but then I wondered if he was just working more."

Sherman craned his neck to see into the interior, not easy with Tom's bulky frame standing in between.

"Thanks for your time, Mr Sherman. If we need anything more from you, we'll call round," Cassie said. She was polite but pointed. Sherman frowned but didn't protest, his disappointment clear to see. He wandered slowly around to the side alley between the two properties, glancing back over his shoulder and lingering at the corner. Cassie smiled her encouragement for him to keep moving and then he disappeared from view. She heard the latch on the gate click into place moments later.

"Irritating man," she said under her breath, stepping into the kitchen to join Tom.

"I doubt much gets past him, though. He might be invaluable."

"Aye, true enough. I'll bet you a tenner he keeps a diary of the neighbourly goings-on."

"I'll take that bet," Tom said, casting an eye around the kitchen.

"You'll lose," Cassie said drawing a laugh from Tom. The blinds to the window above the sink were down and on a winter's day, even a reasonably clear and bright one as they had today, the interior was still dark. The rear garden must face north. "Interesting smell he's got going on in here." Cassie screwed her nose. "Bachelor-itis?"

"I'll have you know my place never smelled like this," Tom said, noticing the large kitchen bin in the corner that obviously needed emptying, judging by the smell of food waste in the air. The kitchen worktop alongside the sink had several plates stacked up alongside some foil takeaway food containers; Chinese, Tom figured, inspecting the dried-on leftovers within. He counted the different containers, plates and forks. He found a credit card receipt dated for the night before, no details other than the total of the order, a little over twenty-two pounds. "Unless he had a very healthy appetite it looks like he wasn't eating alone. Call round the local takeaways and check to see if he collected the order or if they delivered it. You never know, they might remember someone with him."

They moved through the house. The scene was repeated in most rooms they entered, generally untidy and stuffy. Tom felt the nearest radiator and it was hot.

"He likes it warm."

"Hasn't he ever heard of opening windows?" Cassie asked, unzipping her coat as she moved through the living room. Tom indicated for her to carry on and he stayed to examine the room they were in. The dining room and living room were shared, stretching the length of the house. The dining table had several piles of paper on it and a laptop with the lid down. Tom scanned the top sheet of the first pile and then flicked through those below it – printed copies of old newspaper articles. Checking the first few from the top, Tom checked who had the by-line on each article, but none were written by Gavin Felgate. They all had some impressive camera shots attached to them though, depicting military units in active theatre by the look of them. Opening a Manila folder lying next to this collection, Tom found a number of documents that resembled invoices or purchase orders. He didn't recognise the company name but the logo on the headed paper looked familiar to him but he couldn't place it. Lifting the lid on the computer, he stroked the glide pad but the machine was fully shutdown and not in hibernation. Tom closed the lid and flipped the folder, lying alongside it, closed at the same time.

Turning his focus to the living room, he moved over to it. There was a three-seater sofa and matching armchairs arranged around a television in the corner of the room. An electric fireplace was on the far wall with a mantelpiece set into the plasterwork above. Tom went over and looked at several photographs lined up next to one another. Surprisingly, he found several were family shots. They didn't look too old but at the same time not recent either. Gavin Felgate's hair was less grey in one where he was standing with his arm around a woman – his wife? – with two children in front and beside them. The older one was a boy and the girl, with her mother's hands on her shoulders, looked a couple of years younger. Beside this picture was another of the couple taken at a table in a restaurant. The decor in the background looked Mediterranean, perhaps Greek, and they were both recently tanned suggesting they were on holiday abroad. Gavin was raising a glass to the camera, the woman smiling awkwardly as if she was uncomfortable. Tom guessed this was the ex, the photographs didn't look recent enough to be Felgate's so-called lady friend. It struck him as odd to be in a relationship with someone new and to still have such visual records of a previous, failed partnership on show. There didn't appear to be any indication of anything untoward happening in the house. Whatever befell Gavin Felgate most likely didn't occur here.

Cassie appeared at the doorway. "Got something?" he asked.

She shook her head. "Not really. There's a study off the hall but I don't think he used it very much. It's the tidiest room in the house. Your man next door was right though, he's got some framed articles on the wall; looks like he did some work for the tabloids back in the eighties. Nothing recent, though. Trading on past glories, I reckon. A few front pages he appears to be proud of, typical tabloid fodder of the time – or any time – but they weren't even using colour print in the photographs. Hard to imagine that now."

Tom nodded. "I remember. Makes you feel old."

"Not me. MTV was old hat when I was a teenager. I've a long way to go before I feel old."

"Lucky you, wait until you have kids," Tom said.

"That would take some doing," Cassie said, and Tom remembered belatedly that Cassie was in a same-sex relationship, which would introduce a new level of complexity if they ever chose to go down that path.

"What about upstairs?"

"Two bedrooms and a box room. The box and spare room are full of crap, master is as you'd expect from a bloke..."

"Neatly presented and smelling April fresh?"

Cassie laughed. "Close."

"Let's see if we can find a bank statement or something lying around here, see who's paying Gavin Felgate and maybe we'll find out where he works. And have Eric track down his ex-wife, she might still be local." He pointed to the photographs on the mantelpiece. "I don't think he's necessarily moved on, even if she has."

CHAPTER FOUR

Tom walked into the ops room. Cassie stayed behind at Gavin Felgate's home to wait for a uniformed presence to arrive and seal off the house until the CSI team could get there. That wouldn't happen until after they'd processed the scene on Roydon Common. Not that he knew what they would be looking for at his home; it remained unclear as to what they were investigating. Eric was sitting at his desk, a phone pressed to his ear but he waved a greeting as Tom entered.

Upon seeing him, Tamara stepped out of the office and bounded over to speak to him. She seemed much more energetic than she had been first thing in the morning.

"So, what's going on?"

Tom hung his coat up. "A fifty-something male found dead on Roydon Common. He appears to have suffered a blow to the face but the cause of death is inconclusive. No sign of a struggle or altercation on the victim's body, no tears to clothing and no defensive wounds that are visible. The FME suggests we might have some joy with trace evidence but," he shrugged, "she isn't hopeful."

"That's odd," Tamara said, folding her arms across her chest. "But it's not quite the mystery I was expecting."

"Well, that's because I haven't told you the weird part yet."

Tamara opened her hands, palms up by way of encouragement.

"He was found dead beneath a hangman's noose tied to the branch of a tree above."

Tamara frowned. "Botched suicide?"

Tom shook his head. "Only if he managed to fall off a stepladder, die on impact and then pick the ladder up and set it against another tree four metres away."

"I see that as problematic."

Tom tilted his head to one side. "Estimated time of death is around one o'clock in the morning. We've no witnesses other than the man who found him when he went to walk his dog this morning. The victim's car is parked in his driveway, and we have no indication as to why he came to be walking on the common at that time of night – if he was walking."

"You doubt it?"

"Not dressed for it, that's for certain. He looked more like he was ready for a night discussing his handicap at the clubhouse bar to me. I've left Cassie at the victim's place in Heacham to tie things off but it doesn't look like anything out of the ordinary happened there, no break-ins or arguments reported by the local nosy neighbour." Tom glanced over as Eric hung up on his call, spinning his chair to face them. "What have you found out about Gavin Felgate?"

"A fair bit," Eric said, retrieving his notepad from his desk behind him. "I'll skip the home address because you've been there. He was fifty-four, married to his wife, Jane. They have two children, Luke and Kirsten, nineteen and sixteen, respectively. It looks like they are separated, Jane has a registered address back this way in Hunstanton. The children live with her according to the electoral roll."

"Good, we haven't had any luck tracing the next of kin so it would be good to get over there before word reaches them by other means. What about Felgate himself? I understand he's a journalist."

Eric nodded. "I checked out his profile on *LinkedIn*. He's got a number of press accolades to his name but nothing much recent. I get the impression he dropped out of the rat race to lead a simpler life up on the coast."

"Or he wasn't left with any other option," Tamara said with a wry smile. "Who does he work for now?"

"According to his profile he writes for several publications so, at first, I thought he was freelancing but after a bit of digging and connecting the dots, it turns out all the publications listed are actually owned by the same parent company. The business is quite a player in East Anglia, covering all manner of news, politics and lifestyle publications in print and digital formats."

"Where was he based, do we know?" Tom asked.

"Offices in Norwich. I called the reception – unofficially, of course – and they confirmed Felgate works there but said he wasn't signed in today. Obviously, we know why."

"Okay, thanks, Eric. Good work. I'll take a drive down after speaking to the next of kin."

"The estranged wife?"

Tom nodded. "Separated or not, she's still his wife."

"I'll tag along," Tamara said. Tom raised an eyebrow. She mock grimaced. "Writing performance reviews is a bit dry. I could use some human company."

"Eric, can you follow up with forensics and have Felgate's personal effects transferred up here as quickly as possible?"

"Yes, of course," Eric said, making a note. "Anything in particular you want to prioritise?"

"He wasn't robbed as far as we could tell; still had his wallet, mobile and so on. I would like to know who he's been talking to recently as a starting point, help us to build the time-line of his last couple of days."

"Leave it with me."

Tom RECOUNTED the discussion he and Cassie had with Felgate's neighbour to Tamara as he drove them along the coast road. Tom had to admit he was curious as to who the mystery visitor was that Terry Sherman described. It could just as easily have been a work colleague as it could a love interest. He'd explored the rest of the house himself before leaving and hadn't found anything upstairs to suggest a woman stayed over with any frequency at all; there were no feminine toiletries in either the bedroom or bathroom and only one toothbrush in the holder. Tamara listened intently to his description of the scene on Roydon Common, asking occasional questions if she wanted clarification but he had the impression she wasn't as focussed as she would usually be. Once he'd concluded all the details, conversation between them fell away. Tom couldn't help but think she had much more on her mind than just the new case.

"Do you mind if I make a quick call?" he asked. Tamara smiled, shaking her head before returning her gaze back out of the window. Tom activated the hands-free and called Alice. He'd set off so early that morning. Both she and Saffy were still asleep when he left. Alice was due to start her shift in an hour so he might just be able to catch her before she set off.

"Hi Tom."

"Hey, just a quick call to see if everything went okay this morning with you guys?"

"Yes, thanks. Saffy bounded into class. They're starting *Forest School* today," Tamara glanced across and smiled at the thought, "and she's excited. This was such a good idea. I'm pleased we made the move. Are you still okay to pick her up from Mum's after you finish work?"

"Yes, will do. We've picked up a new case... but don't worry, I'll make it over there."

"Sounds interesting."

"That's a good description. I'll tell you later."

"Don't feel you have to," she said and he laughed. "But if you are running behind, please let Mum know. You know how she gets about punctuality and she's got her music lessons this evening."

"She should be getting her hearing checked. That's more pressing."

"That's quite enough of that, Tom Janssen!" Alice said, adopting a mock telling-off tone. "I know she's not got a musical ear—"

"*A musical ear*? I've heard scrapping cats that are more tuneful."

"Speak to you later. Bye!"

"Have a good shift," Tom said, ending the call with a smile on his face.

Tamara glanced at him, smiling. "It sounds like Saffy is enjoying school. I take it it's new. Have you moved her recently?"

Tom nodded without taking his eyes from the road. "After the turmoil of the last year, losing her father like that, it just made sense to put her in an environment that suited her. Where she is now fits that bill. She's thriving."

"Good. I'm pleased for her. She's a lovely little girl." Tamara's smile faded as she looked back out of the window, her own preoccupations settling over her like a thick blanket.

"If there's anything you want to talk about, I'm happy to listen," Tom said. Tamara glanced at him and offered a weak smile but said nothing. "Obviously, if you want me to butt out you can say that too!"

She grinned, resting her head on her hand, her elbow wedged against the passenger window. "Just some stuff I have to work through."

"With your mum?"

"Yes."

"Can I ask one question?"

She looked over, her eyes narrowing. "If you must."

"Since when have you been called Tammy?"

They both laughed, Tamara shaking her head.

"It's taken me thirty-five years to get far enough away from Bristol to lose that name, and if you use it again, I'll have you manning a radar trap on the coast road for the whole of next summer. Okay?"

"Understood."

The remainder of the drive to Hunstanton was made in silence. Tamara sat quietly in the passenger seat watching the fields pass by without saying a word. She seemed preoccupied but Tom didn't want to intrude on her thoughts. She said she wanted human company but that didn't necessarily mean she desired conversation. Tom knew the town well and he bypassed the centre taking a right turn onto Park Road. The road ran downhill almost to the sea which was visible between the small row of houses, almost on the seafront, and the buildings of an indoor bowling green and the Oasis Leisure Centre. But they weren't going that far. Tom pulled the car into the kerb and cast an eye along the row of Victorian semis, looking for Jane Felgate's.

The house was midway down the road, directly opposite the greenery surrounding the community centre. He switched off the engine, an action that drew Tamara out of her self-imposed period of reflection.

"What do you think is going on?" she asked. For a moment he wasn't sure if she was talking about her personal life or the case. "It's early I know, but from what you say it sounds like there was at least one other person present either at the time or prior to Felgate's death. Do you think it was an intentional homicide, a suicide gone wrong or some kind of... weird accident?"

Tom drummed his fingers on the steering wheel. "I agree, he went out on the common with someone else or, at least, to meet someone there. His car is still parked on the driveway at his house and I'll guarantee he didn't walk from Heacham to Roydon in the kit he had on. From what I saw on his dining room table it looks like he was into something but as to what, I don't know." He glanced over to the house they were visiting. "Once we're done here, I'm hoping his boss will have some insight into what he was working on. Beyond that, if we can get into his laptop, we might have a better idea."

"You think it might be connected to his work?"

Tom shrugged. "Right now, not a lot about this is making sense to me. Why there, why the common? It's a daft place to meet, even if you feel the need to be clandestine, I can think of any number of better locations where you won't be seen."

"And what's with the noose?"

Tom nodded, cracking his door open and Tamara, waiting for a car to pass by first, did the same.

CHAPTER FIVE

THEIR KNOCK on the door was answered by a gangly young man. He was almost the same height as Tom, appearing taller by standing on the raised step of the front door, but his build was slight. His complexion was pale and his eyes narrow, staring out at them from beneath a mop of brown hair that stood up and away from his head in every direction; thick and unmanageable. Tom introduced them and the young man was remarkably unfazed, looking back over his shoulder and shouting for his mother.

Jane Felgate, in stark contrast to her son, was shorter and fuller of figure. She had blonde hair running to her shoulders, wide blue eyes and exhibited an anxious disposition as she came to the door, drying her hands on a checked tea towel. Inviting them in, she stood aside and shooed her son indoors and out of the way.

Seated in the front living room a few minutes later, Jane Felgate sat forward, perched on the edge of the sofa, still clutching the tea towel. The whites of her knuckles were visible, so tight was her grip. Her eyes watered a little but aside from that, she displayed little outward emotion but Tom sensed there was a great deal repressed, based on her body language: rigid and controlled.

"I–I can't believe it..." she said slowly, her eyes passing between both Tom and Tamara. "Are you sure?" The question seemed born out of hope more than anything else. "I mean, are you sure it's him?"

"He was carrying photo identification," Tom said, "but we will need a formal visit from his next of kin before we can say for certain."

Her eyes darted to him and away again, looking down at her hands nestling in her lap. "I suppose that's still me."

Tom nodded. "How long have you been separated, if you don't mind my asking?"

She shook her head, drawing breath before answering. "Not at all. Three years ... formally ... but we were apart long before that. Our marriage had become a shell of what it once was."

"Had either of you looked to take the next steps to formalise things?" Tamara asked.

"Divorce, you mean?" Jane replied. Tamara nodded. She shook her head. "No. Not yet. Neither of us are – were – in much of a rush to do so. We talked about it obviously, but we would both be in a worse state if we did."

"How do you mean?"

"Well, initially we went for mediation – trying to find an amicable settlement that would suit us both – and the upshot of that was that Gavin had to sell the house. There was no way he could raise the money to buy out my share otherwise. It would have left him with nothing. He agreed and explored it, even had the place on the market for a time, too. He wasn't perfect, Gavin, by any stretch of the imagination; deeply flawed with a warped perspective of his own importance, but he did make an effort to do right by me and the kids."

"But he still supported you?"

"At first, he did ... but then things got a little ... difficult and the payments stopped coming. Recently, he's been much better; even giving us more than he needed to. He said he was making up for his mistakes, or trying to at least."

The door to the living room cracked open and a pair of blue eyes peered around the frame at them, a face coming into view seconds later. She was the spitting image of her mother, only with the vitality of youth to separate them. Jane held out a hand and encouraged the girl to come and sit with her. She'd been crying, it was clear. Her brother also came into view but he lingered at the threshold, reluctant to enter, despite his mother's encouragement. The daughter, Jane introduced her – Kirsten, immediately put her head onto her mother's chest, Jane putting a supportive arm around her and kissing the top of her head.

"It'll be okay, love," she said in soothing tones. The children must have been eavesdropping from the hall. She turned her attention back to Tamara. "Things were ticking over quite nicely. Gavin was ... finding his feet recently, doing more of what was expected of him."

"How do you mean?" Tom asked.

"Well, it's no secret that he had his demons." She met Tom's eye, forcing an artificial smile. "Gavin liked things his own way. He was the sort of person who needed to feel like he was taking charge of things. Sadly, he didn't work in a field that offered him that; having to dash here and there, trying desperately to make things happen. That took its toll on," she looked between her children, Kirsten staring into her mother's lap, unflinching, and her son Luke, still standing in the doorway, watching on impassively, "all of us, not least Gavin himself. The stress, the deadlines ... he would compensate by ..."

"By?" Tom asked.

"By getting wasted every day!" Luke said flatly. "And the rest!" His mother looked up at him, her lower lip trembling slightly. Kirsten pressed herself further against her mother and Jane responded by tightening her grip. She confirmed what Luke said with a curt nod.

"In the end, I thought it was best for all concerned if we stepped away – me and the kids."

"And the separation ... was it amicable?" Tamara asked.

Jane hesitated. Luke turned his gaze to the hall behind him. Tom noticed.

"Are they ever amicable?" Jane countered. "But things settled down and we made it work for us. Didn't we?" she asked, shaking her daughter in a comforting gesture. Kirsten didn't speak but she bobbed her head briefly. Tom looked up at Luke but he wouldn't meet his eye.

"You said Gavin was doing what was expected of him. What did you mean by that?" Tamara asked.

"Just that," Jane said. "We came to a financial under-standing quite early on and, although it took a while, Gavin did eventually hold up his end of things. Recently, he'd started to make inroads with the children as well. You know, making an effort to be a part of their lives again."

Luke turned and left the room without a word. It was a poignant action. Kirsten lifted herself away from her mother, looking around the room. Tamara clocked what she needed and passed a box of tissues across to her that she found on the table beside her. The teenager accepted them with a grateful smile, wiping her eyes and the end of her nose. Her eyes were still red-rimmed and bloodshot. Tom hadn't noted a similar response from Luke.

He stood up, Jane's eyes following him. "May I use your bathroom?"

"Of course. There's one just through the kitchen."

He made his way out into the hall, casually pulling the door to the living room to as he passed, heading along the hall to the rear. He found Luke sitting on a stool hunched over the breakfast bar with his head in his hands. Hearing Tom's approach, he lowered his hands and sat upright, turning slightly to warily watch Tom as he entered the kitchen.

"How are you doing?" Tom asked.

Luke briefly raised his eyebrows, before glumly nodding slowly and looking at the counter in front of him.

"I know, stupid question," Tom said apologetically.

"It's okay," Luke said. His voice was softer than Tom imagined it to be. He wore the angst of a teenager in the body of someone who looked older.

"I know it's a lot to take in."

"Doesn't matter," Luke said, staring straight ahead. "It makes no difference. I haven't spoken to him in years anyway."

Tom found that quite telling. Although not uncommon for a teenager to fall out with their father, leading to a detached relationship, complete withdrawal was something else entirely.

"The two of you didn't see eye to eye?"

Luke shrugged, then lifted his eyes to meet Tom's gaze. "Something like that, yeah."

"Fathers and sons can have a tough time relating to one another," Tom said, crossing the kitchen and leaning against the wall opposite, facing Luke. The young man tracked his movements with an emotionless expression.

"I'm pleased he's gone."

The nature of the statement and its deadpan delivery caught Tom by surprise. He didn't respond, but watched the boy carefully, his eyes flitting back and forth around the room but focussing on nothing in particular.

"Is that bad?" he asked, turning his head back and staring

at Tom. His eyes seemed to sparkle, almost as if just saying the words aloud had lifted a significant weight from him.

Tom raised his eyebrows, taking a breath and considering his response. "There's only one person who can judge that sentiment, and it's not me."

Luke's expression conveyed disappointment at the answer. Was he seeking approval or reassurance for his feelings towards his father? Maybe his dismissal of the loss was merely a deflection from the need to face it or was it something else entirely? Luke ran his tongue along the outside edge of his lower lip and he looked away.

"My dad was a bully ... and no matter what was going on, what was happening, he always managed to make it about someone else." Luke wrung his hands in front of him, his gaze drifting back to Tom. "You know people like that? They make you feel like it's your fault ... even when it couldn't possibly be."

Tom inclined his head. He'd met a few like that. Fortunately, he'd never been related to any of them.

"And he always goes his way, no matter what!"

"Luke?" Jane Felgate said entering the kitchen, Tamara a half step behind her. Jane shot a dark look at Tom, he read her expression as a curious mix of fear and frustration. Or was it disappointment? She crossed to her son and placed a supportive hand on his back but he shrugged it off, slipping from the stool and pushing past her, making for the hall. "Luke!"

He didn't acknowledge her call or look back, hurrying away. A draught of cold air blew in from the hall and the front door slammed shut. Kirsten held her ground for a moment, standing behind Tamara, and then she, too, melted into the background. Jane's expression switched to embarrassment. Tamara met her forlorn gaze, smiling supportively.

"You'll have to forgive Luke. The last couple of years have been particularly hard on him."

"Because of the relationship with his father?" Tom asked.

Jane was pensive. She nodded.

"Didn't they get on?" Tamara asked. "Luke and his dad?"

"Quite the opposite. Luke loved his father. All he ever wanted was Gavin's approval. He sought it out but no matter how hard he tried; it was never enough."

"I can relate," Tamara said. Tom didn't react but something in her tone made him see Tamara's comment as genuine, rather than a prescribed response to put a witness at ease. She caught him looking at her, suddenly seeming self-conscious. "I think we have enough for now, Mrs Felgate—"

"And you'll be in touch about ..."

"The identification?" Tamara asked, Jane nodded. "I'll call you tomorrow morning with the arrangements. I can send a car for you if you like?"

"Yes, thank you. None of us drive." Tamara failed to mask her surprise. "Oh, Gavin wouldn't allow ..."

She looked down at the floor and Tom exchanged a look with Tamara.

"We'll see ourselves out," Tamara said. Tom took the lead and Tamara stepped forward placing a hand on Jane's forearm. "I'm sorry for your loss." She turned and left the kitchen, meeting Tom at the front door. He looked past her and up to the landing at the top of the stairs where a pair of blue eyes were watching them. Tom smiled at Kirsten and she disappeared from sight.

The doorbell rang. The hallway was too narrow to allow anyone else to pass by them to answer the door, and Jane Felgate hovered behind Tamara craning her neck to see past Tom. He opened it. A woman stood on the doorstep surprised to see two strangers, in Tom and Tamara, greeting her. She smiled nervously and then, spotting Jane in the background, offered her a wave.

"Don't mind us," Tom said to her, "we're just leaving."

"Oh, okay," the woman said, awkwardly moving aside to give them room to pass. Jane Felgate came to the door. The newcomer noticed how upset she was, reaching out to her.

"Jane, whatever is the matter?"

"Oh, Leigh... I–it's Gavin..." she said. "He's dead."

Leigh gasped, a hand raising to cover her mouth as it fell open. "What? How?"

Jane shook her head, indicating Tom and Tamara. "They are from the police."

Leigh's eyes darted between them, settling back on her friend. Jane threatened to cry at any moment, retreating inside and beckoning Leigh to follow. She glanced at Tom and Tamara before doing so, nodding in their direction. Tom returned the gesture with a sympathetic smile. The latch clicked into place and they turned, making their way down the path, heading for the car. Tamara spoke as they walked. "The daughter – Kirsten – is quite skittish. Unless young women always run off when you look at them kindly?"

A smile crossed Tom's face. "You didn't."

"You hardly ever smile at me, though, Tom—" She stopped, gently elbowing him in the ribs and pointing up the road to where their car was parked. Luke Felgate stood there, leaning against their car, arms folded across his chest.

They approached, the young man dropped his arms to his side and slipped his hands into his pockets, looking sheepish. In his haste to leave the house he hadn't picked up a coat. His breath formed massive clouds of vapour around him with every exhale. The wind had dropped which was a blessing.

"Sorry about that," Luke said. "Sometimes... I don't react well to things. Emotional things."

"That's understandable, under the circumstances," Tom said, moving alongside him and leaning his back against the car as well. "How did you know this was our car?"

Luke shrugged, glancing over his shoulder at the car. "It's the only one parked out here that I've never seen before. Not a lot changes around here, you know?"

Tom laughed. He was observant. "Inside, you said your father was—"

"An arse, yeah."

That wasn't what Tom was going to say, but he understood the sentiment. "Did he drink a lot then, your father?"

Luke nodded, staring at his feet. "Some days he wasn't too bad. Other times ... you wanted to be anywhere but near him, you know?" He glanced up at Tom glumly. "On those days you knew it was only going one way."

"Which way?"

Luke shrugged. "One of us would get a good kicking. Usually Mum... unless..."

"Unless?"

He sighed. "Unless I got in the way."

"Did you?"

He nodded. "Sometimes."

"That's harsh."

"I should have done more but," he stared at Tom hard, "I was scared. Let my mum take it while I hid."

"It wasn't your fault, Luke," Tom said, shaking his head. Luke was biting back tears now. "Do you want to go somewhere, grab a coffee or something?"

Luke shook his head, sniffing hard and stepping away from the car. He took a couple of steps back towards the house.

"I should get back inside, see to my mum."

He didn't meet Tom's eye. Tamara, lingering quietly in the background, looked on.

"Luke?" Tom said, the boy turned and Tom passed him one of his contact cards. He nodded towards it as Luke accepted it from him, turning it over in his hand. "You can call me on that number any time you fancy a chat. Any time at all, okay?"

Luke silently accepted with a brief nod and set off back to the house. Tom waited until he was up the steps and passing through the door before he looked over the roof of the car at Tamara who mouthed a silent *wow*.

"What do you make of that?" he asked as the front door closed and he unlocked the car.

"*So* much to unpick there. Families, huh?" she replied, pulling open her door and getting in.

CHAPTER SIX

THEY MADE their way through an open-plan office on the third floor of the building. It was a nondescript office block built sometime in the eighties, Tom figured, uninspiring but functional. The same couldn't be said for the view out of the windows overlooking part of Norwich city centre. Buildings constructed hundreds of years previously, ones that stood the test of time regarding their aesthetics, lined the street opposite. The hustle and bustle of late afternoon traffic filtered up to them.

Their guide glanced back over his shoulder, offering a pleasant smile. His cheeks were pockmarked from acne and, despite making an effort to dress in a formal shirt and tie, he still looked like a little boy. He must be an intern. The shirt was too large for him around the collar, the arms looking far too baggy. Reaching the office, he knocked once and a voice beyond bid them to enter. The lad opened the door, passed through and held it for Tom and Tamara.

"Thank you, David. That'll be all." The escort smiled at the visitors and left, pulling the door closed behind him. Charles Adams, a balding man with a pot belly, rose from behind his desk, offering them a broad smile. "It's a good job you arrived when you did, I was just about to head off."

Tom glanced at his watch; it was only half past three. Adams noticed, the smile fading a little.

"The nights draw in early this time of year and you can't play a round in the dark, can you?"

Tom nodded and smiled. He didn't play; never quite understanding the love of the game but each to their own. They introduced themselves and Adams offered them both a seat.

"We're here to talk to you about a member of your staff, Gavin Felgate. He writes for you?"

Adams rolled his eyes, his mouth falling open. "What's Gavin done now?" He splayed his hands wide in a gesture of supplication. "There's nothing he was assigned to that should be of interest to the police—"

Tamara interrupted him. "I'm sorry to have to tell you, Mr Adams, that Gavin was found dead this morning."

Adams stared at her, open mouthed. It took a moment for the information to sink in. He sank back in his chair, shoulders sagging. "My word. Gavin ... really?"

Tamara nodded. "We are trying to build a picture of his movements in the last few days. Could you tell us what he was working on?"

"Um ... yes, certainly," Adams said, sitting forward again, placing his hands flat on the desk and drawing breath. His eyes turned to the ceiling as he thought hard. He was rocked by the news and seemed to be struggling to process simple questions. "He ... um ... was assigned a couple of stories recently." He shook his head, turning the corners of his mouth down. "None of them were particularly monumental; what we call lifestyle gigs."

"*Lifestyle gigs?*" Tom asked.

"Yes, interviewing prominent locals about their successes, how they do what they do," he said, waving one hand in a circular motion in the air before him. "Sometimes not so prominent, depending on what else we have to run at the time. I like to build up a catalogue of these types of stories, they're cracking filler if you come up a little short content-wise in a slow week."

"And Gavin was working on these, anything specific?"

Adams dragged his hands across both cheeks, his brow furrowing. "Yes, hang on a second and I'll look up what I'd given him." Pulling his keyboard across his desk in front of him, he clicked through a number of folders, his expression lightening as he found what he was after. "Here it is. Gavin was doing a piece on a local businessman in the catering trade. He supplies restaurants, fulfils government contracts and has several restaurants along the coast I believe."

"What was the angle, if you don't mind my asking?" Tamara said.

"Not at all, no. As I said, it was a lifestyle piece and I understand this particular company offers work to those that are perhaps deemed less appealing by other employers; apprenticeships, paid internships ... things like that. I'll give you all the details I have, if you like."

"Thank you. That would be helpful," Tamara said. "Anything else?"

"Erm ... he had a follow-up visit to someone who has become something of a local celebrity in the past twelve months – Greg Beaty – do you know him?"

Tom and Tamara exchanged looks. Neither of them had heard of him.

"Maybe you know him by his pen name – T. C. Boyd?"

Tom shook his head and Tamara apologised. Adams seemed disappointed.

"He used to be a journalist but recently turned his hand to writing crime fiction. His first book has been a runaway success ... I'm surprised you've never heard of him."

Tamara smiled apologetically. "Crime fiction is a bit too close to the day job. I prefer romance, personally."

"Right, yes, of course. I can see that," Adams said, bobbing his head in agreement. "I didn't think of that."

"You said it was a follow-up story?" Tom asked.

"That's right," Adams said, running a hand down the length of his tie and straightening it. He appeared thoughtful. "I commissioned the piece a couple of months ago but Greg was putting a new book together, so I left it on the shelf with a view to running it when the next book was published. That was the beginning of this month, releasing just in time for the run up to Christmas. Gavin had to check in with him just to make sure nothing had changed prior to publication."

"Have you read the piece?"

"Yes, obviously."

"Anything in it that was surprising to read?"

Adams laughed. "Salacious revelations, that sort of thing?" Tom nodded that that was his thinking. "No, not at all. Greg has led an interesting life, a story well worth reading even without the novel, but nothing in the story would be considered contentious. We don't really specialise in investigative journalism, Inspector. No, no, we are – how can I phrase this – the easy-reading Sunday afternoon type of publications." His eyebrows knitted momentarily and he cast a suspicious look between the two of them. "Why do you ask? Just what is it that has happened to Gavin?"

"We are investigating the circumstances surrounding Gavin's death," Tamara said. "At this time, we can't say anything further than that."

"Good Lord. He's been murdered, hasn't he?"

Tamara held up a solitary hand in denial. "That's not what I said—"

"No but it's a possibility, isn't it? Otherwise you wouldn't be here."

Neither Tom nor Tamara denied the possibility but it was true that they didn't yet know what had befallen Gavin Felgate.

Tom sat forward and sought to change tack. "Are you aware of any threats made or arguments Gavin may have had with anyone recently, or noted any change in his behaviour, good or bad?"

Adams blew out his cheeks. "Where to start?" He immediately waved away his own comment. "Please, don't get me wrong. Gavin was all right, not the most popular member of the team, I think it's fair to say, but he hadn't fallen out with anyone as far as I know." He read Tom's expression, encouraging him to elaborate. Adams held his hands up. "He could be," he looked up, searching for the right word, "spiky. Yes, he could be spiky around people and that's not particularly inspirational and doesn't help forge the bonds of friendship, so to speak. Not that it bothered Gavin. I think he'd got used to his own company since his marriage broke down and liked it that way. Not the sort to crave human interaction."

"Makes him an odd choice for a lifestyle journalist, doesn't it?" Tom asked.

Adams tilted his head to one side, pursing his lips. "Maybe, but he was a damn fine writer. He could deliver me a piece needing minimal editing, on time, every time. And he learned to fake it years ago."

"Fake what?" Tom asked.

"His love of people," Adams said, raising an eyebrow along with a pointed finger. "That's the gift journalists need in interviews; the ability to put the interviewee at ease, off guard, relate to them on their level or look up to them if they have the ego requiring it. *Reading people*. It's as important a talent as organising words on a page. Gavin had both. That's why he made it on the nationals."

"Then how come he wound up here?" Tom said, "No offence intended."

Adams smiled. "None taken. The nationals, the tabloids in particular, are like a hamster wheel that never stops spinning. The demand for the next story doesn't let up and it takes a particular type of character to stay in the game for their entire career. The columnists have longevity, the opinion writers, too, but those pumping the stories in day after day ... well, they have to maintain their levels because if not the next guy is champing at the bit for your desk space. It's tough, stressful. And it takes its toll."

"Are you saying Gavin Felgate ... did what ... cracked?"

Adams frowned. "I think the worst of it was behind him, left back in London, but ..."

"But?" Tamara asked.

"I admit I had to speak to him on a couple of occasions when he came into the office having overdone it the night before." He drew a deep breath, letting it out slowly, his brow creasing. "But none of that was recent. In the last month or so I'd say he has had a bit of a spring in his step."

"And the breakdown of his marriage, how did he react to that?" Tamara asked.

"I'm not aware of any specific change in him," he shook his head. "Gavin didn't speak about his personal life in any detail. Not to me, at least. In fact, I'd be hard pressed to give you a name of anyone in the office he was close to. Crying shame that though, don't you think? To go through life alone. You must miss out on so much."

"So, there's no possibility that he was involved with anyone from work?"

"Involved? What, romantically?"

"Yes," Tamara said, smiling, "I'm an old romantic, after all."

"No, not as far as I know but, then again, stranger things have happened."

Tamara looked at Tom. He didn't have anything further to ask and so she glanced over her shoulder through the window towards the open-plan office. "Can we take a look at his desk?"

Gavin Felgate's desk was on the far side of the office, tucked away in a dog-leg section opposite a short corridor linking the office to the communal facilities. Looking at the proximity to other desks, Tom figured it was the ideal spot for someone who didn't wish to interact with nearby colleagues, fitting in with his boss's assessment of him. There wasn't much to look at; the desk was cluttered, but not by anything meaningful, just the detritus that collected over time, Post-it note reminders stuck to the edge of the monitor, stationery and scribbled notes on scrap paper. A framed photograph stood off to the right of his screen, a shot of his wife with their two children. All three of them were smiling and it looked like it was taken at an evening celebration, bunting hanging from the ceiling behind them. The children looked around ten or eleven years old, Kirsten was slight but Luke was already showing how tall he was likely to become. Thinking about it, Tom found it curious. Luke was far taller than his mother and considerably taller than his father as well, which was unusual.

"I don't know what you'll find that's useful," Adams said, standing nearby. "Gavin was old school and didn't make a lot of notes. He liked to keep things in his head."

Tom opened the top drawer of the pedestal, finding a number of loose pens, a stapler and other bits and pieces. Alongside these he found an A5-sized diary; it was worn at the edges, the cover scratched. It had seen some use this year. He slid the drawer closed and opened the two larger ones beneath it but they were almost completely empty, perhaps proving the editor's point. Thumbing through the diary, he found the previous week and then quickly scanned the two weeks prior to that. It was only a week-to-view diary, leaving little room for each day besides the briefest of entries.

"Interesting," he said aloud. Tamara turned to him with a quizzical expression. Tom looked up from the pages at her. "He had two meetings last week, Tuesday and Friday, same time. They were recurring – going back weeks."

"Who with? Does it say?"

Tom shook his head. "Marked with a letter 'M'. Half past two, every Tuesday and Friday."

"Squash partner or something?" Tamara said, only half serious.

"I'll plump for the *or something* there," Tom said. "He doesn't strike me as that type."

Adams scoffed in the background. "Certainly not Gavin, no."

Felgate's boss didn't seem to want to leave them to it. Was it the voyeur in him, an instinctive journalistic desire to stay in the loop or did he think he could help? Tom thought about asking him to step away but, then again, he might be useful.

Tamara didn't seem too concerned about Adams staying with them either. "We'll have Eric cross reference his phone records, see if an 'M' turns up with any frequency. Anything else from last week?"

"Wednesday he was meeting with someone about fish—"

"Fish?"

Tom angled the diary towards her so she could see it herself, placing the point of his finger underneath the entry. "Fish – one o'clock."

"Could he be any more cryptic, do you think?"

Tom briefly raised his eyebrows, turning the page back to show the week before. "A week ago, Wednesday he met with 'Lang'." Tom looked at Charles Adams. "Do you know who that might be?"

Adams frowned, thinking hard. Then he shook his head. "I'm sorry, I've no idea who that would be. But I think the fish appointment you're referring to was probably with David Fysh, the managing director of Fysh Catering; the story I told you about, the one Gavin asked to write."

"I see, thanks."

"That was a surprise when Gavin brought that one to me, I must say."

"It was his idea then?" Tom asked.

Adams nodded. "Yes, it's a great angle, don't get me wrong, but it was not Gavin's sort of thing really." Tom encouraged him to explain further. Adams rocked his head gently from side to side. "Gavin often suggested writing articles a little edgier than I generally cared to commission; criminal cases and the like but as I said, it's not really what we do here. Some of our sister publications carry current affairs, news and so on but, to be honest with you, we are a commercial enterprise, acting as a conduit for advertising revenues and we have spent a great deal of time cultivating a client list of popular, well-paying brands. They want to be associated with ... positive articles and not the dirt and the grime, if you know what I mean."

"And Gavin Felgate wanted to dip his toe into that murky world?"

"Again ... yes, very much so. That's why I was surprised that he wanted to work on this piece, far too upbeat for him," Adams chuckled, although his humour dissipated quickly. "I'm sorry, it's still hard to believe that ... well, you know."

Tom assessed Charles Adams. He thought the man seemed genuine enough but he had to wonder if he, like Gavin Felgate, had that talent he spoke of to project an image to those people he was talking to, presenting himself in a positive light. He was keen to find out who Gavin had been spending his time with recently, hoping to find some answers.

CHAPTER SEVEN

SAFFY THREW her arms around her grandmother, standing on tiptoes in an effort to make things easier. It didn't. There was an awkward hug but the look on Margaret's face showed how much she loved it.

"Bye, Grandma, thanks for dinner!" Saffy said, releasing her grip, scooping up her school backpack, turning tail and running for the car. Tom unlocked it just as she reached the rear passenger door and pulled the handle.

"Do you want to sit up front with me?" Tom called. She looked back, nodded and threw her bag across the rear seats before hefting her booster seat, no mean feat in itself and unceremoniously depositing it through the gap and onto the passenger seat. She then followed herself, clambering between the two front seats and Tom pictured the trail of destruction carried from the soles of her shoes over his upholstery.

"Oh dear," Margaret said with a smile. "She says she was supposed to take wellington boots into school today for their walk around the woods but her mum forgot."

Tom nodded. "Yes, well, it's all still quite a new routine – for all of us. Thanks for picking her up—"

"Tom," she said as he was turning away, "how is she now, Sapphire, I mean?"

He looked at the little girl in the car, she'd already fastened her seatbelt and was watching him with the same impatient expression he often saw in her mother. He smiled at Margaret. "She's doing well. The school has helped, I think."

Margaret nodded along to his words but he sensed she had something she wanted to say.

"It might be nice if she wasn't pushed from pillar to post as often though, don't you think?"

He wasn't sure what she meant. Both he and Alice worked shifts, and sometimes it was hard with their crossovers, but he didn't think they put too much upon family to help out. At least, he thought it was an equitable arrangement and he'd never picked up on any indication that the arrangements were inconvenient. Alice hadn't said anything either. Saffy reached over and gave a short burst on the car horn, although it took her several attempts because she didn't have enough strength in her arms to make it sound. He looked at her and she mouthed the words *let's go* in an overly dramatic manner.

"It looks like I'm delaying her schedule," Tom said. Margaret offered him an artificial smile, clearly she wanted to continue the conversation to make sure whatever point she was making would hit home. He pretended not to notice and walked back to the car. Opening the door, he paused before getting in and looked back. "I'll have a word with Alice about it and maybe we can talk later in the week. Is that okay?"

"Yes, of course."

He got in and closed the door under Margaret's watchful eye. She had her arms folded across her waist, one hand absently toying with her necklace which hung low over her roll-neck jumper. Her expression was stern and he wondered what it was that was really on her mind.

"Can I start the car?" Saffy asked excitedly. He nodded and she unhooked her belt, leaned across him and pressed the button. The engine fired up and Saffy retreated to her seat having let out a delighted yelp.

"If you think that's exciting, you just wait until it starts raining and you get to turn on the variable-speed windscreen wipers!" he said, casting her a wide-eyed knowing look.

"You're so lame, Tom."

He laughed, putting the car in reverse. "Thanks very much. Give your gran a wave." They both waved as he reversed out of the drive, Saffy very enthusiastically with both hands. He was pleased to see Margaret smiling broadly and returning the gesture. Maybe whatever she was getting at wasn't too serious and he'd misread it.

"What can I have to eat when we get home?"

Tom glanced at the clock on the dash, it was nearly seven o'clock. "Didn't your gran feed you?"

"Yes, but that was dinner and I'm talking about snack."

"Ah, I see. Snack. Got you."

"Then we need to have a conversation about *final snack* before bed."

"*Have a conversation*," he said, grinning. "Are you the parent now?"

Saffy seemed pleased with herself finding a new position in the reversal of roles. "But we need to talk about it before Mum gets home."

He knew what she was getting at. He was the soft touch, and he knew it.

"I'll make a deal with you," he said, keeping his eyes on the road. Saffy was all ears. "We get home, I make you a snack – fruit based," he held up a hand to stop the protest already forming, "and you eat it quickly while I run your bath. Then it's bed."

"What about final snack?" she asked, watching him intently and trying to gauge what she might be able to get away with.

"How about I combine both snacks, bath, and then bed ... but with a story?"

Saffy sat in silence. He wondered what objections she might throw at him but after a minute she looked across at him and nodded. "Deal."

That was easy. His phone rang and he answered it through the Bluetooth. It was Eric.

"I'm in the car with Saffy, Eric," he said, keen to ensure Eric didn't say anything likely to give the girl nightmares.

"Okay, cool. Hey, Saffy. How's it going?"

"Brilliant! Gran gave me a Magnum for pudding. Not a mini but one of the big ones!"

"Adult size?" Eric asked.

Saffy nodded, as if Eric could see her, grinning broadly. Tom silently cursed Margaret and her strange obsession with giving children a massive sugar hit shortly before bedtime.

"Are you still in the office?" Tom asked.

"Yep."

"First day back, Eric, you don't need to make up for the last few months in one day!"

Eric laughed. "I know, I know. Becca is coming over to pick me up, she'll be here any minute. I just wanted to run something past you. While I was waiting for forensics to get themselves sorted and send over the vict—" he seemed to catch himself, quickly sanitising his words for Saffy's sake. Although, she'd lost interest in Eric and was now adjusting the climate controls on her side of the car. "Felgate's personal effects are here and the CSI lead promised to give us a run down on their findings first thing in the morning. The body ... sorry ... he's been transported already and we should have preliminary findings by close of play tomorrow. I spoke to

Cassie and we had a chat about the scene. I reckon it's a bit odd."

"You're not the only one, Eric," Tom said, indicating and turning across a line of cars. They were nearly home.

"Forensics told me they were able to lift fingerprints off the rope."

"How did they manage that?"

"Well, not from the rope itself, obviously, but the end was sealed from fraying with electrical tape binding the strands together. They were able to lift a full print and a couple of partials. With a bit of luck, we may have a name tomorrow."

"Good work."

"There's more. I had a thought that the ... use of the rope was a bit suggestive. I mean, if it's not to actually ... suspend ... someone, then what's the significance?"

Tom reached home, pulling into the drive and seeing Alice's car was already here. He realised he was back later than expected. Maybe his deal with Saffy wasn't such a success after all. Saffy must have had the same thought because she frowned at Tom, silently mouthing *Mum's home already*. Tom pulled a frightened expression, she laughed.

"Hang on, Eric." He turned to Saffy. "You go inside and tell your mum I said you could have a snack before bath. If she starts yelling, I'll turn the car around and you run back; we'll make a break for it and go and live on the boat or something." He held up a hand and Saffy high-fived him before getting out of the car and running up to the front door. "Okay, I'm back and the coast is clear. What were you going to tell me?"

"The noose ... well, the location actually. It's off our patch and well before my time, yours too, I should imagine—"

"Eric, I'd like to get something to eat and at this rate I'll be having breakfast—"

"Right, yeah. The location on Roydon Common; I think it's

significant. A few years back a kid hanged himself out there. I've still got to pull up the files on it but I figured it was worth a look."

Tom sat back, rolling his tongue across the inside of his cheek. Eric was right, that was significant and too much of a coincidence to easily dismiss it. Far from making things clearer, it only seemed to add to the mystery.

"Okay. Good work, Eric. First thing tomorrow I want you to get onto the network provider and—"

"I can already tell you about his calls, if you like?"

Tom was intrigued. Eric couldn't have hacked the mobile already, surely? "Go on."

"He made three calls the day he died. One was to a number with no name saved – it's an unregistered mobile."

"A burner phone?"

"Exactly, yes. He has called the same number several times recently. One was to a local takeaway. That one was saved in his contacts list, so he must be a regular of theirs," Eric said. "Cassie was going to call in there on her way home. They'll be open now."

"Good. And the third?"

"Local taxi firm," Eric said. A noise in the background seemed to distract Eric. "Sorry, Becca's here. Do you want me to follow up with the taxi company?"

"No, no. Don't worry. You get yourself off home. I think you've made a strong start on your return. Make it a priority for first thing tomorrow."

"Will do."

"And Eric … how did you get into the phone so quickly?"

"That was easy. His pin code was his daughter's birthday."

"It's good to have you back, Eric."

Alice was waiting for him at the doorstep, arms folded

across her chest. He leaned in and kissed her cheek, she greeted him with a mock-angry expression on her face.

"I'm not sure what I've done, but to be fair you're probably right," he said, leaning back, holding her at arm's length and smiling. She grinned at him.

"Two snacks before bath?"

"Hey, your mother fed her chocolate and ice cream after dinner ... again."

Alice rolled her eyes. "I thought Saffy was a little hyper this evening." She stepped back and he followed her into the house. She closed the door as he took his coat off.

"Oh, and while I think about it, you'd better change your pin code on your debit card."

Her brow furrowed. "Why?"

"Trust me," he said. "Changing the subject; what's up with your mum? She was really odd with me this evening."

"Really, are you sure? How so?"

He shrugged. "I don't know ... just, odd."

"Well, she is odd, isn't she? Probably just Mum being Mum."

"She was talking about us working shifts and disrupting Saffy's life or something."

"I shouldn't worry," Alice said, thinking about it. "What did you say?"

Tom rested a hand on the newel post at the foot of the stairs, his lips pursed. "I did what any self-respecting guy would do in that situation."

"You ducked out of the tough conversation and left as quickly as possible?"

He turned the corners of his mouth down and raised both eyebrows. "You know me well."

She laughed. "Right, do you want to heat through leftovers for us or run Saffy's bath?"

CHAPTER EIGHT

ERIC WAS the first into the ops room the next morning, Tom finding him reading through an old case file as he entered. Crossing the room, he took a look at the white boards and reviewed the information Eric gleaned from Felgate's personal effects that came up late the previous afternoon. What he and Tamara learned from their trip to Norwich the previous day would need adding. Cassie arrived with Tamara a half step behind, Tamara heading straight for the coffee machine. He went to join her. She looked tired, as if she hadn't slept well. He lowered his voice so the others couldn't hear them.

"Everything all right?"

"It will be when I've got one of these inside me," she said, tilting her head towards the machine as she finished loading a capsule, dropped the lid and pressed start. She stared at the machine, watching it kick into life. "How about you?"

"Eric may have turned up a link to an old case."

"Good," Tamara said, sweeping the hair away from her eyes before picking up her coffee.

"You sure you're okay?"

"Fine," she said, striding over to Eric's desk. He turned

when she drew near, smiling a greeting. "What have you found, Eric?"

"A teenage suicide that took place on Roydon Common years back," Eric said, laying out several black-and-white crime scene photographs from both cases next to one another. He angled his head towards his right shoulder and squinted at the pictures as if that made a difference. "The trees would have been much smaller back then but—"

"Same place," Cassie said, craning her neck to see from her own chair. Tamara looked at her for further reassurance. "Definitely."

"Agreed," Tom said, coming over with a cup of coffee in his hand.

"Can't be a coincidence," Tamara said.

Tom agreed. "What do we have that links the two cases, though." He placed a hand on Eric's shoulder and pointed at the folder alongside him on the desk with his forefinger, still holding his steaming coffee cup in that hand. "Anything at all?"

Eric frowned, shaking his head. "Not that I can see. The lad who hanged himself was a fifteen-year-old by the name of Ciaran Haverson. I don't see any link to Felgate at all. They lived in different towns, different ages. Felgate's own children are years younger so they wouldn't have crossed paths at school. However, there is one similarity that is a little scary; Felgate died two days after the anniversary of the suicide."

Tom thought about it, his eyebrows knitting. "Okay, let's look at it from another angle. Assume for now Felgate had no connection with the suicide but he was a journalist. Perhaps he was looking into the suicide, or the events leading up to it?"

"To what end?" Tamara asked.

Tom shrugged. "What do we know about the suicide, Eric?"

Eric picked up the case notes, scanning them to refresh his

memory of the details. "He was found early one morning by a local taking his dog for a walk – so that's the same – he was found naked. His clothes were recovered, following a fingertip search of the area, a quarter of a mile away dumped under some bushes."

"Any sign of foul play?" Tamara asked.

Eric shook his head. "He had some abrasions on the knuckles of his right hand but aside from that, no injuries other than those consistent with death by hanging."

"And Haverson himself; what was said about him at the time?"

"Um … troubled teenager, suffered from depression. He struggled at school … parents had a fractious relationship, so his home environment wasn't positive … found social situations awkward." Eric glanced up at Tamara, "Sounds like the average adolescent to me."

Cassie caught Eric's eye. "You're about five minutes older than that kid was, so you'd know." Eric smiled. The two of them were always keen to mock each other and clearly, since Eric's forced absence from the team, they'd missed one another.

"How did the coroner rule?" Tom asked. Eric snapped back to attention, scanning through the file with his index and forefinger.

"Here it is – the coroner ruled an open verdict," Eric said, surprised. "It's clear to me, from what's written here anyway, that the investigating officers thought it a suicide. Strange. I wonder how he came to that conclusion."

"Presumably an autopsy was performed?" Tom asked.

Eric returned to the file, producing a photocopy of the pathologist's notes and holding it aloft.

Tom looked at Tamara. "Do you think it's worth revisiting the autopsy to see if anything was missed?"

"How long ago was all of this, Eric?" she asked.

"Eighteen years, almost to the day."

"See if the pathologist is still around," she said, eyeing the report. "Although, after this amount of time they'll probably be retired—"

"Norfolk's a lovely place to retire to, though," Tom said, cracking a smile. "It would be nice to get a first-hand account rather than just having to pick over old copy."

"I'm on it," Eric said, looking at the cover sheet. "Paging Dr Alistair Langford—"

"Who?" Tom asked, exchanging a glance with Tamara.

"Lang," Tamara said. Eric and Cassie both looked confused. "Felgate had a meeting the week before last with *Lang*, he'd written it in his diary."

Tom tapped Eric gently on the shoulder. "Quick as you can, Eric. Find us Dr Langford."

THE ADDRESS ERIC gave Tom took him to a chalet-style house in an elevated position on the outskirts of Sheringham overlooking the sea. On the coast it was proving to be a beautiful, crisp winter day. A stiff breeze blowing in off the sea made it feel way below zero but even without it, it was a day to wrap up. A Land Rover Discovery was parked in the driveway and Tom saw a small boat on a trailer undercover, beneath a carport to one side of the house. Cassie joined him as he made his way to the front door.

The door opened before they reached the porch, greeted with a warm smile by an elderly man with wispy white hair.

"You must be Detective Inspector Janssen?" he said.

Tom produced his identification but Dr Langford waved it away without looking at it.

"Do come in," he said, beckoning them to enter and stepping back into the house. They entered, Cassie closing the door. Dr Langford stood to one side, aided by a cane which he leaned on for support. He was dressed in cream trousers and a burgundy woollen cardigan, buttoned up to his chest.

"Thank you for seeing us on such short notice."

"No trouble at all. It's nice to have a foot back in the game, so to speak," Langford said, grinning. The lines on his face were amplified by the smile and Tom noted liver spots forming on his brow close to the hairline. Their host ushered them through the house. The hall was clad in pine, stained a dark brown. The house decor was all very sixties in both style and substance. A large yellow paper lantern, in the shape of a ball, hung above them illuminating the hall. It was necessary despite the bright sunshine outside because the combination of the pine cladding and matching Sapele doors sucked the natural light out of the narrow passage.

Langford took them through to an open-plan kitchen and dining room, wrapping around the rear of the house, with floor-to-ceiling windows overlooking the garden. The sixties feel continued in here, the kitchen looking like it hadn't been updated since the house was built. They declined the offer of tea and took a seat before an open fire.

"When did you retire?" Tom asked, while Cassie took out her notebook.

Langford eased himself into his chair, looking unsteady on his feet while doing so and let out a relieved sigh when he was able to set aside his cane.

"Fifteen years ago." He frowned. "I still miss it. I shouldn't have let myself be pushed out of the door."

"They made you retire?" Tom asked.

Langford grinned. "Not work, no. My good lady wife thought it time I took it a little easier."

"Ah, I see," Tom said smiling and looking around. He hadn't seen anyone else. Langford followed Tom's gaze, then reached to his right and picked up a framed photograph, offering it to Tom. It was a picture of a woman, she had long blonde hair and a kind smile.

"I'm afraid Sally passed a few years ago now. This was her favourite spot," he pointed to the fireplace, "right here beside the fire. You can't beat it on a winter day like this."

"I'm so sorry," Tom said, returning the photograph. Langford put it back in the same spot, repositioning it several times. Tom guessed he was a man of detail, unsurprising judging by the profession he worked in. "We would like to talk to you about one of your old cases."

"Yes, yes. Your young detective constable said that." Langford, elbows on the arms of his chair, brought his hands together and formed a steeple with his fingers. "But he was reticent to tell me which one. It was all very cloak and dagger."

"I wouldn't quite put it that way," Tom said, smiling.

"Oh, please don't take this away from me, Inspector. It's the most excitement I've had in years. Lawn bowls and weekly bridge games don't really cut it anymore."

"What about sailing?" Tom said, looking to his left as if he could see through the walls of the house towards the boat outside.

Langford laughed dryly, gently tapping his knee. "Sadly, those days are behind me. When my children visit, in the summer, we often take the boat out but even they tell me I should sell it and be done with my time on the water! If I had my choice, when the time comes," his expression took on a faraway look, "I think I would rather like the prospect of being buried at sea."

"Why?" Cassie asked. "If you don't mind me asking?"

"Not at all, young lady. I'm not sure really, but I think it looks like fun, don't you?"

"I–I suppose so," Cassie said, evidently amused.

"Now, which case can I help you with?"

"Ciaran Haverson," Tom said. Langford's smile faded.

CHAPTER NINE

"REALLY? The young Haverson suicide; popular choice," Langford said, the lines in his forehead deepening further. "You're the second ones to ask me about that case recently. It's like waiting for a bus to come along. Not that I do that very much. Public transport – predictable, functional but expensive and not very comfortable." Tom held out his hands, encouraging him to continue. "It was a journalist who visited me, a chap called Farthing or something … now, when was it?" He pursed his lips, cupping his chin with thumb and forefinger and thinking hard. "I believe it was a week, maybe ten days ago. Something like that anyway."

"And he was asking about Ciaran Haverson?"

Langford nodded enthusiastically.

"What was he asking about specifically?"

"He wanted to go over my conclusions based on my autopsy notes, but he didn't reference anything specific that I recall." He frowned. "I don't know why, I couldn't tell him anything different to what it said in my write-up, and it was all read out at the poor boy's inquest by the coroner."

"Do you know if he was also planning to speak to the coroner?"

"Not that I'm aware of, but he wouldn't have had any joy there. Colin passed away a number of years ago."

"Colin being the coroner?" Tom asked. Langford confirmed it with a nod. "As we understand it, this journalist was usually writing lifestyle pieces rather than following up on this type of case. What was his angle, do you know?"

"No idea whatsoever, I'm afraid," Langford said, splaying his hands wide. "I asked him, of course, but all I could get from him was that he was coming at it from a new angle."

"What angle?" Cassie asked.

Langford sat forward, meeting her eye. "Didn't say." He sat back again. "I imagine he was writing a book about it or something. Isn't that what journalists do? Particularly when they are bored with writing fluff pieces."

"*Fluff pieces*?" Cassie repeated.

"Yes, all that guff about interior design and homemade candles and the like will drive anyone mad." Tom offered him a quizzical expression. "I looked up this Gareth Furlong chap after he'd left. You can find most things online now. I would be looking for something more interesting to write about if I were him too."

Tom couldn't help but notice Langford's short-term memories suffered with accuracy issues; he could only hope those from the past would fare better.

"One thing that stood out to me regarding the Haverson suicide was the coroner's verdict..."

"An open verdict rather than suicide?" Langford asked. Tom nodded. "Well, that's not so hard to understand when you think about it. Although every indication pointed towards the poor lad having taken his own life, the lack of the deceased's clothing being found anywhere near the body – along with the graze to the knuckles – indicated the possible presence of another person. That possibility left Colin with no alternative but to deliver an open verdict."

"I see," Tom said, putting his hands together, gently rubbing one palm against the other. "I've read your autopsy notes already but it pays to hear things first hand."

"That's exactly what Fulford said too."

"Right. So, in your mind, you didn't have any doubts as to the case being a suicide?"

"Well … your notes can't always convey all of your thoughts, can they, Inspector? I mean, people like us, we deal in facts and leave supposition to others, don't we?"

Tom fixed his eye on the retired pathologist. "Humour me if you don't mind? I know what you wrote but what did you think?"

"An amateur job, I must say… to put it bluntly." His expression clouded. "A good hangman's noose should be able to break the neck," he demonstrated with his hands, pulling one clenched fist away from the other in a rapid upward motion, "but this one was nowhere near up to the task. The rope was neither tightly pulled against the neck nor thick enough, in my opinion. Not that I am an expert in such endeavours. I fear the poor lad slowly strangled to the death … until the delight of asphyxiation finally took him." Langford sat in silence for a few moments, seemingly lost in thought. He looked at Tom. "To answer your question candidly, I cannot say with any certainty whether young Haverson took his own life, but I was left with an uneasy feeling. And that hasn't left me to this day."

"What troubles you about it?"

"Although the tying of the noose was all wrong, therefore indicative of a novice which adds weight to the theory of suicide, there were other factors that led me to speculate otherwise. For instance, the boy's clothing."

"It was found some distance away."

"Quite right, Inspector," he wagged a pointed finger in the air before him, "a quarter of a mile away, hidden under some brush according to the search team. Why would Ciaran remove his clothes on a chilly November night and walk, or run, naked to his chosen spot. Couple that with the lack of mud on the soles of the boy's feet, irrespective of the frosty ground, I find it surprising that he was considered to have covered the ground from where his clothes were found to the location of his death barefoot. I've seen all manner of suicides over the years – and some are indeed bizarre – but this one stood out for me."

"Giving weight to the suicide theory, however, was that I could find no evidence of trauma elsewhere on the body; no sign of a struggle, defensive wounds or trace evidence under fingernails, no sign of sexual assault … nothing that one could reasonably expect to find in the event of a suspicious death. There were abrasions on his neck, caused by the rope, but they were at the correct angle to denote a hanging, as opposed to a strangulation and then a subsequent hanging. It is quite easy to tell the difference from a professional point of view." He shook his head. "No, no, Ciaran Haverson went to that place willingly, or at the very least without putting up a physical argument about it."

"What about the graze on the knuckles? Couldn't that be considered a defensive injury; the result of a scuffle maybe?"

"Possibly, yes," Langford said, nodding. "But with no other DNA or signs to reinforce the idea, it is unlikely. How could a teenager be forced up a ladder or clamber up a tree without there being more evidence for it. The absence of a ladder or other method of getting into the air was also troublesome. Maybe he climbed the tree and jumped from the branch but the abrasions on his neck, particularly with such a loose rope, didn't support that theory, so how did he do it? Then there were the contents of his stomach."

"What about them?"

"He'd recently eaten. Not a full meal but he'd filled up on junk food, crisps, chocolate bars and the like. That's not the behaviour of someone planning a suicide attempt – an impulsive overdose in a fit of depression perhaps, but not a scenario like this one. He also had alcohol in his bloodstream, but it was only point zero four, certainly not enough to consider him intoxicated to the point of impaired thought or irrational bouts of behaviour, regardless of how young he was. I recall he was a slightly-built young man, below average height for his age but, in my opinion, he would easily be able to process what he had in his system."

"Just so that we are clear," Tom said, "you don't believe Ciaran was alone on Roydon Common that night?"

Langford shook his head. "Unlikely ... but it is speculation. I cannot prove it either way. That is a conclusion drawn only from viewing the evidence within my scope though. Colin, the assigned coroner, had access to much more information than I did, the boy's background, his interpersonal relationships along with his state of mind at the time. He was ... a mixed-up child."

"And did you speak of all of this with Gavin Felgate?"

"Who?" Langford's eyes narrowed momentarily. "Oh, the journalist. Yes, yes, I did. I appreciate dragging all of this up again after this amount of time will be traumatic for the relatives, but if the man was writing a book anyway, then I may as well be as open and frank as possible. Particularly if someone else was present that night."

Tom passed him one of his contact cards. "I appreciate you taking the time to speak to us. If you remember anything else you think might be pertinent, please give me a call."

Langford accepted the card, holding it aloft and squinting to read it. "Haven't got my glasses on," he said, frowning. "No matter. I'm happy to be of use. It's been a long time since I could say that. Are you reopening the case?"

"Haverson?" Tom asked. Langford nodded. "No, we are investigating something else."

"How delightfully interesting, Inspector. And this ... Felgate fellow is doing likewise?"

Tom shook his head, standing up. "We are following a different inquiry. Again, thank you for your time."

They showed themselves out. Tom mulling over what they'd heard, trying to decide how credible the retired patholo-gist's speculative thoughts were.

"Penny for them?" Cassie asked, drawing her jacket about her, as they walked back to the car.

"I'm thinking just as much about what was going through Felgate's mind as I am about Langford's theories."

"How so?"

"What was his interest – Felgate's? I mean, a teenage suicide is undoubtedly tragic, but statistically quite common, so why this one and why now?"

"True, a lot of time has passed. What's brought it to mind?"

Tom stopped, turning himself away from the wind and thrusting his hands into his pockets. "We need to revisit the Haverson suicide."

Cassie shook her head. "That'll not be easy. There wasn't a lot to go on back then and it was *ages* ago."

"I know," Tom said. "But specifically, where did he get the alcohol from? It was probably the same place he bought the food; that's not the type of snacks you take with you when you head out for an evening. You'll pick that type of thing up when you're out and about."

"I didn't see many convenience shops around Roydon

Common," Cassie said. "What about the actual village? I've never been, is there a shop there?"

Tom shrugged. "Petrol station, sure, but we'll have to see if it has a licence to sell alcohol ... and whether it did back then. There's a village shop in nearby Grimston as well, but it's not the place to sell to minors."

"So, we're looking into an eighteen-year-old suicide as well now?"

He smiled, gesturing for them to resume their walk to the car. "Do you still think it was a suicide?"

Cassie grimaced but didn't press it. When they came to the car, she looked back at the house, nodding her head towards it.

"Why didn't you tell Langford what happened to Felgate? He was itching to know what we are investigating."

Tom smiled. "I know he was but," he followed her gaze back to the house, "we're police officers. We ask more questions than we give answers. Until we have a better handle on what this is all about, I want to keep it that way."

CHAPTER TEN

THE PATHOLOGY LAB WAS COLD, every movement creating an exaggerated sound reverberating off the solid surfaces. A body lay on a stainless-steel post-mortem table in the centre of the room covered in a light blue sheet. Cassie, standing next to Tom, shuddered.

"These places give me the creeps," she said quietly.

"You'd be a bit strange if they didn't," Tom said.

"How long is Dr Death going to keep us waiting do you think?" she said just as the door opened and a flustered Dr Tim Paxton hurried through, a clutch of papers and two folders under his arms.

"Sorry ... sorry, to keep you waiting, Tom," he said in passing, crossing to a desk against the far wall and carefully unburdening himself. "I had a quick call to make which led to a longer call, more questions and ..." He waved away his excuse, coming back to stand with them and smiling at Cassie. "DS Knight. Lovely to see you again."

"And you, Dr Paxton." She deferentially bowed her head slightly, a motion the pathologist eyed warily. The polite acknowledgements of one another aside, they didn't get on.

Tom judged that Cassie was a little too outspoken for Dr Paxton, him having made several references to her nature on previous occasions. Only to Tom, mind you, and never in front of Cassie herself. Tom figured he wasn't brave enough to do that. He was confident the feeling was mutual. Tom indicated the body on the table.

"Gavin Felgate?"

"Indeed, yes," Paxton said, walking to the head of the table and pulling back the sheet in a slow, controlled manner. "Not the most interesting of specimens you have ever delivered to me, Tom."

"Sorry about that," Cassie said dryly, "we'll try to find a more interesting victim for you next time."

"Sarcasm, DS Knight, will get you nowhere. Didn't your parents ever tell you that?"

"Often gets me a free drink at the bar, though," she retorted with an accompanying wink. Paxton turned his back on her, Tom casting her a disapproving look that only she would see. She whispered, "Well, it does, depending on who's behind the bar anyway."

"Gavin Felgate; a fifty-four-year-old male with no significant underlying health condition. However," Paxton said, clicking his tongue against the roof of his mouth, "with that said, he was not exactly a supreme example of the species for his age." He looked at Tom with a sideways smile. "He was generally in a poor state of health; early signs of cirrhosis in the liver, indicative of being a man prone to bouts of overindulging."

"We are led to believe he drank a fair bit," Tom said.

"That would be my guess, but the lack of inflammation or swelling suggests he hasn't been doing so recently."

"That's interesting," Tom said. "How about on the night of his death?"

Paxton shook his head. "Sober. There was no alcohol in his blood at all. Fiona was correct regarding the time of death; I have set it at between midnight and one in the morning. The lack of cloud cover and freezing temperatures leave a little leeway to the timings, so that is my best guess."

"Cause of death?"

"The result of a single blow to the head," Paxton said with a forlorn expression, leaning in to Felgate's face and pointing to the man's nose which was depressed and very obviously broken."

"One blow?" Cassie asked, sceptical.

"Oh yes, my dear. Believe me, one blow can be more than enough and it doesn't even need to be a particularly forceful blow if delivered correctly. And when I say correctly, I only mean in a manner that could lead to this eventuality." Cassie frowned. Tom had heard it was possible but had never come across such an instance in his career. As he understood it, these outcomes usually resulted from a victim falling to the ground and suffering a severe concussion from their impact with a kerb or a wall as they fell, not likely in an open field, even if the ground underfoot was deeply frozen. Dr Paxton glanced between them, the beginnings of a smile edging up at the corners of his mouth. "Is this a day for forensic scepticism, Detective Inspector?" Tom shook his head. "Good. It isn't so hard to comprehend once you understand how the brain works in conjunction with the spinal cord and its protective casing – the human skull." He straightened up, holding his left hand out flat in front of him, palm up. He placed his balled right fist on the left. "Imagine the brain as a jelly on a plate. If you shake the plate hard enough the jelly will also shake, slamming back and forth into the surrounding bone of the skull, and after a time it will begin to tear. When the brain *rattles* around inside the skull in this way, like a bouncy ball in a small irregular space – the skull with its facial bones – the neurons and cells that make up the soft brain tissue can be damaged. In this instance, the trauma of the blow and probably an awkward fall caused the victim's brain stem – a small part of the brain no larger than your thumb," he offered them the thumbs-up sign to visualise, "to tear away from where it connects to the spinal cord."

"And that was enough to kill him?" Tom said, looking down at Felgate.

"Oh yes, easily enough to kill him. Among other things the brain stem is responsible for autonomic nervous system functions such as regulating the body's breathing, heartbeat and digestion. Such damage can be life threatening if not dealt with immediately."

"Fiona Williams didn't find any evidence of a struggle prior to death. Does that still hold?"

Paxton nodded his agreement. "I found no other wounds, bruises or abrasions, no cuts or visible damage to the knuckles on either hand to imply a trading of blows. Nor was there any trace evidence under the fingernails that might tell you who else was with him that night ... sorry," Paxton said, smiling apologetically. "I would even hazard a guess that the first blow was the only one in this exchange," he paused, looking thoughtful, "although if it was the only blow, then it can't really be labelled an exchange, can it? Never mind. At any rate, one blow and he would have died shortly afterwards."

"Can you at least say whether he was struck with a weapon, and if so what type?" Cassie asked. The two of them were quite capable of remaining professional, setting aside personal feelings for the sake of their work. Paxton thought hard.

"I've considered this," he said, scratching absently at his chin. "I found traces of soil in the face wound and I did wonder if someone had picked up a branch from the ground and used it to strike him," he made a downward motion with his right arm, "but I put the presence of it down to him landing face down in the earth and rolling. If he'd been struck with a branch or log, a spontaneous attack, if you will, then there would also be minute splinters of wood in the wound. If he was struck with a weapon brought to the scene by the killer, it would need to have been heavy, smooth, and probably easy to conceal."

"Why do you think so?" Tom asked, his curiosity piqued.

"The lack of defensive wounds of any kind ... the solitary blow ... points to a surprise attack for me. I don't think this poor soul saw it coming."

"Lured there unawares, perhaps?" Cassie said.

"Conjecture," Paxton said, with no admonishment attached to the comment. "I couldn't say that either way but no one stands there waiting to be struck. If they do, then they are very foolish indeed."

"True," Tom said, "or they felt unable to act in their defence for some reason." Paxton inclined his head, acknowledging the logic. "Other than that?"

"Other than that," Paxton said, frowning, "I can tell you what Mr Felgate had for his dinner at approximately eight o'clock that evening – a tandoori chicken meal, vegetable fried rice – Basmati no less, if I had to guess – and a naan bread, but the fried aspect makes it rather less healthy than the boiled alternative."

That confirmed what they already thought giving the purchase of the takeaway meal added importance. They could do with finding the person who took the order or made the delivery.

"How much had he eaten?" Tom asked. Paxton looked at him quizzically. "We know a takeaway was purchased and consumed at his address the night he died, but if he ate alone then he—"

"Would have had a healthy appetite, yes I understand," Dr Paxton said, crossing to his desk and returning with his notes. He put his glasses on and began reading through his hand-written notes. "I'm sorry, I transcribed these from my voice recording only an hour ago and forgot some of the finer details. Ah ... here we are." He stood in silence, his brow furrowing as he went back over what he'd written. "I would say he consumed an above-average portion. Bearing in mind what he was already digesting and what was left in his stomach I would expect there to be leftovers. Does that match with what you found?"

Tom shook his head. "Not from what I saw in the containers although we'll have forensics go through the bins and check it wasn't thrown away."

"That would be a waste of a rather tasty meal, if that was the case."

"Sacrilege," Cassie said and both men looked at her. "Throwing away a takeaway. I enjoy a decent Indian."

"So do I, young lady," Paxton said, leaning forward and addressing her over the rim of his glasses, "but a home-cooked one is far more preferable to that of a takeaway."

"I wouldn't disagree," she said. "My Butter Chicken recipe is a culinary delight."

"Be advised, though, you should always rinse the rice prior to cooking, whichever method you choose," Paxton said. Cassie raised an eyebrow in query. "Arsenic. The natural levels found in rice are rather high. Rinsing prior to cooking reduces it. Heavy metal content should be restricted to musical prefer-ences for those desiring a longer life."

Cassie nodded slowly. "Thanks for the tip."

They left pathology, Dr Paxton promising to have the

formal report completed and sent over to them as quickly as possible.

"Dr Death was even weirder than usual today," Cassie said.

Tom glanced sideways as they walked. "I thought the two of you got on better today, or was that just me?" She shrugged. "What is it with you and him anyway?"

"I don't know," Cassie said. "I guess I'd find anyone who seems to take so much pleasure in death quite creepy."

"I wouldn't say he takes pleasure in it, but he's diligent in his job."

"Yeah, exactly – creepy," she said, pushing open the door to the car park and allowing Tom to go first. He smiled as he passed, shaking his head. The breeze was picking up but the skies were still clear. It was going to be another cold night. "Never trust anyone who surrounds themselves with dead people, that's what my old mum used to say."

"Did she?" Tom asked, his mobile ringing. He took it out of his pocket, looking at the screen and seeing it was Eric.

"Nah, not really," she said with a smile. "My mam would never be so profound. She'd probably recommend a good take-away, mind you."

"Hi Eric, we're just leaving pathology and heading back in. What's up?"

"We've got forensics back from the crime scene. I thought you'd want to know as soon as possible. The rope – the one used to tie the noose with – the fingerprints have come back and we have a match."

"Excellent. What's the name?"

"That's just it," Eric said, sounding dejected. "One set of prints and they belong to Gavin Felgate."

Tom stopped in his stride, almost lost for words. Cassie looked over at him, curious.

"Okay, do me a favour would you, Eric? Can you tell me

how much food waste was dumped in the kitchen bin, if any?"

"In the … um … right, hang on." The thump of the receiver being put down on a desk was followed by typing on a keyboard. Then Eric was back. "The bins hadn't been emptied for a few days based on what was in them. D–Do you want me to run through the contents?"

"Specifically relating to the takeaway food purchased on the night."

"Ah, right. Yes, of course," Eric said, his tone lightening. "Er … minimal. Is that what you were … expecting?"

"Someone was with Gavin Felgate at his house that night."

"Yes, we have more fingerprints taken from the cutlery, plates and a glass but there are no matches in the system for them."

"I want family members fingerprinted for comparison and dismissal. And I want to know who the mystery woman was who has been seen at his home recently."

"And every contact in his mobile phone call history, I'm with you," Eric said.

"That's it, Eric. Keep going."

He hung up. Cassie waited expectantly.

"Felgate tied the noose himself," Tom said, slipping his mobile back into his pocket.

"Say that again," Cassie said. "Why would he do that? You don't think he was going to kill himself, do you?"

Tom shrugged. "If he was, then why would someone try and kill him? Why kill a man about to kill himself?"

"You wouldn't, obviously," Cassie said. "How about accidentally killing a man when trying to stop them killing themselves? That's beyond ridiculous."

"And from what I've seen so far, Felgate doesn't strike me as a man looking to end it all."

"Weird," Cassie said, opening the car door and getting in.

CHAPTER ELEVEN

DCI TAMARA GREAVE hesitated as she raised her hand to knock on the door. Never one to experience apprehension when summoned to come before a senior officer, this was unusual. The same could be said for the chief superintendent's tone when he'd called her shortly after the morning briefing. Taking a breath, she gently knocked and received a call to enter. Opening the door, she walked in purposefully; grateful to only see Chief Superintendent Collins present in the office, sitting behind his desk.

"Good morning, sir."

"Tamara, excellent. Come in," he said, offering her a warm smile by way of greeting. "Do sit down."

She picked up the nearest chair and set it down opposite him, feeling a measure of anxiety. Something about Collins was wrong, his demeanour, tone... something.

"What can I do for you, sir?"

He sat forward, resting his elbows on the desk before him, making a show of shuffling some papers on the desk. "I just wanted to ... touch base with you on this suspicious death down in King's Lynn."

"Roydon Common?"

"Yes, indeed. How is the investigation coming along?"

The question was fairly open, not particularly probing but she sensed hesitancy on his part.

"Early days," she said, not wishing to pre-empt the direction of the inquiry. She was keen to hear what Tom and Cassie would have learned from their trip to pathology and the early forensic reports were intriguing, if a little baffling. They certainly weren't in any position to be definitive on any aspect at this time. The fact the chief superintendent was so interested was curious. "But we have several lines of enquiry to follow up on."

"That's good to know." Collins frowned, pursing his lips and absently touching the mouse next to his keyboard, moving it to the right. "It was ... my understanding that this could well be a suicide gone awry. Is that a feasible hypothesis?"

She was curious as to how he came by this theory as it wasn't given serious consideration by her team. She shook her head. "Early signs would indicate that isn't the case. May I ask what your interest is?" The question was asked more directly than perhaps it should have been, particularly in light of the stern expression that came her way from Collins and she tried to recover by adding a smile. It didn't soften the look he gave her.

"I would like you to remember we took that case as a favour to our colleagues," he said pensively. "And when we do favours it doesn't pay to make a mess, if you follow."

"Not really, sir, no." Tamara's reply was genuine.

"Your team have been asking questions related to a former investigation, into the suicide of Ciaran Haverson. Why is that?"

Tamara was caught by surprise. How on earth did he know that? Her facial expression must have conveyed the unspoken question. "It may be related to the suspicious death of Gavin Felgate."

"Am I correct in thinking that he was a journalist?"

She nodded. "Yes, he was."

"And his interest in the Haverson case was what exactly?"

She shook her head. "At this time, we can't say, sir. But he was asking some questions and he died—"

"At the same location," Collins said, chewing on his lower lip.

She confirmed it with a nod. "It would appear so."

"That was a traumatic investigation for everyone concerned. It would be a shame to have to rake all of that up again."

"I agree, sir. We are still building a picture."

"Please ... tread carefully, Tamara."

"We will, sir."

He held her gaze for a few moments, and just as she began to feel uncomfortable under his scrutiny, he slowly lowered his eyes to the papers on his desk.

"Keep me advised."

HESITATING at the entrance to the ops room, Tamara could hear Tom speaking with Cassie and Eric. The brief chat with the chief superintendent had left her with an uneasy feeling but she had no idea why. Her mobile beeped. It was a text message from her mum. She swiped it away from her screen without opening it and entered ops. Tom looked up, pausing, but she waved him on, perching herself on the edge of a desk at the rear intent on catching up.

"Right," Tom said, "we have two lines of approach I want to take at the moment. Eric, I want you to find out what Gavin

Felgate was working on. His editor has told us what he was assigned to. In the meantime, Cassie and I will do the rounds speaking to the people he'd interviewed recently. Have you had Felgate's tech brought up from his house yet?"

Eric nodded. "We have his mobile, as you know, and I've already been onto his service provider. They're gathering his data together for us and sending it over later. I'll have his call and text message records going back three months by this afternoon. Anything beyond that and they'll have to access their archives but that shouldn't be a problem." Eric looked over his shoulder to where several archive boxes were set aside. "And I have the laptop from his house along with his work files to go through. What do you want me to focus on?"

"Look for the pieces he was supposed to be writing and also anything recent that no one else is talking about. His interest in the Haverson case may be purely journalistic or ... he might have had a different reason."

"Hold on," Tamara said. The three of them turned to her. "Are you suggesting there could be another reason, other than investigating the suicide?"

Tom nodded. "I know it is easy to think he was investigating it afresh, as per Dr Langford's suggestion, but his fingerprints being found on the noose suggests his interest could have been something altogether different entirely."

"That he was what – involved somehow?"

"Possibly," Tom said. "What was he doing tying that noose to the tree?"

"Recreating it?" Cassie asked. "To experience the scene for the writing of his book—"

"Or reliving it," Eric said quietly, "before doing another one."

Tom pointed to Eric. "We can't rule anything out."

Tamara was perplexed. "What did Dr Paxton have to say?"

"He's of the opinion that Felgate was not alone on the common, and that he was most likely assaulted," Tom said.

"But there's no evidence to prove it," Cassie added, pursing her lips. "And he had some food safety advice." Tamara shot her a quizzical look. "I'll tell you later, if you're interested?"

"So, Eric," Tom said, returning his attention to assigning tasks, "I want a list of Felgate's contacts, who he was talking to and how frequently. Then I want you to cross reference them against the Haverson suicide: family, school friends, neighbours ... if he had a paper round, everything you can find. How did you get on with the calls he made the night he died?"

Eric nodded. "No joy with the unregistered number. I called the taxi firm, though, and spoke to their coordinator. She told me a taxi was booked to pick him up from his home at ten-thirty that night."

"How far ahead of time?"

"Three days before, so it was planned and not booked on the fly."

"Destination?" Tom asked, eyeing the map pinned to the white board.

"Hunstanton," Eric said, shaking his head, "but no specific address, just heading to Hunstanton. She checked with the driver and he dropped him off on Sandringham Road just after eleven."

"That's close to where Felgate's family live," Tom said. "That places him almost a half -hour drive away from Roydon Common a couple of hours prior to his death."

Tamara came forward, hovering in front of the white board. "What about this takeaway order?" she asked.

"I spoke to them," Cassie said. "Felgate's order was phoned in by a man. Felgate's name was given and payment was made over the phone and the food was delivered three quarters of an hour later. Only one person was seen by the delivery driver; matches Felgate's description."

Tamara scanned the information once more before turning to Tom. "What are your plans regarding the Haverson suicide?"

Tom splayed his hands wide in an open gesture. "I think we've no choice but to review the original findings and try to work out Felgate's interest."

"I agree," Tamara said, "but do bear in mind this will attract a lot of attention. It already has done."

"Really? We haven't released Felgate's name to the press yet or described the manner in which he was found. Who's asking?"

Tamara glanced over her shoulder, seeing Cassie and Eric paying attention. She inclined her head. "We're stepping onto old ground; a closed case deemed a suicide by the initial investigators. That's all."

Tom held her eye for a moment and something unsaid passed between them. She was confident he understood when he didn't turn his attention back to the boards and didn't make further comment.

"Eric," Tom said, "where are you with gathering all the information on the Haverson case?"

"I've got the headlines here," he said, tapping a folder on his desk, "and the rest have been archived but I've requested them."

"Good. I thought Cassie and I should go and speak with David Fysh seeing as he was Felgate's current assignment. Then we have an author to speak to," Tom said, glancing at his watch.

Tamara was lost in thought. She realised Tom was watching her.

"Sorry, Tom, what did you say?"

"Cassie and I will go and speak with Felgate's last two interviewees, unless you have an alternative approach you'd rather we take?"

"No, you go ahead," she said. "Let me know how you get on."

CHAPTER TWELVE

CALLING in at the registered office of David Fysh's catering business saw Tom and Cassie redirected to a restaurant located on Hunstanton High Street. The business must have been undergoing a refurbishment because they had to squeeze past a painting and decorating team packing up their gear as they arrived. Tom identified themselves to a member of staff who politely disappeared from view towards the rear, returning a couple of minutes later with a man in tow.

Tom took his measure. He was younger than expected for someone with numerous successful businesses to his name, in his early to mid-thirties and athletic. Dressed in a slim-cut light-grey suit, a pristine white shirt with the top two buttons undone, and a hint of a necklace beneath, Tom wondered if it was summertime on the Algarve rather than progressing through a bitter Norfolk winter as they currently were.

"Hello," Fysh said, offering his hand and shaking both of theirs in turn with an accompanying warm smile. "My office called to say the police had been round but," his eyes darted between them, "I thought it must be a wind up. What can I do for you?"

Tom returned the smile. "We would like to talk to you about an interview you gave recently."

"The one with Gavin?"

"You remember?"

"Of course," he said. "Believe me, I don't get interviewed very often and it was a cracking piece of free advertising for the opening of this place."

"It's new?" Tom asked, looking around. "Not a redecoration?"

"Just the exterior signage to go up," Fysh said. A clatter came from out of sight, presumably in the kitchen. Fysh frowned. "And some teething problems with the chef." Tom raised his eyebrows in query but the comment was dismissed. "Gearing up for a soft opening later tonight; last minute jitters."

"Soft opening?" Cassie asked.

"Yes, we open officially this coming weekend but we have a few chosen guests coming for dinner tonight, to test the menus, build up a head of steam and so on. Call it a trial run."

"So, if anything goes wrong, it doesn't matter," Cassie said.

"I wouldn't say that. Some of those coming tonight will be leaving reviews or recommending us to their circles of influence. There's still a lot riding on it."

He gestured for them to take a seat at one of the tables, offering them a coffee but both declined.

"Shame, the machine is brand new. It produces a lovely espresso."

"How many restaurants do you have, Mr Fysh?" Tom asked.

"This will be our third," he said, beaming. "Up until fairly recently, we've been focussing on supplying to the trade. My father used to be a greengrocer, doing a little bit to supply local restaurants but when he handed me the reins, I really pushed it." He sat back, flexing his arms in a way to loosen his shoulders. He was evidently proud of his success. And why shouldn't he be? "Once the business expanded, I picked up several government contracts to supply care homes, local schools and council premises. Then I saw there was room in the market for us to do more; bring it all in house so to speak, from the supply to production and finally hospitality itself. The first restaurant was more of an upmarket cafe-cum-brasserie and it did well, so we moved to a restaurant and now here. I have to say we have been very fortunate."

Tom cast an eye around the interior. "It's looking good, I must say. May I ask what the thrust of this article was going to be?"

"Gavin's?" he asked, nodding. "Sure. He was keen to look at our approach to employment." Another round of clattering sounded and Fysh glanced back over his shoulder, shouting emanated from somewhere. Fysh shook his head. "Sorry about that. I hope they get their game faces on later!" He shook his head. "Lost my train of thought…"

"Staffing," Tom said.

"Right, yeah. Well, we see ourselves as a core element of the community. This is a small town and although we get seasonal workers from all over, we need to operate all year round and not just in peak season. Things invariably slow down in the winter, so we just have to tick over with the locals but people need jobs, have families to feed and so on. You hear it all the time, right; coastal communities losing their youth to the draw of the bigger cities with their opportunities? We think you need to create jobs for local people from all walks of life and give them opportunities."

"Do you find a lot of young people want to work in catering?" Cassie asked. Fysh met her eye, seemingly assessing whether her question was genuine. Cassie noticed. "I just mean the hours aren't exactly sociable, are they? And hospitality hasn't got the best reputation for meeting the living wage, has it? Besides that, it's damned hard work."

Fysh inclined his head to one side, rolling his tongue across the inside of his cheek. "Fair comment, but we pay above the market rate to our staff, wherever possible. But," he wagged a pointed finger in Cassie's direction, "we don't only offer opportunities to the local youth. We have partnership links with a number of organisations and charities who help people back into the workforce."

"What type of people are you referring to?" Tom asked.

"We offer paid work experience, internships and apprenticeships to all manner of people from children with disadvantaged backgrounds, those recovering from substance abuse or addictions ... and some of those who you have crossed paths with, in your line of work."

"Some people would consider that to be a brave policy?" Cassie asked.

Fysh shrugged. "Some might say that but let's face it, we can all use a bit of help from time to time and show me someone who has never made a mistake in their life and I'll show you a liar!"

Cassie tilted her head to one side thoughtfully. "Admirable ... but still a gamble."

He laughed. "That's fair comment, but remember, we didn't do this all-in-one hit, it was a gradual process. I approached a local charity to see if there was anything we could do to work with them and it went from there. Last year I was shortlisted for a *Developer of People Award*."

"Has Gavin Felgate provided you with the draft of his article?" Tom asked. "And do you retain any editorial control over what gets published?"

Fysh sat back in his seat, focussing on Tom. Lifting his

hands from the table he turned them palms up, his lips parting slightly. "Why on earth would I need ..." He looked between them. "What's all this about?"

"Gavin Felgate has been found dead and the circumstances leading up to it require investigation. As we understand it, you were the last person, professionally speaking, who he came into contact with.

"Wow!" Fysh said, shocked. "I–I ... just, wow." He shook his head, then raised a closed fist to his mouth and absently bit the end of his thumbnail. "I don't see how that could be related to me." He met Tom's eye. "Gavin spoke with me for an hour or so and then spent a bit of time talking to the staff, hearing their thoughts about what we do around here."

"And was it here that you met with him, here in the restaurant?" Tom asked, looking around.

Fysh nodded. "This place has dominated my time recently. I've barely been anywhere else, to be honest."

"It must be hard," Cassie said, "managing multiple separate enterprises, even if they broadly operate in and around the same field? Stressful. Spinning a lot of plates."

Fysh sniffed hard, angling his head to one side. "Yes and no," he said quietly. "I have a terrific team working with me. And I have learnt to delegate."

"Whose business is it?" Tom asked. "You said you took over from your father."

"Yes, I did. He is in semi-retirement now; although," he laughed nervously, "he was supposed to be *in retirement* but maybe I won't care to step away when the time comes and my son is champing at the bit."

"And how does he feel about your radical approach to expanding his life's work?"

"People don't like change," he said, raising an eyebrow. "Sometimes I think he would have been happier if I was still knocking out fruit and veg from single premises but," he shook his head, "times have changed and people don't shop like that anymore. You either adapt and evolve or you go under. As long as his dividends keep coming, I'm sure he'll be fine."

"How old is your son?" Cassie asked.

Fysh smiled. "My son? He'll be two in three weeks."

"That'll be tough for him growing up." Fysh looked at her quizzically. "Having a birthday so close to Christmas. That happened to someone I knew, born around Christmas and I think he felt pretty hard done by over the years."

Fysh smiled but it struck Tom as artificial. The pride and confidence were less visible now, but Tom couldn't fathom why?

"We will need a list of all those employees Gavin Felgate spoke to," Tom said. Fysh frowned but then he accepted the request with a curt nod. "We need to know what was said. And we would like that before we leave."

"Really? I mean, I am very busy."

"One more question before you get that for us," Tom said. "Can you tell me where you were between eleven o'clock and one in the morning this past Monday night into Tuesday morning?"

His mouth fell open, lips moving slightly but making no sound. "I–I beg your pardon."

"Where were you?"

"At home ... in bed." Fysh smiled, incredulous. You can't think I—"

"We have to ask," Tom said. "And where do you live?"

"Wiveton," he said, scoffing. "Ask my wife, if you must."

"Thank you," Tom said. "We may well do that in the coming days." Tom held the man's gaze until Fysh looked away. A member of the kitchen staff hovered in the background, seemingly nervous about coming over and interrupting. The restaurateur drummed his fingers on the table, glancing up at Tom.

"Is there anything else," he said, looking over his shoulder, "or can I—"

"Just that list of staff members," Tom said.

"Right, yes." He patted the flat of one hand on the table. "Of course." He stood up and Tom caught his eye.

"As well as their contact details, address and telephone numbers, please."

Fysh rolled his tongue along the edge of his lower lip. "Yes, of course."

He walked into the rear of the restaurant, the member of staff falling into step alongside him and asking questions as they went. Tom watched them go, mulling over the conversation. Cassie blew out her cheeks.

"That article never seeing the light of day may be a blessed relief."

David Fysh disappeared from view and Tom glanced at her. "How do you mean?"

"Not exactly interesting, is it? Maybe use it as a sedative."

"Cynic!"

"Oh, come on!" she said. "Guy goes from selling fruit and veg to selling more fruit and veg, along with a few restaurants – selling fruit and veg alongside hot food. A fascinating read."

"Creating opportunities for those who might otherwise be overlooked, though," Tom said. "Commendable."

"Did you catch the *we pay the living wage where possible* bit? Ten-to-one he exploits people who can't find work anywhere else."

Tom looked at her with a sideways smile. "You're making bets lavishly at the moment. Am I paying you too much?"

"No danger of that, is there?" Cassie said, grinning.

"The person you mentioned – the one born around

Christmas – is that true?" Tom asked as he caught sight of
David Fysh stepping out from the kitchen, a sheet of paper in
his hands. He met Tom's eye, glanced at the paper in his hand
and hesitated.

"Sort of," Cassie said.

"Sort of?" Tom watched as Fysh started towards them. He
said under his breath, glancing at Cassie, "It was Jesus,
wasn't it?"

"Yep," Cassie whispered before Fysh came within earshot.
They both rose from their seats and David Fysh passed Tom
the piece of paper. He nodded towards it as Tom scanned the
names. The list was short, only four names on it and only two
with further contact information.

"That's all I have at the moment, but I'll get the other telephone numbers and addresses and send them over. I don't
keep personnel records here. They're in the office. If that's
okay?"

Tom thanked him and they made to leave the restaurant.
Cassie stopped at the entrance, looking back at Fysh.

"Did you win?" she asked. He looked at her blankly. "The
award for developing people; did you win it?"

Fysh shook his head. "No. No, I didn't."

Cassie tilted her head, adopting a conciliatory expression.
"Maybe next year, hey?"

Outside, the sign makers were hanging the new name plate
from the front of the building. David Fysh lingered near the
front window keeping an eye on them but trying hard to
appear casual as they walked away.

"He's nervous," Cassie said, focussing straight ahead.

"Yes, he is but what about? Maybe you're right, and his
staff can't stand him."

She shrugged. "Could be. He's come a long way in a short
time, so maybe he has something to hide."

"Similar age to you, isn't he?"

"Yeah, I'd say so. Why?"

"I just wondered if he made you contemplate your life choices, that's all."

Cassie laughed. "I'm not rising to that. Besides, there's something about him that's wrong."

"Such as?" Tom asked as they walked.

She shook her head. "I don't know exactly, but there's something about him that I don't like." She looked to their left and eyed the traffic on the narrow high street, crossing in between cars. "He's too good to be true. No one's that squeaky clean and philanthropic."

Tom shrugged. "Maybe you've been in the job too long and your cynicism is clouding your positivity?"

She laughed again. "Yeah, maybe. We'll see."

CHAPTER THIRTEEN

TOM JANSSEN KNOCKED on the door for a second time, stepping back and taking a peek through the window adjacent to the front porch but there was no movement from inside. The wind drove at them in the way you could only appreciate if you spent time on the north Norfolk coast, gusting in off the sea and battering you much as the waves did the cliffs. The veranda, stretching the full width of the property's frontage, offered them shelter from the rain that had come in on the stiff easterly early afternoon. Cassie, hands thrust into her coat pockets looked around.

"Car's in the drive," she said.

"And you're sure he lives alone?" She nodded. "But he knew we were coming this afternoon?"

Cassie didn't get a chance to answer, the front door creaking open. A man greeted them, standing awkwardly with two crutches supporting his weight. He was tall, not quite as tall as Tom but still comfortably over six foot, dressed in joggers and a loose-fitting hooded jumper.

"Sorry to keep you," he said, smiling and revealing stained

yellow teeth and shrinking gums. "But I'm not as quick on my feet these days," he said, nodding towards the crutches.

"No problem," Tom said, offering him his warrant card. "DI Janssen and DS Knight, Norfolk Police."

"Yes, yes, I was expecting you," he said, shuffling backwards to give them room to enter and keeping the door open with his back. "Greg Beaty," he said, offering his hand, now off balance and putting all his weight on one crutch. He was breathing hard, trying to maintain his composure as Tom shook his hand and entered. "You'd think I'd be used to these by now, but I swear they have a mind of their own some days."

Cassie entered, offering to close the door. An offer Beaty accepted with an appreciative smile.

"Do come through," Beaty said, setting off in loping bounds with an abnormal gait which must be down to more than merely using the crutches.

"Have you had an accident?" Tom asked, entering the living room and noting the fantastic view of the coastline and the sea. The rain clouds were driving in from the north-east, dark swathes moving like huge flocks of migrating birds dipping and swerving on the wind, but further along the coast the skies were a lot brighter and Tom could make out the turbines of an offshore wind farm in the distance. "If you don't mind my asking, of course?"

"No, not at all." Beaty levered himself into an armchair next to the large picture window Tom had been looking out of with a pained expression, sweat beading on his brow, his cheeks burning. The house was detached and situated towards the end of Cliff Parade in Hunstanton, barely a stone's throw from the Old Lighthouse. The room not only had a large picture window but there was a door out to a covered balcony offering further impressive views due to their elevated position on the edge of the town. Beaty grimaced, stretching out his right leg and sucking in a sharp intake of breath as he rubbed furiously at his thigh. Tom glanced at Cassie who was casually looking at an array of framed photographs on the wall of the room. The entire wall was a collage of photographs seemingly depicting a lifetime's experiences. "Ah … sorry," Beaty said. "Just give me a moment, would you?"

"Take all the time you need," Tom said.

Beaty soon looked more settled, taking a deep breath and putting his head back. His right leg remained outstretched. "I tell you, this doesn't get easier," he said, reaching for a blister pack of tablets and popping one. He put it in his mouth and swallowed it with a mouthful of water. Tom raised his eyebrows in query, not wishing to ask the same question twice for fear of intrusion. Beaty realised, breathing easier. "War wound," he said, eyeing his own leg.

"I didn't realise you served," Tom said.

He shook his head. "I didn't. Not in that sense." Beaty waved a hand in Cassie's direction. "That there is my service." Tom crossed the room to join Cassie, perusing the pictures. On closer inspection he found artistic shots of local areas he recognised, but many of the photographs were taken overseas in military theatre. By the look of the terrain and the paint chosen for the armoured vehicles and uniforms, most likely Iraq or Afghanistan. Seeing the mountainous terrain in several, Tom looked back over his shoulder at Beaty.

"Afghanistan?"

He nodded. "Most of them."

"What about these," Cassie said, pointing to a couple taken in a jungle setting.

"A brief spell with the Colombian military and a US special task force; counter-narcotics. Those were the days! I hated the jungle; hot, damp, and it never went to sleep – always something alive and picking at you. The jungle will eat you alive; literally. I'd love to be able to do it all again, though."

"You were injured in Afghanistan?"

"Unfortunately," Beaty said, sighing and glancing out of the window as rain lashed against it. "The Scimitar I was riding in lost an argument with a roadside IED." He grimaced again, only this time with a mock smile. "Attached to the ISAF Quick Reaction Force at the time; I was chuffed to land it – I could see the award ceremonies already – little did I know." He tapped his leg. "Nine surgeries and at least a dozen associated proce-dures ... and the bloody thing still doesn't work properly."

"I'm sorry to hear that," Tom said. Beaty acknowledged the sentiment with a brief smile. Tom looked along the line of images, finding some shots of his hometown, Sheringham. There were children playing; by the haircuts and clothing they were not recent and leaning in he saw several shops that he knew were no longer there. He found a class photo of a year group towards the far end, recognising the school crest. He pointed to it, smiling. "Is this where you went to school?"

"Yeah," Beaty said, sipping at his glass of water. "Why do you ask?"

"I went there myself. I didn't realise you were from Sheringham."

"Ah, a long time ago," he said. "I left shortly after that photo was taken; went to live with my dad in London for a bit before coming back to north Norfolk, but not Sheringham. When I finished school, I followed in his footsteps."

"He was a photographer too?" Tom asked, coming to sit down on the sofa opposite their host.

"Yes." Beaty nodded. "Not a war correspondent, mind you. He was more into the natural world, wildlife photography. He did a lot of stuff for the BBC." He sniffed, taking on a faraway look. "A long time ago. He retired out here and – after all of this – I came back too." Tom looked around, half expecting Beaty's father to appear. "He passed away a couple of years ago."

"I'm sorry."

"That's okay. He got to see me pick up a lifetime achievement award from the Press Photographers' Association. I know he approved of my work, if not where I chose to do it."

"And now you've turned your hand to writing, we understand?"

"That's right. I can't run around dodging gunfire and mortar rounds anymore, so I had to do something else."

"Is it something you'd always wanted to do?" Cassie asked, sitting down next to Tom.

Beaty laughed. It was a dry sound, one without much genuine humour. "No, it never entered my head. All I've ever wanted was to be behind a camera." He turned in his chair, reaching behind and stretching for a picture in a frame. Tom felt like he should help but refrained from offering just as Beaty's fingers curled around what he was after. Turning around, he passed the frame to Tom. It was a picture of a man, whom Tom presumed was his son, looking around eight years old, clutching a camera with a massive grin on his face. "Me and my dad. That's my first camera; on my ninth birthday. I never looked back. I always had a camera with me pretty much from that day onward. I guess photography was in my blood from birth."

"You know why we're here?" Tom asked.

Beaty nodded. "Yes, the woman told me on the phone earlier. It's a shame. Gavin struck me as a good guy."

"Can I ask you about your interview with him?" Beaty nodded. "He interviewed you a while back."

"Yes, back in early summer. My book was proving successful and the local press wanted to run a feature."

"And he came back to see you now because ...?"

"Routine follow-up," Beaty said, shrugging. "Check nothing had changed, that sort of thing."

"Did it bother you that they hadn't already run the article?"

Beaty waved the notion away. "Nah. A few extra eyes on my book from around here won't make it a success or a failure but, I must admit, a little hometown recognition would be nice, I'm sure. Besides, I have a follow-up ready to go soon, so it's played out well. Not that I expect they'll run the piece now anyway."

"Why not?"

He shrugged. "Good point. They can publish it posthumously, I suppose."

"Have you read it?"

"Yes, of course. Gavin was very open with me about it. Look, I'll level with you," Beaty said, sitting upright with obvious discomfort in the movement, "the article isn't very interesting. He – Gavin – could have played up my photography but that isn't the angle they were looking for. I think they liked the crippled guy writing a best-seller. It's no secret that the author lives in these parts, but no one really knows it's me." He sighed, then smiled. "But," he glanced around as if worried someone would overhear him," I was kind of looking forward to people finding out that *T.C. Boyd* isn't a sixty-something woman, but me, a crippled thirty-something!" He sat back again, the smile widening.

"Why the pen name?" Tom asked.

"I already had a couple of non-fiction works out there; collections of my photographic work, you know? I was advised not to confuse things. I sort of wish I'd used my own name now but that's just the vanity in me." His brow furrowed momentarily before his expression lightened. "I'm only human, after all."

"And can you confirm when Gavin Felgate was last here?"

His eyebrows knitted, sucking on his lower lip. "I want to say Thursday of last week but... it may have been Wednesday." He raised a hand apologetically. "The days tend to be meaningless for me at the moment. Nothing really changes. I don't sleep... I get up, wander around a bit, take a few painkillers – repeat." He shrugged. "It's not rock and roll, but it's the way it is."

"And how did he seem to you when he was here?"

"Fine, I guess," Beaty said, casually. "It was only the second time I'd met him though and I think we spoke on the phone a couple of times to check details and for me to give him feedback on the piece. But those conversations were short. I didn't really know him."

Tom nodded solemnly. He took out one of his contact cards and passed it across, Beaty took it, glancing at it before putting it on the table next to his chair. "If anything comes to mind you think might be useful."

"I'll be sure to call, Inspector."

They saw themselves out. Beaty's movements were restricted and Tom wondered whether he had been asleep when they first called. Beaty's hair was greasy and uncared for, his personal hygiene was entirely questionable. The routine management of day-to-day tasks everyone else took for granted must be quite challenging.

"What a change that guy's had to deal with," Cassie said as they briskly walked back to the car, thankful the passing rainstorm was easing. "I know he was a pro photographer but you'd have to get some sort of a buzz from the adrenalin rush of being on the front lines of war zones otherwise you couldn't do it, surely?"

"Yes, I'd say so." Tom unlocked the car, tasting the salt spray in the air on his lips before getting in and shutting the door, the deafening roar of the wind suddenly muted. "Credit to him, though, for finding a new challenge."

"Whilst still dealing with the last one." She looked over at him. "I don't know about you, but I don't feel like we're getting anywhere." Pensively, Tom nodded his agreement. "Where to now then?"

CHAPTER FOURTEEN

TOM TOOK out his mobile and called Eric. The detective constable answered swiftly.

"Are you having any luck with Felgate's computer?"

"No, not really," Eric said. "I have a support call with tech services in a little bit. Hopefully, they can help me get into it. How did it go with Beaty and Fysh?"

"Open and forthcoming ... but no smoking gun, so to speak. Maybe we'll try a different approach. Ciaran Haverson, can you send me his next of kin details." Tom's mobile beeped to notify him of another incoming call. He glanced at the screen. It was Alice. "Hang on a second, Eric." He switched between calls. "Hi Alice, everything all right?" he knew she was already at work, the second night of her evening shift roster.

Her voice was strained. "I've just had a call from Mum. She can't collect Saffy from school today; she feels ill ... or something and doesn't want to drive."

"She seemed okay yesterday evening."

"Yes ..." she hesitated and he heard voices in the background as people passed by her. "Tom, I can't collect her. I would, you know I would—"

"I'll sort it," Tom said, glancing at the clock on the dashboard. It was approaching two o'clock. Saffy finished school at ten past three. He could feel her relief.

"Thanks, Tom. I–I'll make it up to you."

Tom's eyes flicked across to Cassie who was attempting to look as if she couldn't hear what was being said, casually watching the world go by.

"No need. Do you think – and I might be going out on a limb here – your mum is trying to tell us something?"

"I had the same thought. But she sure can pick her moments. Why she can't have a conversation about it like normal people, I'll never know."

"We'll talk about it later," Tom said. "I'll let you know when I've got her."

He ended the call, holding the mobile in his hand and staring at it. Cassie looked over. "Relatives, huh?"

"You heard?"

"Alice is great, you know?" she said, turning to look out of the window again. "But she's loud."

Tom laughed. "True. The result of needing to be heard over *Cbeebies* and YouTube running simultaneously in the background."

"Hah! You have to love Saffy. The girl's going places." Tom smiled. "So ...?" she raised her eyebrows and nodded at his mobile.

"What?" he asked.

"Eric?"

Tom tutted; he'd completely forgotten Eric was on hold. "Sorry, Eric. That was Alice. I wanted to go and speak to Ciaran Haverson's parents, but it looks like I'm on the school run this afternoon."

"To pick up Saffy? Becca could help."

Tom was momentarily puzzled but then remembered Becca was a teacher at Saffy's school. "Do you think she'd mind giving her a lift over—"

"No, I'm sure it'd be fine. Becca's coming to pick me up from the station this afternoon anyway. You'll have to call the school and give them permission though."

"I'll do that, Eric." Eric was on light duties, and restricted hours. Both Tamara and Tom were committed to ensuring he didn't push himself so soon upon his return to work. "Do you have Ciaran's parents' address?"

"Just the father. There's another son as well but he's not on the electoral roll. I'll text you the address and then I'll call Becca."

Tom's screen blinked into life with a text from Eric. Ian Haverson lived in Ingoldisthorpe, a small village located between Dersingham and Snettisham on the edge of the Sandringham estate. They should be able to get across to speak to him and back to the station before Becca arrived with Saffy in tow.

"Let's go and see what Ian Haverson makes of all this," Tom said to Cassie.

THE HOUSE WAS A NONDESCRIPT SEMI-DETACHED, opposite a T-junction at the end of a quiet lane. A large hedgerow spanned the frontage lining the road, stretching across the adjoining house as well. An old caravan was parked on the small patch of lawn to the front of the house, blocking the window, but it looked like it hadn't moved in years. The tyres were flat and green moss grew on the walls, roof and windows. Cassie peered through them, shaking her head to indicate there was nothing of note. A car was parked down the side of the house underneath the overhang of established trees on the boundary with next door. Tom rang the doorbell, hearing the muffled tune inside. The curtains were closed. Tom checked his watch. It was quarter past two in the afternoon. He rang again.

"All right!" someone shouted from inside.

Tom and Cassie exchanged a look. "Sounds like he's in a good mood," Cassie whispered. The door was hauled open to reveal a man in a pair of jogging bottoms and a dressing gown, which he hastily drew about him as soon as he felt the cold breeze on his bare chest. He was a tall skinny man, pale with a drawn face and dark beady eyes. His nose appeared to be offset to the left of his face and Tom wondered if it'd been broken years earlier.

"Mr Haverson?" Tom said. The man squinted at him, stifling a yawn.

"Who wants to know?" he asked, looking away from Tom at Cassie and then beyond her towards the road. The question wasn't asked aggressively, more like he was uninterested.

"Detective Inspector Janssen," Tom said, indicating Cassie with a flick of his hand. She brandished her warrant card as well. He gave both of them a cursory examination. "Can we please have a word?"

"About what?"

"May we come inside?" Tom asked, feeling spots of rain on his face.

Haverson looked nonplussed but he acquiesced, stepping back and beckoning them in. The house had a strange odour to it, stale air and a hint of damp which wasn't unusual in old houses like these. Haverson showed them through to the front room, pulling open the curtains to allow in what little light there was from an overcast and showery winter afternoon. One of the curtain hooks stuck in the runner and despite several shakes it wouldn't budge. Haverson gave up, leaving it swaying back and forth and turned to face them. The caravan didn't help matters. Rubbing at his cheeks, Haverson yawned, making no attempt to shield his mouth.

"Sorry," he said, "but you woke me up."

"Afternoon nap?" Cassie asked.

"I work nights," he said, sinking down into an armchair next to the window and reaching for a packet of cigarettes on the table alongside him.

"Ah, right," Cassie said. "What is it that you do, Mr Haverson?"

"Driving."

"I'm sorry to have woken you," Tom said. Haverson didn't reply, he was too busy searching for a lighter, a cigarette dangling from his lips as he did so. Cassie saw the lighter on the mantelpiece above the open fireplace and picked it up.

"Here," she said. Haverson looked up, smiled – still with the cigarette in his mouth – and deftly caught the lighter as she tossed it to him.

"What's this all about?" he asked, sparking the lighter and taking a steep draw on the cigarette, exhaling away from Tom and Cassie.

"I appreciate this might be difficult for you but we wanted to speak to you about your son."

"Ah … bloody hell! I knew it. What's he been up to now?"

"Excuse me?" Tom asked.

"Jimmy. What's he done?"

"No, I'm sorry. I should have been clear; it's Ciaran we wanted to talk about."

Haverson stared at Tom for a moment, unflinching. After a moment passed, he licked the outside of his lower lip and inhaled another drag on the cigarette.

"Well, I'm sure Ciaran hasn't done anything wrong," he said, dryly. "What's going on?"

"Two days ago, a man was found on Roydon Common," Tom said. Haverson watched him intently. "The man was found dead, most likely murdered. This happened at the same place where your son was found."

Haverson's eyes drifted to a photograph hanging on the wall. Tom followed his gaze. It was a family photo; two adults with their children who couldn't have been more than six or seven years of age.

"That's ... very sad. Murdered, you say?"

Tom nodded. "We believe so."

"And what's that got to do with Ciaran? He ... he died eighteen years ago."

"You must be aware of the date," Haverson nodded, holding Tom's eye, "and there was a," Tom hesitated, "noose hanging from the tree. It seems too coincidental to ignore the possibility of a link to your son's passing."

Haverson looked at the floor, the smoke gently curling up from the end of the cigarette in his hand. "Who was it – the dead man – what was his name?"

"Gavin Felgate. He was a local journalist."

Haverson slowly shook his head, slowly releasing a cloud of secondary smoke from his nose. "I don't know him."

"Might he have known your son? I know it is going back some years."

"Never heard of him," Haverson said, looking up. "What was he doing out at Ciaran's tree?"

"His tree?"

"Yeah," he said softly, staring straight ahead and chewing on the thumbnail of his free hand, gently rocking back and forth in his chair. "That's what I call it, *Ciaran's Tree*. He chose it, after all." His eyes lifted to Tom. "That's the last place he decided to be, where he chose to leave this world. It deserved marking; wouldn't you say?"

Tom inclined his head. "I'm sorry for having to bring all of this back to you."

"It's all right. I live it every day, you know. Have done for years."

"What can you tell me about the days or weeks leading up to what happened?" Tom asked, sitting down opposite him. Haverson looked to the ceiling, took a deep breath and then stubbed his cigarette out in an ashtray already fit to overflow. The action caused ash to fall from the edge and onto the table. Haverson ignored it. He took another breath, putting his hands on his thighs and setting himself.

"Not a lot, if I'm honest," he said quietly. "I was ..." he scratched at the stubble of his chin, "not the most attentive of parents if I'm brutally honest. Not a great husband either. But, in my defence, things weren't great between me and Susanne. Rocky, you know?" He looked up at nothing in particular. Tom saw a haunted sadness in his eyes. "Anyway, things weren't great at home and both Ciaran and Jimmy spent as much time as possible away from the house." He rolled his eyes. "As did I."

"Did you notice a change in his behaviour at all in the days leading up to ... his death?"

Haverson sat there with a blank expression, staring straight ahead. Tom wasn't sure if he'd registered the question. He was about to ask again when Haverson sniffed hard, sat upright and touched the heel of both hands to his eyes. He was barely holding it together.

"I should have. Looking back, the signs were there. He'd become withdrawn ... but it was hard to see because he was ... different ... to other children."

"Different, how?"

"When he was nine, Ciaran was diagnosed with Asperger's. That answered a lot of questions for us ... why he seemed unable to form friendships with the kids at his school, why he struggled to socialise." He shook his head, drawing a hand across his face and rubbing at his eyes. "We kept pushing him when he was little; thinking he'd just fit in if we kept at it but ... he didn't settle. It just led to more and more outbursts. We couldn't understand it at the time. I mean, he was an intelligent lad, far brighter than his brother. Even though there was only a year between them, Ciaran was streets ahead in their schoolwork. He was so quick to pick things up; not like a boy genius or anything, but smart. After the diagnosis we thought things would improve and they did ..." he looked at Tom and then Cassie, "sort of."

"Knowing the cause of something doesn't always lead to knowing how to deal with it, right?" Tom said. Haverson agreed, nodding slowly and turning the corners of his mouth down.

"True. Susanne and I carried on fighting." He sighed. "It turns out Ciaran's condition wasn't the cause of our troubles, merely something else to add another layer of complexity to."

"Is your wife still local?" Cassie asked. Haverson's eyes darted to her. Tom was taken aback by the way he looked at her. He looked ready to snarl at her but it dissipated and he shook his head.

"After ... what happened to Ciaran, the stress we were under became too much and things unravelled. Me first, then our marriage ... and her." He took a deep breath. "Susanne took an overdose four years after Ciaran ... four years after he died."

"I'm sorry," Cassie said, sheepishly glancing at Tom. "We didn't know."

"That's okay."

"And Jimmy?" Tom asked. "How did he cope with it all?"

"He lost his brother and then his mum, all before the age of seventeen. He may as well have lost his dad as well, for all the good I was for him. I hit the bottle ... felt very, very sorry for myself," Haverson said, rubbing the back of his neck. "I'm surprised he turned out as well as he has. He has a steady job, stays off the sauce, unlike his old man."

"Do you see him often?" Tom asked.

He shook his head. "From time to time. But I think there's still a lot of anger there, which is fair enough. I wasn't there for him when he needed me, and I'll have to live with that. But that was me all over; at least I was consistent." He met Tom's enquiring look and sighed. "Ciaran wasn't like other kids, he was big for his age; not tall but overweight. The children at school – some of them, not all – used to tease him mercilessly. That's what kids do, isn't it? They isolate the weak, the vulnerable and pick them off to make themselves look bigger." He shook his head. "All he ever wanted was to fit in, have friends. He was rubbish at fitting in but he did try; he tried ever so hard." Haverson interlocked his fingers, Tom seeing the whites of his knuckles. "I should have helped him more ... been there, done something. Anything. He was such a sweet kid, even in his teens. There was none of the attitude you'd expect, not like me when I was that age. Jimmy made up the shortfall, though. He had attitude in spades!"

"Do you know who his friends were?" Tom asked.

He shook his head. "If I'd been a better father, I might do ... but no."

"You blame yourself for your son's death?" Tom asked.

Haverson met Tom's eye with a steely gaze. "Who else should we blame when a child takes their own life?"

Tom accepted the comment, choosing not to respond.

Whatever he said would be inadequate. Haverson looked at the clock.

"I'm sorry, but is there anything else? I need to start getting myself ready for my shift, and …"

Tom also looked at the time. He needed to get back as well and they'd covered what he'd wanted to know. Ciaran Haverson sounded much as Eric had described, a typical teenager who could conceivably have taken his own life.

"I think that's all for now, Mr Haverson. I'm sorry to have brought this to you unannounced."

Haverson smiled glumly.

Tom closed the door behind them. Cassie, hands deep in her pockets, turned and walked down the drive backwards looking at the house as she spoke. "Poor guy. His life fell apart in quick fashion, didn't it?"

Tom nodded. "Do I sense a moment of compassion bursting from that steel heart of yours?"

"It does happen from time to time," she said, smiling. She turned away from the house, falling into step alongside him. "He's in no doubt his son killed himself, though."

Tom glanced back over his shoulder, seeing a curtain twitch. He couldn't see Haverson at the window and it might have been the curtain catching a draught. "Yeah, seems so."

CHAPTER FIFTEEN

"THE NOOSE HAS REALLY GOT me puzzled," Tamara said, folding her arms across her chest. The presence of the noose in the tree above where they found their victim could be there for a practical purpose – to hang someone – or could be merely symbolic, put there for another, as yet undetermined reason. The scenes of crime officers could only find evidence of one person present and that was Gavin Felgate.

"I don't understand," Eric said. "Why would he tie a noose to the branch ... was he looking to kill himself?"

"Was who looking to kill themselves?" Tom asked entering ops with Cassie in tow.

"Felgate."

Tamara turned away from the information boards towards Tom. "We're trying to think *why* Felgate would hang the noose on that tree. A couple of hours earlier he's sharing a takeaway with someone. It doesn't point to a confused mindset."

"Maybe the takeaway was *just that* bad," Cassie said. Tom shot her a disapproving look and she held up a hand by way of apology. "For what it's worth, I don't see Felgate as suicide material."

"Neither do I," Tom said, hanging up his coat and coming to join Tamara and Eric.

"Then what is the purpose of it?" Tamara repeated.

Tom bit his lower lip. Tamara waited patiently. Tom was methodical, resistant to idle speculation but she could almost see a theory ticking over in his mind. He was staring at the pictures taken at the scene of where Felgate was found on the common. "The way I see it, either someone forced him to hang that rope from the tree, possibly under duress, or he did it himself but not for the obvious reason. But I am certain there was a reason. If we can figure that out then the rest will fall into place."

"So … was he planning to hang someone else?" she asked.

Tom shook his head. "Not the way it was tied. Fiona Williams was right, at the scene; it was amateurish. My guess would be to put the frighteners on someone."

"On Felgate, or someone else?" Tamara asked.

"That, I can't say." Tom looked away from the boards and down at Eric. "How did you get on with the background surrounding the Haverson suicide?"

Eric sat up in his chair. "I looked up the other members of Ciaran Haverson's family. His mother—"

"Had a breakdown and committed suicide a few years after her son," Tom said, glancing at Tamara. "We had that confirmed by Ian, the father, just now."

"Right, Jimmy Haverson – Ciaran's brother – fared only slightly better. Following the suicide, social services got involved because Susanne – the mother – suffered bouts of mental health collapse. She was sectioned twice in the subsequent months after Ciaran's death, on one occasion for a weekend but later for several weeks. The father struggled – he has a record by the way – and to cut a long story short, Jimmy found himself a ward of the state on numerous occasions, bouncing between foster homes." Eric frowned. "It was always planned as temporary, until his mother died and then it ended up being permanent. When he was eighteen, he stepped out on his own, despite his age the local social services were still able to offer him residential care. By all accounts he turned it down."

Tamara listened to Eric, thinking hard. "You said the father has a record?"

"Yes. He was done for burglary in his twenties, served three months inside and also received a caution for assault five years ago."

"Who did he assault?"

Eric glanced at his notes. "An altercation in a pub car park; alcohol related by all accounts. The son – Jimmy – also has a record. In his teens he was arrested for shoplifting. The arresting officers figured he was selling the stuff to pay for his drug habit – nothing major – a bit of weed and some ketamine was found on him when he was picked up. It was deemed he had it for personal use, and was in care at the time, so prosecution wasn't considered in the public interest. He was referred to a community outreach programme. Later, aged sixteen, he was arrested again for burglary and, on that occasion, it did go to trial and Jimmy Haverson was convicted of several break-ins and was sent down for two years."

"Where is he now?" she asked.

"I can't find him registered locally but there's no record of him re-offending," Eric said.

Cassie cleared her throat. "The father said he was still living nearby and also that they didn't see much of one another. He cites rubbish parenting as a causal factor in his son's death and feels he didn't do right by Jimmy either. He said Jimmy sorted himself out."

Eric nodded. "Perhaps he wanted to cut himself off from his past, make a fresh start."

"I think we need to speak to the brother—"

The door to the ops room opened and a uniformed constable stepped through, holding the door for those coming behind. Saffy was first to enter, seeing Tom her face split into a broad smile and she ran to him. He scooped her up in his arms and gave her a hug.

"Hello, munchkin!" he said and she squealed. "How was school?" She leaned away from him, still in his arms and gave him a thumbs-up. Tamara smiled at Becca, who acknowledged her before waving to Eric. Tamara's smile faded as her mother came through the door, with a wide smile on her face and arms full holding a large plastic cake carrier. She hurried across the room as her mum thanked the constable for escorting them.

"Mum, what are you doing here?" she asked, glancing over her shoulder and lowering her voice. Her mum offered her a withering look.

"Tammy, darling," she said, looking past Tamara and at the others, "I just thought I'd stop by—"

"With…?" Tamara said, eyeing the cake carrier. She could see cupcakes or something through the plastic cover.

"I just did a little baking, dear," her mum said, brushing past her. "And it's a good job I made plenty!" she said, raising her voice and placing the cake carrier on the nearest desk, smiling at everyone. Cassie moved towards the desk to see what she'd brought with her. The lid came off. "Mince pies!" she said triumphantly.

"Mum!" Tamara hissed but no one seemed to notice. Her mother looked round at her.

"Well, it's nearly Christmas and I thought I'd get in early before everyone else. People are sick of mince pies by the second week of December—"

"Mum—"

"It's okay, Tammy," she said, holding up both hands, "I made a trip to the supermarket especially and they sell vegan mincemeat now, so you needn't worry."

Tamara frowned, putting aside her irritation, and came to join the group.

Saffy eyed the mince pies warily, looking at Tom. "Mince is meat, isn't it?"

Tom smiled. "Not this type of mincemeat. It's made up of fruit and spices."

"Urgh."

"And sugar," Tom said. "Lots and lots of sugar. I expect you'll love them."

"Can I try one?"

Tom lowered her down and Saffy chose carefully, ensuring she picked the largest available. Cassie and Eric took one each as well. Tamara caught Tom's eye and she knew he could tell she was annoyed.

"Nice of you," Tom said to her mum who beamed at him which only served to annoy Tamara more. Tom found the tray offered to him and he took one. Tamara thought he was just being polite.

"Mum, can I have a word?"

"Yes, Tammy, of course."

There was that name again. She could feel the flutter of anger in her stomach, was it anger or just frustration? She caught Tom's eye, silently asking to use his office and he didn't object. She allowed her mum to go first.

"Bring a mince pie with you."

Tamara was about to object but her mother gave her that look, the same one she always managed when wanting to appear vulnerable and needy, rather than her usual over-bearing self. Tamara took a deep breath, and swiftly picked up a mince pie. Her mum smiled gratefully and headed into Tom's office closing the door behind them.

"Mum, you can't just turn up at my work with a bloody picnic."

"Well, there's no need to take that tone, young lady."

Immediately, Tamara felt bad. She took a breath, calming herself and ensuring she spoke kindly. "Mum, this is my work. We are in the middle of a—"

"Yes, you are. And it's conveniently ensured you leave home early and come back late," her mum said, tilting her head to one side. "It's like you're avoiding me."

"I'm not avoiding you." Her mum raised her eyebrows, shooting her a knowing look. "All right, maybe I am... a little. But you've turned up unannounced, and I have a life—"

"If you called home every once in a while, or invited me to visit, then maybe it wouldn't be necessary for me to drop in on you like this... at home or work."

Tamara sighed. She was right; annoyingly. Her mum looked at her with a weak smile.

"Is it so bad for a mother to want to spend time with her daughter?"

The tone. The victimhood. It was so practised and so effective. "No, of course not, Mum—"

"Good." Her mother smiled, gesturing to Tamara's hand. "Try the mince pie, let me know what you think. I've never made them vegan before."

Tamara rolled her eyes and took a bite to avoid another potential cross word. She had to admit, it tasted divine. Raising her hand to cover her mouth as she spoke with food inside, Tamara frowned. "Which supermarket did you go to? There isn't one within walking distance of the house."

"No need, darling. I borrowed your car."

"What, you took the Healy?"

"You weren't using it, dear." Her mum turned and headed back into the ops room, Tamara hurrying to catch up.

"Mum…"

"Mrs Greave," Cassie said.

"Francesca, Cassie dear, please."

"How did you make this pastry so light?" Cassie asked. "It's delicious."

"Good quality lard."

"Mum!" Tamara said, grabbing a tissue from a nearby box and trying to politely spit the contents of her mouth into it. "If the pastry is made with lard, then it's not vegan, is it?"

Her mum looked at her, incredulous as Tamara theatrically dropped the mince pie into the nearest bin. "Well, of course it's made with lard, love. It makes the best pastry! How else am I supposed to make shortcrust pastry?"

"Give me strength," Tamara muttered under her breath.

Without skipping a beat, her mum turned to the others. "So, what is everyone doing for Christmas?" she asked smiling.

"Mum, Christmas is over a month away."

"We're going to my mum's," Eric said, smiling.

Becca looked at him quizzically. "Since when?"

Eric shrugged. "I always go to my mum's."

"Not this year, you're not."

The news came as a hammer blow to him and he appeared ready to argue only to see Becca's expression and drop it.

Cassie smiled at Eric's discomfort. "Lauren is going to her folks, so I'll be flying solo. Her parents don't know about us yet, and I'm not pushing it."

"That's a blow," Francesca said and then she smiled. "Why don't you come to ours?"

"What?" Tamara said. Her mum waved her comment away.

"There's an idea," Francesca said, "you're obviously such a close-knit group. Why don't we all do something together?" She grinned. Tamara wanted to object but didn't get the chance. "We have space. You could all come to ours, I'll cook." She looked at Tamara. "I'm sure I can do some sort of roasted nut-thingy for you."

"Mum, it's Christmas – it *will* be Christmas – and I'm sure people have plans."

"I want to have Christmas at Aunty T's house!" Saffy exclaimed, putting a hand in the air in an imaginary show of casting a vote.

"Ah..." Tom said, meeting Tamara's desperate look and giving Saffy a gentle shake by the shoulder. "We'll have to speak to your mum about that."

"Right!" Tamara said. "Eric, you're finished for the day, so you'd best get off home. I'm sure Becca wants to put her feet up." Eric smiled at his heavily pregnant fiancée, who was still shooting daggers at him. "And Mum, thank you for popping in with ... the non-vegan, vegan treats but we have work to do."

Francesca made ready to protest but Tamara's steely glare, for once, intimidated her into silence. Tamara assertively escorted her mum to the exit.

"Christmas? Just how long are you planning on staying?" she asked quietly, leaning in so no one could overhear.

"I–I don't know. I've not decided yet. Is it a problem, my being here?"

Tamara heard something in her tone. It was different, a genuine vulnerability where she feared the answer. "No," she said softly. "Of course, it's not a problem," Francesca visibly relaxed "but... what about Dad. He'll be missing you terribly and you know how poorly he copes without you."

"We've separated."

Tamara stopped, stunned. For a second, she thought she'd misheard, shaking her head. "Y–You've... what?"

"I–I've left your father," Francesca whispered pensively, turning towards her and chewing her lower lip, nervously looking back at the others gathering themselves together nearby. Thankfully, they seemed oblivious to the conversation. Tamara was lost for words. All of a sudden, she felt numb, awkwardly looking at her mother, open mouthed.

"I–I..."

"We'll talk later," Francesca said, reaching out and patting the back of Tamara's hand. She turned and hurried out of ops, disappearing from view. Tom came alongside, Saffy holding his giant hand in her tiny one.

"I have Saffy, so I'm heading home," he said. She glanced at him, lost in thought. "I'm heading off," he repeated.

"Yes, of course. We'll pick this up in the morning. Maybe Eric could go out and about and try to track down Jimmy Haverson?"

Tom grimaced, glancing towards Eric, currently fussing around Becca.

"Problem?" she asked.

He shrugged. "No, I just wanted to keep Eric in the office for a—"

"I understand, Tom, really I do, but you can't keep him locked indoors forever. You've got to let him back out sooner or later."

He nodded glumly. "I know." Saffy let go of Tom's hand and threw her arms around Tamara's waist, looking up and smiling at her. Tamara returned it, ruffling her curls, then released her and Saffy skipped away to the door. Tom followed. "I'll see you in the morning."

Eric and Becca made to follow, Eric pausing as he slipped

his coat on and eyed his partner. "Are you okay?" he asked. Becca seemed lost in thought.

"Yes, yes, I'm fine. It's just someone at work – a colleague." She shook her head.

"What?" Eric asked.

"She was upset, very upset but she didn't want to talk about it. I felt for her. I feel like I should have helped more."

"How?"

"Oh, I don't know. Forget it."

They said their goodbyes and departed leaving only Cassie with Tamara in ops. She went to join her. Cassie smiled. "Where should we start?"

Tamara thought about it. "There's so much I want us to unpick in Felgate's life; for example, who he had the recurring meeting with that was recorded in his diary along with this mystery woman who has been visiting."

"Yes, of course. Obviously … all of that …" Cassie was smiling and weaving a circular motion in the air with one hand "… but I was thinking of Eric not realising that his mum is no longer the primary woman in his life." Tamara smiled as well, shaking her head. "And not to mention how Mrs Greave senior—"

"Don't even go there, Cass, I beg of you." Tamara waved a pointed finger at her DS.

Cassie shrugged, the smile widening playfully. "Christmas at the Greaves' sounds fun to me…" she ran her tongue along her bottom lip, watching Tamara whose smile also broadened as she looked at the floor. "But, yes," Cassie bobbed her head, "Felgate … much more pressing."

The telephone on Cassie's desk rang and she answered. Tamara turned her attention to the information boards. There was every possibility that Felgate's life would open up to them once they were into his laptop, but so far, he hadn't left much of a trail as to whom he mixed with.

"Right, thanks," Cassie said, replacing the receiver. "Fancy a trip over to Heacham? Gavin Felgate's house has been broken into."

CHAPTER SIXTEEN

THEY WERE MET by a uniformed constable on Gavin Felgate's driveway, getting out of his patrol car when they pulled up alongside.

"Evening Ma'am," he said, nodding to Cassie. "They got in through the patio doors at the rear. The chap next door heard them leaving and they scrambled over the perimeter wall."

He led them around the side of the house, the path illuminated by a handheld torch. Reaching over the gate, he slid the bolt across and pushed it open. The path ran between Felgate's house and that of the neighbour, Terry Sherman, who Cassie met the previous day. Coming into the rear garden, the access point was clear to see. The access into the house from the patio came via a set of sliding doors. They were not particularly new, unpainted silver aluminium-framed but evidently fitted decades previously. Contemporary frames looked vastly different. Someone had taken a wrecking bar and wedged it beneath the door, levering it up and away from the runner it nestled into. It was an old burglary trick that most homeowners weren't aware of. The weight of the door neutralised the lock by snapping the mechanism, allowing the door to be set aside.

It could be done in a matter of seconds without any of the associated noise that breaking such a large pane of double-glazed, toughened glass would generate.

"Have you been inside?" Tamara asked.

"Yes, but they're long gone. The neighbour who called it in," he pointed towards Sherman's house, "says he saw a man going over the side wall, there." Tamara looked across the garden, following the beam of the torch. The boundary wall was a little over five foot high, climbing ivy ran along the length of it. From memory, she realised Felgate's house backed onto a lane cutting, allowing pedestrians through to the next road. "The internal lights are out for some reason. Must have tripped or something."

"Okay, thanks. Can you call forensics and ask for someone to come down here? I want prints taken from the tool and the door. Maybe whomever it was got careless. Can we borrow your torch?"

The constable passed her the torch and she entered with Cassie, taking care to keep to one side and hopefully not disturb any evidence that might be left for them to find.

"What do you reckon, opportunistic burglary or something else?" Cassie asked Tamara as they cast their eyes around the room. The dining room area was largely unchanged from when Cassie and Tom were last there; the room looking much as it did in the photographs the technicians took when they processed the house. The paperwork on the table was sitting in an archive box on Eric's desk along with Felgate's laptop.

"One thing," Tamara said, stepping into the kitchen and opening several cupboards, casually inspecting the layout and not finding what she was expecting. "His wife – Jane – said he was a massive drinker, didn't she?"

"I think so, yes. So?"

"His boss at the paper said so too."

Cassie shrugged. "What of it?"

"I don't see any booze around here; not in the dining room there, or here in the kitchen."

Cassie looked around, walking into the living room area and finding the sideboard – doors open – with the contents strewn across the floor. She found some pint and wine glasses but no alcohol. "Yes, that is odd. And Dr Death didn't register any alcohol in his blood in the autopsy either, come to think of it."

"So why did he have to order a taxi when his car was parked on the drive?"

Cassie's brow furrowed. "Good point. I missed that."

Tamara pointed towards the hallway leading to the front of the house. "Home office that way?" Cassie nodded and they went through. The office overlooked the driveway, accessed by a door adjacent to the front door of the house. It was open and Tamara stood at the threshold, peering in. "Someone's had a right go in here."

The office was a mess. Every drawer of the desk had been pulled out and turned over, the contents lay all over the floor. The search hadn't been methodical by the look of it. The cupboard and filing cabinet on the far side of the room had been given the same treatment, as if the contents had been hastily thrown to the floor. It was more reminiscent of a demolition rather than a search.

"Standard burglary fare, if you ask me." Cassie said.

Tamara angled her head to one side. Cassie was right, it was certainly how a burglar would leave a property. A seasoned thief could be in and out of a property within six minutes, leaving a trail of devastation in his wake and with everything of value missing. She turned, shining the light up the stairs. "Do me a favour, go and see what's been done upstairs. Has the bed been stripped?"

"On it," Cassie said, setting off. Burglars often arrived empty handed, aside from the tools they use to gain access, and use whatever comes to hand to cart away their finds. This could be bags left by the homeowners or, what was often the case, bedsheets or duvets. Speed was everything in a burglary which was why houses are usually turned upside down. The perpetrator doesn't have the time for a meticulous search, fearful of discovery and locating what they can easily sell, gathering it all in one place – in a bed sheet or a duvet – allows them to flee in quick time.

Cassie returned a few moments later, shaking her head. "I don't think they made it upstairs. Everything looks like it did before. Maybe they were disturbed."

"Neighbour saw him going over the wall; not in here."

Cassie pursed her lips. "Went straight for the office, then?" She looked back towards the living room. "Couldn't find what he wanted and turned out the sideboard en route."

"That's my thinking. Aside from some tech, home offices aren't usually where you keep your valuables in my experience. Watches, jewellery … even wallets are usually found elsewhere."

"So, what were they looking for?"

"That's what I want to know, Cass. We'd better have a word with that neighbour. You can lead."

They made their way back out to the garden intending to walk around to the front of the house but the head of a figure in the next-door garden caught their attention, just visible above the fence line.

"Is that you, Mr Sherman."

He appeared, peering over the fence. Cassie could tell from the movement of his face around the eyes that he was smiling.

"We'd like a word, if possible."

"One second," he said, disappearing from view. Moments

later, a latch clicked and the fence two metres along from where they stood swung away with a scrunch and rustle as the vegetation was pulled from the fencing. A clematis plant had grown across the opening, but the leaves were gone, leaving only a tangle of branches hanging over it. In summer, the gate wouldn't be visible at all. Sherman appeared, the white of his teeth reflected in Tamara's torchlight. She raised the beam to his face and he shielded his eyes with one hand.

"You have a gate into someone else's back garden?" Tamara asked.

"Yes, yes, I do," Sherman said, waving his hand frantically until she angled the beam away from his face. "It's an old right of way."

"Not one that it seems to get a lot of use very often, by the look of it," Cassie said.

"No, that's true," Sherman said, looking back at the gate. "I suppose not."

"What did you see earlier this evening?"

"Um ... see? Nothing. I heard noises and automatically assumed it was your colleagues. But I couldn't see a police car outside and when I looked over the fence, it didn't look like anything you would do. I called out."

"Did anyone answer?"

"No, so I waited and then he came out. When I challenged him," Sherman puffed out his chest, tilting his head, "he took off and vaulted the wall." He pointed to where the burglar clambered over, seemingly using the garden furniture as a makeshift ladder.

"Did he have anything with him?"

Sherman thought about it, frowning. "Not that I could see, but it was dark." He sounded apologetic and defensive in equal measure.

"Can you tell us what he looked like?" Cassie asked.

"I only saw his face for a second ... and then he took off, as I say. And it was—"

"Dark. Yeah, you said that. Can you tell us anything at all?" Cassie asked.

"Tall. Big fella. Taller than that inspector you were with before."

"Six three?" Tamara asked, surprised. She had barely met anyone as tall as Tom in her life, let alone since she came to Norfolk.

"Well, maybe not that tall, but he was taller than me."

Cassie looked Sherman up and down. "What are you, five nine?"

"Five seven ... and a half," Sherman said, raising his eyebrows.

"Makes all the difference," Cassie said. "What about his clothing?"

"Dark. Jeans and a hooded top."

"That's ... really helpful, Mr Sherman." Cassie glanced at Tamara. The man appeared to swell with pride. "Thank you."

"I think he had a car waiting for him as well."

"You do?" Tamara asked. "What makes you think that?"

"A few seconds after he vaulted the fence, I heard an engine revving, and then a car roaring away. At least, I think it was a car ... but could have been a van, I suppose. Either way, definitely a diesel. You can tell the difference."

"You said *waiting for him*. Do you think he wasn't alone?"

"Oh ... I don't know, thinking about it. Maybe," he hesitated, "I don't know. Sorry."

"That's okay, Mr Sherman," Tamara said. "You've been very helpful. I'll have one of my officers stop by and take a full statement from you in a little while."

Sherman nodded, smiling and then trying to look serious.

Tamara politely returned the smile. The man stood there looking between the two detectives.

"You can go home now, Mr Sherman," Cassie said.

"Yes, right. Will do."

Sherman returned to his gate and left, struggling to close it again, having disturbed the clematis. He persevered and eventually managed to drop the latch into place.

"Keen, isn't he?" Tamara whispered, believing him to still be outside and probably listening. Cassie agreed. This might be the most exciting moment of the man's year. She motioned for them to head around to the front of the house. Once crime scene techs arrived, Tamara instructed the constable to take down a statement. The two of them got into their car. She looked at Cassie.

"I'm not buying a random burglary."

Cassie shook her head. "Me neither. He – or they – were after something specific. If they thought it might be in the office then I reckon it's safe to assume it could be on his laptop."

"We need to get into that. What did Eric say?"

"He has an IT tech coming up tomorrow. But – and feel free to shoot me down – I know someone who could probably help us a bit quicker." She mock grimaced. "It's a guy I ... worked with before ... sort of."

"I don't want to know," Tamara said. Then she thought better of it. "Actually, I do want to know."

"I nicked him."

"Cassie—"

She held her hands up in supplication. "He's legit now, I swear. He got a job with an IT firm after," she grimaced again, "he got out." Tamara rolled her eyes. This was getting worse. "No, he's a good guy now. That's what happens, you know? People who are good at hacking are actively headhunted.

Some are offered jobs to help with getting parole. Who better to set up security than those who are most adept at bypassing it, right?"

"Fine," Tamara said, holding a hand up. "Don't tell me any more." She rubbed at her eyes, suddenly feeling tiredness catching up on her. She could do with getting an early night but somehow, going home, she thought would only increase her stress levels.

CHAPTER SEVENTEEN

DS CASSIE KNIGHT YAWNED, stretching out both arms above her head. Her eyes were strained, feeling enlarged and painful. Shutting her eyes tightly, the relief from the glare of the screen felt pleasant. Reaching for her coffee, she checked the clock as she raised the cup to her mouth. Six-thirty in the morning. The others would be arriving soon and she'd promised she'd get this done. If not, it wouldn't be the end of the world but her pride would be dented.

"Connor," she said, turning the microphone of her headset back to her mouth, "how much longer is this going to take."

"Not long."

The soft voice, audible now with an American east coast twang, remained calm and unflustered.

"You said that an hour ago."

"And the hour before that, too," he said.

No matter how long she watched, it was still an odd sight to see the cursor moving across the screen in front of her, seemingly with a mind of its own. Connor Harris was as gifted with computers as anyone she'd ever met. Such a talent, developed and fuelled by his own ambition to do what others couldn't, put him on a collision course with company firewalls and ultimately, the police. Much of his illegal activities were focussed on breaking into systems ahead of his peers, if only to be the first rather than with any malicious intent. What got him into trouble was using credit cards to make purchases, selling them on through online auction sites and making a tidy living. Unfortunately for Connor, the cards weren't his and he'd obtained them through the hacking of company records of multiple businesses. And this was how Cassie came to know him.

For the last four years, Connor had been working in cyber intelligence, at corporate level, achieving special dispensation from US authorities to obtain a work visa. As she understood it, this was virtually impossible with a criminal record. Connor had a way of getting where he needed to be. Getting into Felgate's laptop hadn't been an issue. He'd achieved that in a matter of minutes but it was the encrypted files that proved troublesome. There was little else of any interest to their investigation, but these files must be significant and it was this that Connor had been attempting to gain access to for the last six hours.

"There, we're in."

Cassie opened her eyes, fearful she'd dropped off to sleep again just as she had done earlier. She looked at the screen.

"That's it?"

"All yours," Connor said. "I told you it wouldn't take long. I'll hand control back to you."

"Thanks, Connor. Stay out of trouble, yeah?"

"Always."

The line went dead and Cassie suddenly felt alone for the first time that night. Gently slapping her cheeks to wake herself up, she sat forward and opened the first of the folders she had until now been unable to access. Inside were multiple MP4 files and she randomly double clicked on one. The media player opened and she was pleased to see it was a video file but there was no audio. The recording was made at night, in the early hours and six months previously, according to the date stamp in the corner of the screen. The area was dimly lit with the only light creeping beneath the metal shutters of a nondescript building. It looked like a light industrial area but she had no idea where it might be. A white lorry came into the shot; a six or seven tonne one and possibly refrigerated.

The lorry approached the building, coming to a stop. A man got out from the driver's side but she couldn't see his face; the vehicle obscuring the camera's view. Moments later he hammered on the shutter and within seconds it was raised. Two men greeted the driver. They were familiar with one another, sharing a joke and a few smiles. Two of the men walked around to the rear and opened the truck, setting about unloading crates stacked in the rear. The third man ducked back inside, returning with a sack truck. They made swift work of unloading, the driver furtively looking around with regular frequency. At one point he appeared to stare directly at the camera but from the distance that he was being filmed his features were not distinguishable. He wore jeans and a hooded jumper, the hood up over the top of a baseball cap. He was white and Cassie assessed him to be around five foot ten inches tall.

The men didn't stand on ceremony; as soon as the lorry was unloaded the doors were shut and the shutter dropped before the driver had a chance to bid them goodbye. Not that he seemed to mind. The driver got back into the cab and a cloud of smoke blew from the exhaust and the lights came on. Illuminated by the rear lights, the camera zoomed in on the licence plate. It was clear. Cassie made a note of it. Nothing else happened of note and the footage ended as the lorry drove away, out of shot. She closed the file down and clicked on another. It was another video file, this one filmed three weeks after the one she'd just viewed. The location was different this time and filmed earlier in the night shortly after eleven o'clock.

The footage was focussed on a building but not an industrial location. This place looked more like a shop front with a large glass window with gold stencilled writing. The angle the footage was recorded at made it difficult for her to read the signage, though. She was about to abandon this one and select another, but then an exterior light came on and there was movement from within. Two figures stepped out of the shadows and into view beneath the light. The first she didn't recognise but the second was unmistakably David Fysh, the businessman she and Tom had spoken with. The two men shook hands, broad smiles on both their faces. They parted company, Fysh locking the door to the building they'd just left, before turning to watch the other man leave, calling after him and sharing a joke. Fysh laughed, presumably at his joke or the response. His companion got into a car. Cassie paused the recording to make a note of the registration, then she clicked play and watched Fysh walk away. The camera, footage shaking, tracked him until he got into a blue Land Rover Discovery parked nearby. The vehicle moved off, and as it approached the cameraman the footage abruptly turned to the interior of a car, the flash of passing headlights indicated the car's passing. The recording ended.

Cassie turned to her own computer and accessed the police national database, typing in the lorry's licence plate from the first video. She hit return and waited. The results came up within seconds. The lorry was registered to a business in Thetford, *QualM*. Opening a new search, she put in the second registration number she'd noted down. The car was also registered to the same company. She opened a Google search page and entered the company name. The company was a meat wholesaler but the website was basic to say the least and appeared tailored towards industrial clients as opposed to the general public. The addresses for both the business and the registered keepers of the vehicles were identical. She sat back in her chair, putting an elbow on the arm and resting her chin on her hand. Certain that she'd never had dealings with the firm before, the name seemed familiar but she couldn't place it. Resolving to figure it out later, she checked to see when each of the files was created, sorting them and arranging them into date order. There were nine files in total, all in MP4 format and the first was created seven months earlier, the last, five months ago.

Playing the first file, she found it was another recorded at the industrial building with a very similar turn of events, although the vehicle used was different. The driver could have been the same man but it was impossible to tell. This video was filmed in May on a rainy night and none of the people involved were recognisable. She closed it down and went to the last. This one was different. The camera was placed in the footwell of a car, angled up so that the passenger seat was clearly visible. The man in the driver's seat, she assumed, was Gavin Felgate although his face wasn't on camera. A man appeared at the passenger side door, looking through the window and was beckoned in.

The newcomer got into the car. He was in his forties, slim and with receding sandy hair that was parted to the right. It was raining outside, drumming on the roof and windows, and the man sniffed, wiping his nose with the back of his hand as the two men greeted one another. They were amicable but the newcomer appeared tense, glancing around outside of the vehicle. The two men talked briefly before the one out of shot asked flatly, "Do you have it?" The second man reached into his back pocket and took out a white envelope. It looked thick and he reluctantly handed it across. The envelope remained in shot and was opened. Inside was a wedge of notes and the man in the driver's seat thumbed through it quickly before moving to his left and off camera. "That'll do." The sandy-haired man was hesitant. "Is there something else?" He shook his head. "Good. Then I'll see you in a couple of weeks." They seemed to make eye contact, held it for a moment before the man in view nodded, cracked open the door and got out, slamming the door before disappearing into the rain again.

The driver waited thirty seconds or so before reaching for the camera and pulling it out of the footwell. There was a fleeting glimpse of the operator. Cassie ran the footage back and paused it. It was definitely Gavin Felgate. She wasn't certain but the man who'd just handed Felgate an envelope of used notes might have been the same one recorded leaving the restaurant with David Fysh.

"Morning."

She turned to see Eric, beckoning him over. He hung up his coat and crossed the ops room, eyeing her suspiciously.

"You look dreadful ..." He looked at her, his eyes narrowing. "Have you been here all night?"

"Never mind that," she said. "Have you ever come across a company called *QualM*?"

Eric focussed, his brow furrowing. "No, not that I recall. Why?"

"We need to find out what their connection is with David Fysh and his catering business. From what I can see they are meat wholesalers."

"That sounds like an obvious connection."

"But why would Gavin Felgate be clandestinely recording

them making deliveries late at night and, for that matter, taking large cash payments from an associate of Fysh's." She pointed to the screen. Eric came to stand behind her and she replayed the clip of what looked like a pay-off.

Eric watched in silence until it was complete. "Who is this guy?"

Cassie shrugged. "I should imagine he has some connection with this *QualM* but, as a minimum, he met with Fysh at what I suspect will turn out to be one of his businesses. What their relationship is, mind you," she shook her head, "I have no idea."

"When were these recorded?"

"Over a couple of months – early to mid-summer." Cassie thought about it. "Do we have access to Felgate's bank accounts yet?"

"We do, yes, but I haven't been through them yet."

"Make a start, would you? See if there are any random cash deposits coming in. We certainly didn't find evidence of Felgate hoarding cash in shoe boxes or anything when we searched his house. The money had to go somewhere."

"Will do," Eric said, pulling out the chair before his desk and turning on the monitor.

"How did it go last night, with Becca, I mean?" Cassie asked, changing her tone. Eric looked at her, his lips parted slightly as he made to speak and then he didn't. "That bad, huh?"

He looked glum. "She's really crabby when she's pregnant."

Cassie chuckled. "Yeah, I'm sure that's what it was." She turned back to the screen, planning to go through each of the videos in turn to see what else might be in them. First, she needed more coffee. Looking to save the battery, she locked the computer. Connor had already reset the passwords, so there would be no issue returning to it. The lock screen image was a photograph that caught her attention. It was a picture of three boys hanging out in the sunshine, smiling at the camera. She figured one of them must be Felgate's son; the quality of the image as well as the style of the boys' clothing indicated it wasn't a recent picture. She stifled another yawn, closing the lid of the laptop.

CHAPTER EIGHTEEN

PETER BARNARD WAS a man who'd recently turned forty but looked a decade older. Perhaps it was the thinning blond hair, rapidly in retreat from his forehead, his slim frame and almost skeletal features with the pronounced cheekbones that gave him the appearance of a man older than his years. His suit jacket was off the shelf and a poor fit, a cheaper and far inferior copy of a tailored tweed blazer. Cassie Knight, fresh from a quick shower, if not a fresh set of clothes lifted her coffee cup, inhaling the aroma as deeply as she could without appearing to do so; anything to get the smell of Barnard's business premises out of her nostrils. It didn't work; the stench of what was, quite frankly, rotting meat lingered as badly as that of a three-day old corpse. Thankfully, it was November and not August otherwise it would no doubt have been worse.

"So, let's recap shall we?" Cassie said, smiling. Barnard looked uncomfortable. He had good reason to be. "What is the nature of your relationship with David Fysh?"

Barnard shifted in his seat. When Cassie and Eric visited him at work that very morning, he'd denied knowing Fysh or having any relationship. Eric, sitting alongside her, opened a folder and passed her a clutch of photographs blown up to A4 size. Keeping her eyes fixed on Barnard, she slowly and methodically laid them out side by side in front of him. Keen to avoid her gaze, he looked away from her, analysing each picture as she put it down but he didn't comment. When Cassie placed the last one on the table – an enlarged picture of the driver making a delivery – she tapped it gently with her forefinger. The image was a little pixelated because of the enlargement but it was clearly Peter Barnard; a distinctive mole on his left cheek stood out.

"Are you in the habit of making late-night deliveries to people you don't know?" Eric asked. Barnard's upper lip twitched as he glared at Eric but still he said nothing. Cassie took another image from Eric, laying it on top of the others; a screenshot of Fysh and Barnard shaking hands.

"Or having meetings at a restaurant while it is closed?" she said. Barnard closed his eyes. "Pet food."

"What?"

"You manufacture pet food, I understand?" Cassie asked.

"Yes."

"Much call for pet food in restaurants these days, is there?" Cassie said with deliberate sarcastic emphasis. "I shouldn't imagine so."

"I'm looking to expand … branch out," Barnard said flatly. "Nothing wrong with making a living. That's still allowed in this country, isn't it?"

"Provided it's legal, yes."

Barnard sat forward, aggressively pointing a finger at her. "That's all I'm doing, earning a crust."

"QualM is your business, right?" Barnard nodded. "And what is it that you do?"

He shrugged. "We have contracts with pet food companies; to manufacture and package their products. Then they are shipped into distribution centres before going into the supply chain."

"Gather food, blend it ... package it up?" she asked. Barnard nodded. "Presumably, the raw ingredients aren't as expensive as when we pick them up in our local supermarket, right?"

"Of course not!" he scoffed. "Otherwise, a tin of dog food would cost five quid."

"So where do you find your profit margin? Beef, pork, lamb ... doesn't come cheap."

"Well, it's not fresh, is it?"

"I see," Cassie said, remembering the walk through the processing facility to Barnard's office. Just the thought of it seemed to rejuvenate the residue in her nose and she felt queasy. How Tamara would have coped, a vegan in such a place, she had no idea. "*Unfit for human consumption* is the phrase, I believe."

"If you know, why do you ask?"

"And it's your business; QualM?"

Barnard nodded again, rolling his eyes. "Yes! I've already—"

"But you were disqualified from being a director or running a business two years ago, according to Her Majesty's Revenue and Customs." She stared at him. "A fraud conviction doesn't go down well, does it? The ban extends beyond this year and into next. That would make your *earning a crust* illegal."

"It's my wife's business!" Barnard said, sighing and folding his arms across his chest in defiance.

"Convenient. However, if it's just a paperwork exercise to get around the ruling, it's still illegal but that's not our concern.

Someone else will look into it in due course. In any event, I'm sure your wife will be able to explain why a pet food manufacturer is making deliveries to a business selling food into restaurants, schools and care homes."

"Like I said," he splayed his hands wide, smiling, "we're looking to branch out."

"You mean, your wife is?" Cassie said, reading through the notes in front of her. She didn't look up at him. "We're carrying out a search on Fysh Catering Supplies later today and no doubt they will be able to provide us with invoices and delivery notes to qualify what you were delivering. I'm sure they'll match up with your records as well."

Barnard chewed his bottom lip, taking a deep breath.

"And Gavin Felgate."

"Who?"

Cassie looked up. "Gavin Felgate, a local journalist. You knew him, didn't you?"

Barnard hesitated, his cocky demeanour shifting slightly as he focussed on her, perhaps trying to figure out what she might already know.

"It's not a tricky question, Mr Barnard. You either know him or you don't."

He slowly shook his head and then tried to play the question with a straight bat. "If I did, then it isn't by name."

Cassie bobbed her head knowingly. She glanced sideways at Eric, who picked up his mobile phone – the case holding it folded out to allow the phone to stand up of its own accord – and set it out in front of Barnard. Eric pressed play. Peter Barnard's mouth fell open as he watched himself getting into the car. Eric paused the playback.

"So, Mr Barnard," Cassie said, "tell us about Gavin Felgate."

He absently scratched at the top of his head before sitting

back and exhaling heavily. He stared at Cassie. "Okay. What do you want to know?"

"What was the money for?"

He sniffed, picking at something underneath one thumbnail with the forefinger of his other hand, ignoring Cassie's scrutiny. "He lent me a few quid. I had to pay him back."

"A few quid? I see. A guy you don't know lends you what looks like hundreds, if not thousands ..." Barnard shrugged. "Here's the curious thing," Cassie said, receiving another printout from Eric. She placed it in front of Barnard. It was a bank statement with several deposits highlighted in yellow. "Regular cash deposits at weekly intervals ... similar amounts, too. They begin a couple of days after this video was recorded. Would you care to explain that?"

Barnard's eyes drifted to the statement and up to Cassie, shaking his head. "I'd be bankrupt if I gave away that amount of money."

"Why do you think Felgate recorded you?"

He turned the corners of his mouth down, exaggerating his expression. "Maybe he had a fetish for balding men? Who knows?"

"Where were you last night, Mr Barnard?"

"At home," he said, angling his head forward so his chin almost met his chest, "watching telly with my wife."

"Not in Heacham, then?"

He took a deep breath. The question seemed to irritate rather than unsettle him. "Why would I be in Heacham?" Cassie stared at him, raising her eyebrows. He sighed. "No, I wasn't in Heacham. I don't recall ever going to Heacham, nor can I imagine doing so in the coming days. Satisfied?"

Cassie pursed her lips. "No. Far from it. When was the last time you met with Gavin Felgate? And before you answer, remember we have more candid camera episodes that you haven't seen yet."

Barnard sat in silent contemplation.

"And I'll take this opportunity to remind you that we are investigating a murder here."

"Well, I didn't kill anyone, for crying out loud!"

"When did you last meet with Gavin Felgate?"

His throat must have run dry because when he spoke, his voice was hoarse. "Ten days ago. That was when I last paid him ..." his eyes darted to Cassie and away again "the last instalment of what I owed him."

"Sticking with the loan story, are we?"

Barnard smiled at her but his eyes remained distant and cold. He inclined his head. "That's right. You can ask him yourself."

"I would," Cassie said flatly. "If he wasn't dead, obviously."

CASSIE STEPPED out of the interview room, pulling the door to behind her. Tamara Greave came from the adjoining room, where she'd been watching the interview unfold, and the two made their way back to ops.

"He seemed genuinely surprised to be the star of his own TV show," Tamara said.

"Agreed. I think that came as a shock. We've no idea what the full context of the transaction was between them, though because it's not directly spoken of. It has to be a pay-off, though, surely?"

They entered ops. Tom was there waiting for them. Tamara nodded towards Cassie.

"Cass thinks Barnard was paying Felgate off."

"What for?"

"Looking at his bank account, Felgate has been receiving multiple cash payments for months," Cassie said. "Similar amounts on a regular basis, all cash deposits. Unless he was having phenomenal success at the bookies every week, we have to assume the money came from this type of thing. What if the products Barnard has been supplying to David Fysh turns out to be dodgy meat?"

Tom perched himself on the edge of a nearby desk. "I doubt he'd get away with it in the restaurants. Maybe if they were prepping Indian food; the spices would mask the poor quality."

"True," Cassie said, "but let's not forget Fysh fulfils multiple contracts to provide food to local schools, care homes and the like. It'd be much easier to hide it there."

Tamara shuddered. "That ... leaves me with a queasy feeling. How could someone do that to children and the vulnerable?"

Cassie laughed, flicking a hand towards Tom. "Those shoes he had on when we spoke to him would've cost at least three hundred pounds. The suit was pretty sharp, too. The money has to come from somewhere."

Tom nodded, his face a picture of concentration. "So ... Felgate figures it out and, rather than run a story on it, approaches Barnard and solicits – or is bribed with – money in exchange for his silence?"

"That's what I'm thinking, yes," Cassie said. "The recording is insurance, just in case he either needs leverage to guarantee his safety at some point in the future."

"Or more money?" Tamara said. She turned to Tom. "Do you remember Jane Felgate telling us he'd started paying her and the children more money recently?"

"And that he'd stopped supporting them for a time prior to that. He also couldn't afford the hit to his finances if they divorced; didn't she say that he would lose the house?"

Cassie smiled. "Maybe he found a way to pick up a little extra. Blackmail is a healthy motive for murder."

"But why now?" Tom asked. "If we're looking at Barnard for this, why did he wait until now?"

Cassie shrugged. "Maybe Felgate got greedy and asked for more? Barnard was unhappy about it and killed him. He is local, so he could have known about the Haverson suicide years ago ... dressed the scene to tie it into a sketchy case from years ago and throw everyone off."

Tamara shook her head. "Do you see Felgate going down so passively to a man like Peter Barnard? He doesn't strike me as the most intimidating of people."

"Unless your daughter brought him home on a date," Cassie said. She shrugged. "But I take your point."

"Whether it was Felgate who initiated the exchange, it stands to reason Fysh would be aware, though, wouldn't it?" Tom said. "Barnard would tell him."

"Or Felgate would tap Fysh for the same deal and go for double bubble," Cassie said, nodding her approval. "He'd be daft not to, seeing as Fysh is bound to know anyway."

"Which gives both of them the motivation to silence him," Tamara said. "And two people would make overpowering Felgate that much easier. Where did Fysh say he was at the time of the murder?"

"At home, in bed," Cassie said.

"Right, keep Barnard here for the full twenty-four hours while we search his premises and execute another search warrant on David Fysh and his businesses," Tamara said. "If we need more time, we can apply for an extension."

Tom frowned. "We don't have anything to tie him to the murder. The footage on Felgate's laptop is damning, but even if we can prove what we think he's been up to, it still doesn't prove involvement in a murder."

"No, right enough. But we can use it to apply pressure on him. If we bring in Fysh as well, maybe we can play them off against one another. You never know, one of them might feel threatened enough to throw the other under the bus." She looked at Cassie. "Get the warrants and gather as many bodies for the searches as you can."

CHAPTER NINETEEN

Tom Janssen stepped to one side, allowing an officer carrying another archive box to pass by. The handful of customers frequenting the restaurant this lunchtime soon finished their meals and left after Tom served the warrant; uniformed officers scouring the building destroyed the ambiance of dining out at a swanky establishment. The building was small with the majority of the space given over to the front-of-house operation and well laid-out kitchen facilities. Fysh had a small office to the rear but the first floor of the building was a self-contained flat which was let out to a private tenant and unrelated to the business. Once the last customer left, the shift manager, a woman called Sally, swiftly closed the restaurant, turning prospective customers away rather than have them witness the police presence. She stood behind the bar now with her arms folded, scowling at him.

"Is this going to take long?" she asked for the fourth time.

"As long as it takes, I'm afraid. When do you expect Mr Fysh to come in?"

She shrugged.

"Thought so," he said, turning to a constable approaching him.

"That's the last of the files from the office, sir."

Tom thanked him and crossed to the small bar where Sally seemed implacable.

"Do you know what you've done by coming here like this?" she said, a flash of anger in her eyes. "You're ruining us before we've even got going! This is a small town and people talk."

If she thought this was bad, then she'd be in for a shock when environmental health and trading standards turned up to investigate the source and quality of their meat products, if the investigation threw up links to Peter Barnard's pet food supply business as they suspected. Tom looked around at the empty space. "A soft opening, I think David said it was. When is the grand opening?"

"Friday evening, if it goes ahead."

Tom didn't respond. It wasn't his concern. "When did you last see him, David, I mean?"

Her expression softened a little. As much as she was frustrated, she didn't seem to be taking the situation personally. "I've had the last couple of days off – seeing as it would be my last time off for a while – so I haven't been around. James would know."

"James?"

Sally nodded towards the kitchen. "The head chef. He's been here all week working on the menus and organising his team for the opening, ironing out the kinks," she rolled her eyes, "although we didn't expect you lot."

"Can I speak to him please?"

She scoffed. "Might as well, seeing as you've emptied the place anyway."

She disappeared into the rear and a few moments later a man stepped out from the kitchen in a white chef's jacket and blue and white checked trousers, but Sally was nowhere to be seen. He looked around and met Tom's eye, walking over to him and removing his hat to reveal dark and wavy hair, shoulder length, but tied at the nape of his neck. Tom recognised him as the man who'd spoken to Fysh on Tom and Cassie's previous visit.

"Detective Inspector Janssen," Tom said, smiling.

"James Cook," he replied with a curt nod. He seemed nervous. Tom recalled the name from the list of staff Fysh had given them. "You were here the other day."

"That's right, talking to David. Do you know where he is?"

James shook his head. "Sorry. I half expected him to be here today, but he hasn't shown."

"Why did you think that?"

He shrugged. "Because he wasn't here yesterday, which surprised me. We've all been living and breathing this place," he looked around the restaurant, "for weeks, if not months and then he does a disappearing act this close to opening! It's not like him to duck out when the hard work is underway."

"How did it go with the local dignitaries?" Tom asked, remembering they had a special evening planned to help raise the restaurant's profile before the big opening.

"It went well. The kitchen was a bit hectic – new staff and all – but feedback was positive."

"Sally tells me you're designing the menu?"

"That's right." He half-smiled. "Mr Fysh has put a lot of faith in me with this place." Tom encouraged him to explain. "Previously I worked in his bistro, the one in Sheringham. I'm head chef here, though." He frowned. "I don't want to let him down."

"You've worked for him for some time then?"

James nodded enthusiastically. "Yeah, quite a while. I

started on an apprenticeship a few years back. Mr Fysh saw something in me when no one else did."

Tom understood, and that went some way to explaining why he might be nervous. "He talked to me about his recruitment policy."

"Gave me a shot," James said. "Not easy getting a second chance in a place like this ... a town like this, you know? Everyone knows everyone else's business." He was pensive, running a tongue along the inside of his cheek. "I owe Mr Fysh a lot. I don't know where I would've ended up if it wasn't for him; back in prison probably." He briefly met Tom's eye before looking away, shifting his weight between his feet.

"Tell me, what do you know about Mr Fysh's business and how it operates?"

James frowned, looking up at him. "How do you mean?"

"How involved are you in the sourcing of ingredients, not just for here but for the bistro and his other enterprises? If you've worked for him for a while, you must know who he deals with on a regular basis?"

James thought about it. "He gave me free rein with the menus, allowed me to show him what I could do, you know?" He shook his head, his eyebrows knitting. "We source local produce where possible, seafood in particular. We have long-standing ties with Cromer in that respect."

"Any change recently?"

He blew out his cheeks. "Not here, not really. I think things run a bit differently in his larger operation, the mass-produced meals for the schools, NHS and care homes and the like. But I don't really get involved in that side of things. Sorry," James said, gesturing with open hands. "Can I ask you something?" Tom nodded. "What's all this about?"

Tom declined to answer. Until they got hold of David Fysh

himself, he didn't want him getting wind of what they were investigating.

"I'm glad you're here today," Tom said. Cook suddenly looked nervous again. "I understand you were interviewed by Gavin Felgate, a journalist writing a piece on your employer."

"About Mr Fysh's community work and stuff? Yeah, yeah, I remember."

"How did that go?"

He shrugged. "Okay, I guess. I mean, it was all standard stuff … what do I like about working here, type of boss David is … that sort of thing? Why?"

"Just trying to get an impression of what tone the article might have, that's all," Tom said. "I'm sure you're aware that the journalist was found dead earlier this week?"

His mouth fell open. "No… really? I–I've been working here so much, I hadn't caught that. I mean, I heard a guy was found dead but not… wow! That's mental."

"Mr Fysh didn't mention it to you after we left the other day?"

He shook his head. "No, he didn't. But then again, why would he? We're not mates or anything."

"I see. And Gavin Felgate – the journalist – was on good terms with your employer as far as you're aware?"

"Yeah, I don't think there was any issue. Is that what this about; that guy's death?"

"I'm sorry, I really can't say." Tom took out one of his contact cards and handed it to him. "If Mr Fysh appears, please let him know to call me straight away, would you? It would be in his best interests." James Cook scanned the card and nodded. Tom looked towards the rear as if he could see through to the kitchen beyond. "Is there anyone else here who Felgate spoke to?"

James followed Tom's eye, thinking hard. "No, I don't think so. I think he was just going through the motions to be fair."

"How so?"

"Well, it was incredibly dull stuff. Why anyone would pay someone to write it, let alone get someone to pay to read it is beyond me."

Cook returned to the kitchen. Tom was the last officer to leave the restaurant and the manager, Sally, hadn't reappeared as he stepped out. Once outside, he took out his phone seeing a text message from Eric asking him to call in. First off, he phoned Cassie, overseeing the search of David Fysh's head office. Tamara Greave was picking over Peter Barnard's business address at the same time. Although confident they were onto something with the relationship between the two of them, Tom wasn't sure how easy it would be to prove impropriety if Barnard was adept at hiding the origin of the products he was supplying.

"Any sign of David Fysh?"

"No," Cassie said. "No one here claims to have seen him for a couple of days. How about you?"

"Same."

"Do you think he's gone to ground?"

Tom thought about it. "It does seem out of character for him not to be around. Go over to his house and see if he's there. He mentioned his wife when we spoke to him and, if he's not around, have a word with her. If anyone knows where he'll be, she should."

"You'd hope so," Cassie said with a dry laugh. "Unless he's already taken off with her in tow."

Tom looked back at the restaurant. "His entire life is here. Where would he go?"

He hung up and immediately called Eric.

"Hi, Tom. I've finally got hold of the data from Gavin

Felgate's mobile phone service provider. Regarding his mystery woman, I think we might be getting somewhere."

Tom reached the car and got in. "Can they put a name to the unregistered number?"

"Not quite as good as that but I have the transcripts of text messages exchanged between the two of them and despite sometimes being a little cryptic for reasons you'll understand soon enough, there is a mention of someone called Leigh—"

"That name rings a bell," Tom said, racking his brain to figure out why it stood out to him.

"Yeah, I cross referenced the name with Felgate's list of colleagues and interviewees, those we're aware of anyway; drew a blank. But then I extended it to known friends and associates, which was a short list."

"Any time today, Eric," Tom said.

"Right, okay. Leigh Masters. She's listed as a social media friend of Jane Felgate's and the two interact quite reg—"

"That's where I know her from!" Tom said, excitedly. "She came to Jane's house the day Tamara and I visited to notify the family of Gavin's death."

"More than that, she and Jane Felgate go back a long way; she is tagged in multiple photographs in the Felgate's wedding album. She was one of the bridesmaids."

"Now that is interesting."

"Yes, I also went to her social media page – which is public – and from what she shares it appears she's happily married; lives in Old Hunstanton."

"Great," Tom said, checking the time, "can you text me the address and I'll stop by on my way back to the station." His phone beeped.

"Way ahead of you," Eric said. "And you might not want to go alone. I looked up her husband – Rhodri Masters – and he has two convictions: one for affray and a second for actual bodily harm. Nothing recent, but I'm looking at his picture on Leigh's profile page... and... he's a big guy."

Tom smiled. "I'll be tactful, Eric. Good work."

He hung up and opened the text message to check the address. Hamilton Road. He knew it well.

CHAPTER TWENTY

WIVETON WAS a small village set back a mile or so from the coast, between the coastal villages of Blakeney and Cley. Having left the coast road, DS Cassie Knight turned left onto a narrow lane at the village boundary and kept her eyes open. Mature trees and overgrown vegetation lined the lane to either side of the road and anything beyond them, even in late November, was obscured from view. Even paying attention, she missed the house and had to pull in at the next passing place and make an awkward three-point-turn, all the while praying that an overconfident local wouldn't come flying around the corner at speed as they were prone to do in these parts. The narrow lanes didn't bother Cassie as much as they did others not familiar with the area – Tamara Greave for instance – because in her native North East, once out of the cities, you could easily find yourself on single track roads heavily used by agricultural vehicles in the blink of an eye.

The entrance to the property was through a five-bar gate, located almost on the roadside, which she was grateful to find open. The house was of traditional brick and flint construction, two storeys high and Cassie thought she caught sight of skylights in the attic, suggesting a conversion. The house was set back from the road and secluded even with many of the trees stripped of their greenery. In the spring and summer, you could probably drive by without realising there was a house there at all. The driveway curved around to the rear and Cassie parked alongside a dark blue Audi saloon, barely a year old with run flat tyres on massive rims that Cassie figured would ensure the driver recognised every bump and depression in the road each time the car met it.

She walked towards the house. A dog barked, alerted to her presence, but she didn't worry. It sounded like a yappy dog – a terrier or similar, one of those little things like Tom's that suffered from short-person syndrome, making up for its lack of stature with an exaggerated woof. There was no doorbell, just an old bell and clapper mounted to the right of the door. She rang it twice, the shrill sound making her wince as it reverberated. Moments later the door was opened by a flustered young woman. Cassie was surprised by her age, initially wondering if she was an au pair rather than David Fysh's wife, she couldn't be far into her twenties.

"Mrs Fysh?" Cassie asked. She nodded, blocking a light-coloured border terrier from getting out of the house with her left foot. Cassie took in her measure. She was five two or three tall, slightly built with blonde hair hanging to her shoulders. Her make-up was fastidiously applied, hair styled and her fingernails were equally well presented. Her clothing was just as stylish. Cassie wondered if she was on her way out. "I'm sorry to bother you," she held up her warrant card, "but I'm Detective Sergeant Knight and I'm looking to speak with your husband. Is he around?" She looked past the woman into the interior. She could see a child playing in the background.

"I'm sorry. David's not here," she said, her eyes narrowing. "Is there something I can help you with?"

"Perhaps, yes. May I come in?"

The door widened, allowing the dog to get past despite its owner's best efforts. Cassie didn't mind. The dog lifted itself up on its haunches, front paws in the air, to sniff her. Finding nothing untoward about Cassie, it turned tail and ran ahead of them as they walked through into a large kitchen-dining room. The child Cassie saw was a boy, no older than three, and he seemed to have taken out every toy possible in order to fill the available space, Cassie tentatively picking a path through.

"Do you know when your husband is likely to come home, Mrs Fysh?"

"Anna, please," she said, raising her eyebrows and striking a thoughtful pose. "I'm not sure, to be honest. He's away on business."

"Oh, right. Anywhere nice?" Cassie asked, looking around. The house was presented much as she might expect having met David Fysh. They'd managed a coherent blend of modern and traditional in the space. The kitchen was a Shaker style, white, with complementary marble worktops and copper fixtures and fittings. It made the space contemporary but blended well with the tradition of the envelope.

"I'm afraid he didn't say. I'm not expecting him back for a couple of days, though."

"Odd timing."

Anna looked at her quizzically.

"To go away," Cassie said. "What with the opening of the new restaurant."

"I guess. David doesn't talk to me about his work very much, though."

Cassie was disheartened but she didn't show it. If Anna was truthful, she wouldn't be likely to offer up anything damning on her husband's business enterprise. The little boy dropped something, startling the dog, who barked. A baby cried out. Anna visibly deflated, looking up forlornly at the ceiling.

"Sorry. I'll be right back."

Cassie smiled sympathetically. "No problem." She should have realised that Anna couldn't be the au pair. Despite Anna's outstanding efforts in personal presentation, no amount of make-up could hide the dark shades beneath her eyes that only came from being the parent of a newborn. Cassie moved closer to the boy, dropping to her haunches beside him and looking at his assortment of figures he was playing with. They were set up in two rows, superheroes, cartoon characters and small soft toys – even a couple of racing cars – appearing ready to face off in some sort of duel.

"What's going on here then?"

He looked at her, smiling. "War." He turned back to his game. The conversation was over.

Anna Fysh soon reappeared with a baby in her arms, bouncing it gently in her arms to calm it. Cassie rose and smiled as she looked at the child, unsure if it was a boy or a girl. "Cute," she said. Anna smiled. Cassie was lying, but it was what you said to parents with babies. They seldom were cute – perhaps the odd one or two – but most looked Churchillian or something akin to one of his descendants at least. "How old is…?" she stopped short of defining a gender.

"She's five months."

Definitely a girl then.

"She's lovely." Anna fawned over the baby. Her son began smashing the figures he was playing with against one another. "How long have you and David been together?"

"We knew each other for a long time before we were in a relationship," Anna said, putting her daughter down in a Moses basket on top of the dining table. The dog was fussing around her feet and she shooed it away.

"How did you meet?" Cassie asked, roughly calculating the age difference between the two of them, Anna must be at least ten years younger than him.

"We used to work together."

"He employed you?"

She nodded. "Yes, I used to wait tables at his Sheringham bistro."

"Are you sure you've no idea where your husband went? It is important that I speak to him."

"I can give you his mobile number if you like?" she said, reaching for her own. "Not that he's answered it the last couple of times I rang him."

"Is that unusual?" Cassie's curiosity was piqued.

Anna thought about it, nodding. "Yes. I mean, he often doesn't answer but he always calls back sooner or later as soon as he gets a minute."

She brought up his number on her screen and Cassie took a quick photograph of the display with her own mobile.

"How has he been recently?"

"What do you mean?"

"Stressed, unhappy... preoccupied, maybe?"

She shook her head. "No, I think things have been going well. David's been working a lot, but that's nothing new. He is a bit of a workaholic. It doesn't surprise me that he found his wife in a work environment." Cassie smiled politely. Anna's gaze lingered on her. "I know you will have noticed."

"Noticed?"

"That David is a lot older than me."

Cassie shook her head. "Not at all." She was lying again.

Anna smiled knowingly. "You'd be the first. Half of the staff at the bistro were pleased for me – for us – but the rest split their opinions between me being a gold digger and him being a dirty old man." Cassie inclined her head but said nothing. "We are neither, by the way."

"People always have to talk about something, don't they?" Cassie smiled politely. "So, David's been quite normal, no change in his behaviour at all?"

Anna started to shake her head but hesitated.

"Anything at all? No matter how minor."

"Well, he's been busy, as I said, and I put it down to that, but..."

"But?"

Anna looked at the baby and her son. "What with the new restaurant opening, as well as our new addition to the family, I figured he's just found himself spread a little thin recently. Thinking about it, I suppose he's been – what did you say? – a little preoccupied recently. A bit snappy."

"I see." Cassie made a note. It was a bit vague for her liking, though.

"Could that be related to what you want to talk to him about?"

Cassie smiled. "Maybe, who knows? But he hasn't said anything to you, mentioned something he's been worrying about?"

Anna scoffed. "You've met David, right?" Cassie nodded. "He's not exactly backward in coming forward."

"I see that, yes."

Anna watched her intently. "He's not quite as arrogant as you think. I know he comes across that way but underneath that exterior he really is quite vulnerable."

"Right," Cassie said, bobbing her head. "What about when he told you he was going away? How was he then?"

"I didn't speak to him. He texted me."

"*Texted you*? To say he was going away on short notice?"

"Yes. I wasn't pleased but... you have to know David to

understand. When he's preoccupied, he can be a bit closed off. It's just the way he is."

"Doesn't that bother you?"

"Besides," she shrugged, "he wouldn't choose to be away if he didn't need to be, would he?"

"I guess not, no. When did he send you the text?"

Anna looked thoughtful. "The day before yesterday, I think." She sought out the text on her mobile, checking the date and holding it up for Cassie to see. "Yes, he sent it at four-thirty the day before last."

"And you've not heard from him since?" She shook her head. "And he was driving his Discovery?" Cassie asked, making notes.

"Yes. Why? What's all this about?"

Cassie smiled broadly. "Just background, Mrs Fysh – Anna – nothing to worry about, I'm sure. Is there anyone local your husband is close to who might know where he has gone? I know his father is local."

"You'll get nothing useful from him, I'm afraid."

"They're not close?"

"It's not that so much but they don't spend a lot of time together these days. David's father had to take early retirement from the business, and David was forced to step up. The way he talks about it, I don't think he was ready for the responsibility. I've always had the impression David was quite a... I want to say *player* a few years ago, but I wouldn't want to give you the wrong impression of him."

"A flamboyant character?"

"Yes, that's apt. A happy-go-lucky kind of guy, by all accounts. Not that I knew him back then."

Probably still in primary school, Cassie thought.

"His father wasn't able to carry on, his illness came on quite suddenly and he went downhill."

"What is his condition?"

"Early onset dementia." She read Cassie's expression. "You seem surprised. Why?"

Cassie had to admit she was. David Fysh talked about his father, and his taking over the business, but implied he was still keen to be involved. "Your husband said his father was still seeking to be involved or at least questioned the expansion plans."

"That's David, I'm afraid. Covering it up, downplaying it. He's struggled to get to grips with his father's illness. I think he is embarrassed about it. I'm not sure, but he certainly doesn't like to speak about it. Not even with me. Maybe he's fearful of what it might mean for his own future." She looked at the baby and her son playing nearby. "And for our family?"

"Anyone else then, friends, other family members?"

"There isn't any other family, I'm afraid. David is an only child. He's close-ish to a couple of old friends," she said, shrugging, "but I don't know them personally. I've met one once, he stopped by the house. He lives abroad, though and David doesn't see him much." She looked thoughtful. "I think David has a postcard from him in his study."

"Worth a check," Cassie said. "Please can I have the details?"

Anna began scrolling through her mobile, quickly abandoning it and asking Cassie to keep an eye on the baby whilst heading to David's study to look for the postcard. Cassie couldn't help but find David's rapid disappearance concerning, but she couldn't figure out whether he was running from police scrutiny or something else entirely? She walked over to the dining table and peered into the basket. The baby was sleeping, blowing tiny spit-bubbles as she exhaled. She had to admit, the child looked cuter than she'd first thought.

Anna returned with an orange sticky note in hand. She

passed it to Cassie. The note had one name written on it along with a mobile phone number. It was an international code but not one she recognised, unlikely to be European. It wasn't a name she recognised but Eric was back in ops, so he could look him up. She resolved to call him as soon as she left.

"You said there was another friend. Any idea who that was?"

Anna shook her head. "Sorry. Like I said, David doesn't really keep in touch."

Cassie assessed the woman. She was seemingly unperturbed by all of this.

"Forgive me, but you don't seem very concerned," Cassie said.

Anna met her eye. "Why should I be? It's all very David."

"Really?"

She laughed. "Yes, you'd have to know him to understand." Cassie encouraged her to explain. "My husband is the sort of man who loves to be married but still needs his freedom every once in a while." She read Cassie's expression, hastily clarifying what she meant. "Not in that way. It's just," she looked up, searching for the right words, "he is like a wild bird that needs to fly free. To be caged would stifle his creativity... make him less of the man he is. Do you know what I mean?"

Cassie nodded slowly but, internally, she wondered if that was Anna's take or the one her husband instilled in her. Thanking Anna and leaving her with a contact card in case her husband returned, Cassie left the house. No sooner than the door closed on her, she took out her mobile and called Eric whilst walking to the car. She let it ring but he didn't answer, the call diverting to a message box.

"Eric, it's Cass, can you give me a call as soon as you get this?" She glanced at her watch; he should still be in the office. "I need you to look into someone for me."

CHAPTER TWENTY-ONE

Eric Collet stared at the monitor, absently grazing on a packet of cheese and onion crisps, hoping for some inspiration. *Surely it shouldn't be this difficult.* He'd been trying to locate Ciaran Haverson's brother, Jimmy, for several days now. Speaking to him was a low-level objective in the hierarchy of tasks but Tom had tasked him with it and he was stumped. Jimmy Haverson had been in trouble as a child, not much worse than the average teenager until he edged towards adulthood. That was when things had developed for him. Having been cautioned for shoplifting and possession, referred to community outreach programmes, it was following Ciaran's death that Jimmy stepped up a gear being arrested for burglary before his sixteenth birthday and was subsequently sent to a juvenile detention centre. He was released just prior to a potential transfer to an adult facility as he approached the age of eighteen.

Then, shortly afterwards, Jimmy Haverson disappeared.

Eric found him listed on the electoral role as residing with his father but the following year that was no longer the case. The last census, almost a decade ago, didn't have any mention of Jimmy Haverson at all in the local area. There was no Council Tax entry in his name, or PAYE account on HMRC's database. Jimmy Haverson was a ghost. On the off chance, Eric even looked up the register of deaths to see if Jimmy featured there, despite the father's information that he was working locally. Tom said the two weren't close. His death wasn't recorded. Maybe the father was very out of touch and Jimmy had moved on.

A knock on the door.

Eric looked over his shoulder, a uniformed constable leant on the door frame with one arm.

"Hey, Eric." The constable looked around the empty ops room. "Just you today?"

"Everyone's out and about. Is there something you need?"

"Yeah. We've got a suicide that the duty sergeant wants one of you to take a look at."

"Why? What's odd about it?"

The constable's brow furrowed. "I don't know. Marcus is there and he has one of his *feelings*." Eric found that intriguing. PC Marcus Weaver was an experienced officer, coming close to his thirty, and if he wanted CID to take a look then it must be necessary. "Any chance you can get someone round there?"

Eric experienced a flutter of excitement. He was supposed to be desk-bound for the foreseeable until Tom said otherwise, but no one else was around. Cassie was out tracking down David Fysh's whereabouts and Tom was heading out to Old Hunstanton to speak to Leigh Masters, and Eric had no idea if he'd be back into the station before clocking off. Where Tamara was, he didn't know. He glanced at the clock.

"Where is it?"

"Heacham. One of the holiday homes on the seafront."

"Really? At this time of year? They're pretty much locked down until spring."

"I know. A passer-by on the promenade called it in."

Eric thought about it. The promenade, atop the mammoth concrete sea defences, ran from Hunstanton down the coast to Heacham's South Beach. Behind the sea wall were a line of holiday homes of varying size and style from old timber cabins – held together by a fresh lick of paint every now and again or by pure hope – to more impressive contemporary additions, raised on stilts with an expansive deck to capture the sea view. The homes gave the seafront an upbeat atmosphere during the summertime with parties and barbecues happening all along the promenade; beach-goers and thousands of tourists flocked to stay in the holiday parks set back from the beach beyond the houses and altogether gave Heacham a vibrant feel to it. At this time of the year, though, that stretch of the promenade was more like a ghost town. The facilities, small businesses serving coffees and ice cream, were shuttered until April and the only people who passed by were locals exercising themselves or their dogs. In winter, that stretch of the coast could be brutal with the wind channelling up The Wash from the North Sea. It was barely visited aside from the hardiest.

"Give me the address. I'll take a pool car, head over and have a look," he said, standing up and lifting his jacket off the back of his chair. He flicked the switch on his monitor to turn it off and headed for the door. Falling into step alongside his colleague, Eric heard a telephone ring from ops. He stopped, hesitating and looking back.

"Do you want to get that?"

Eric bit his lower lip. He should but if it was Tamara or Tom, he'd have to explain where he was going and they'd stop him; at least Tom would. Feeling for his mobile in his pocket, he held down the power button knowing it would switch it off whilst nodding towards the end of the corridor.

"Nah. If it's important they'll call me on the mobile."

CHAPTER TWENTY-TWO

TOM JANSSEN FOUND the house in Old Hunstanton, an Edwardian residence set within extensive gardens and shielded from the main road by a mixture of mature trees. His arrival was noted by the incumbent who was visible in the bay window of the living room. The man watched him with a curious expression as Tom left his car and walked to the porch and rang the doorbell. He was surprised a few moments later when a woman opened the door. It was Leigh Masters. He remembered her from their brief meeting at the Felgate family home but she had clearly forgotten.

"Mrs Masters, I'm Detective Inspector Tom Janssen," he said, holding up his warrant card for her. Her surprise grew. "Do you remember we met recently, in passing, when you visited your friend, Jane Felgate?"

She stood there, open mouthed for a second before realisation dawned and she nodded. "Yes, sorry." She shook her head. "I forgot."

"That's okay. May I have a word?"

"Who is it, love?"

Tom looked past her to see the man who'd watched his

arrival step out from a doorway further along the hall. Leigh looked over her shoulder.

"I–It's the police, Rod."

Tom presumed he was her husband. He was built in the manner Eric had described, comfortably over six feet tall and powerfully built. He approached them both, placing a hand on his wife's shoulder. She appeared to flinch. It was an almost imperceptible involuntary action but Tom saw it nevertheless. He looked Tom up and down.

"What is it? What's happened?" he asked.

Tom smiled. "Nothing to worry about, Mr Masters. I'm looking for a little help."

"Rod," he said, offering his hand. Tom accepted. "Rhodri Masters. It'd be a pleasure to help. What can we do for the police?"

His tone was measured and polite, keen to assist. It was exactly what one would hope for when faced with a police visit. However, in Tom's experience, it rarely happened. He was too accommodating.

"I'd like to speak to you about Gavin Felgate."

"Gavin?" Rod said, frowning. "Yes, terrible business all that."

"All what?"

"Well... his death."

He glanced down at his wife, easily a foot shorter than him but she looked at her feet, wringing her hands slowly in front of her.

"Yes," Tom said. "It's certainly a tragedy."

"Murder, we heard. Didn't we, love?" Rod said. Leigh nodded solemnly. "Have you," he hesitated, rolling his lips together, "got anywhere with finding out who did it?"

"Investigations are continuing, Mr Masters."

"Please, do come in." Rod eased his wife back into the

house, both hands now placed on her shoulders guiding her. Tom followed, closing the door behind him. "As I say, a nasty business," Rod said, pushing open a door to the front-facing living room. His wife entered but he held back, allowing Tom to pass through first. "We knew Gavin quite well, you know?" Tom met his eye with a backward glance, nodding. "We were friends since he and Jane were married. I wonder how she's coping with all of this?"

He offered Tom a seat on a floral-print sofa, the Masters sitting down opposite him. Tom looked between them, feeling the need to speak to Leigh alone but realising he'd need to engineer a way for that to happen. Rod Masters looked to be settling in for the duration.

"You were a bridesmaid at the Felgates' wedding, weren't you?" Tom asked. Leigh nodded, forcing a smile but it only served to make her appear nervous. "So, you say you go back a long way with the couple?"

"Yes, many years," Rod said. Tom had directed the question at Leigh, but he didn't seem to notice, choosing to answer. "We used to spend a lot of time together. Two couples, getting along." Rod's face split into a broad smile and he shot a quick glance sideways at his wife. "Not so much these days. Not since their split. Isn't that right, love?"

Leigh nodded, smiling weakly.

"I don't really know how much help we can be to you, Inspector," Leigh said, looking between Tom and her husband, all the while one hand fiddling absently with the pendant hanging from her necklace. "I mean, we hadn't really mixed with Gavin for a long time."

"That's right. A long time," Rod said quietly.

"I see." Tom took out his notebook and flipped through a couple of pages. "But you remain close with Jane?" He looked at Leigh directly, ensuring they both realised the question was meant for her to answer. That didn't stop Rod.

"You saw her from time to time, didn't you, love? We still live in the same town."

"I was hoping to speak to your wife, Mr Masters. If you don't mind?" The tone was such that Rod knew he'd been slapped down, politely. Tom fixed his eye on her. "Mrs Masters?"

She bit her lower lip, nodding. "We kept in touch, yes."

"And Gavin?"

Rod flinched, making ready to answer but thought better of it as Tom stared at him.

"N–No... I've not really seen much of Gavin for a long time."

"Right, that's what your husband just said." Tom looked at Rod. "I've been on the go all day. Would it be terribly inconvenient to trouble you for a cup of tea, Mr Masters?"

Rod's brow furrowed and he exchanged a look with his wife.

"I–I guess not, no." His gaze narrowed momentarily and his lips moved without uttering a sound.

"White, no sugar for me, please," Tom said, smiling and glancing at the door. It was clear what he wanted. Rod Masters wasn't keen but he rose and slowly made his way out of the room. He didn't close the door but Tom followed, listening to ensure he'd actually left, hearing his footfalls on the wooden floor making his way into the kitchen. Tom gently closed the door and returned to the sofa. Leigh was watching him, wide-eyed.

"You were saying... about the last time you saw Gavin Felgate?"

She shook her head. "I–It's been ages."

"Right," Tom said. "But here's the thing," he leafed through his notes, "we have multiple text messages exchanged between Gavin and an unknown person over a prolonged period, and it's quite clear that the person in question was in a relationship with Gavin Felgate."

Leigh shook her head, her lips pursed, before nervously glancing at the closed door.

"Any idea who that person might be?"

Again, she shook her head.

"And then there's Gavin's diary," Tom said, holding her gaze, "where he has pencilled in regular meetings with an unnamed individual, the same times each week. Now we've checked with his boss, asked around his work colleagues... neighbours... and we're stumped."

She averted her eyes from his.

"Although one particular neighbour was very helpful. A stereotypical nosy parker," Tom said softly. Her eyes darted up to meet his and away again. "He describes one particular frequent visitor to Gavin's home – a woman – and I dare say he could pick her out if needed."

"I–I don't understand why—"

"Because it's you, Mrs Masters."

She scoffed, attempting to appear dismissive but failing and looking flustered.

"Gavin mentioned you by name in one of the texts," Tom said, glancing at the closed door. "And I think I can see why you made use of an unregistered mobile. You were both very careful, but just that one little lapse, that one moment of care-lessness by Gavin and here I am."

Leigh closed her eyes, taking a deep breath as the colour drained from her face.

"I'm not here to cause trouble for you, Mrs Masters, nor am I passing judgement. It isn't my place, but I need you to be straight with me."

The door opened and moments later, Rod Masters backed into the room carrying a tray bearing three mugs. He'd made the brew quickly. Tom guessed the tea would look like dishwater. He swiftly got up and crossed the distance between them. As Rod turned, Tom lifted two mugs from the tray, nodded his thanks and blocked the man's path into the room.

"I need to speak to both you and your wife separately if you don't mind? It's for the best, professionally speaking."

Rod hesitated, shooting a look at his wife who didn't return it. She had her hands clasped together in her lap, perched as she was on the edge of the sofa staring straight ahead.

"Well, I might have something to say about that."

"And I'll be delighted to listen, Mr Masters. Once I'm done speaking to your wife. If you'd care to wait in another room."

Tom gestured to the door with an open hand leaving the man in no doubt that it wasn't a request. Grumbling, Rod Masters retreated but not before holding a lingering gaze over his wife. She didn't look at him once. Tom placed both mugs down on the coffee table between them as the door's latch clicked upon the husband's departure. Leigh didn't register its presence. He sat down again, watching her expectantly, but allowing her a moment to gather herself. She closed her eyes and took another deep breath before opening them and meeting Tom's eye.

"Gavin was an intriguing man," she said, pensively. "I always thought so. Difficult, certainly," she tilted her head to one side, "but he could be witty and charming... and his knowledge about the world was a joy to engage with. Time with Gavin was altogether very different to my average day." She pursed her lips.

"And when did your relationship begin?"

Leigh sighed, wringing her hands and looking to the ceiling, her eyes watering. "A year ago, perhaps? I'm not sure. We bumped into one another... hadn't seen him for ages." She smiled nervously. "And it was great to see him, to catch up. He looked different somehow, vibrant! He hadn't been like that in years. We went for a coffee a–and we got chatting." She looked away from him, fearful of his judgement maybe. "And it... it just went from there really."

"And you used to meet him regularly?"

She nodded. "Yes, at his place in Heacham."

"I'm not particularly interested in your personal life, Mrs Masters. You're a grown adult but I need to know if you were with him on the night he died?"

She swallowed hard. Her throat must be dry. She nodded again. "Rod was working. He's a rep for a pharmaceuticals company and he had a deadline for something or other," her tone was dismissive, as if his work was a source of friction in their marriage, "and I knew he'd be back late." Leigh took a deep breath, lifting herself upright and adjusting the way her long skirt sat over her legs. She was on edge. "We didn't often get to spend an evening together – Gavin and me – and so it was nice to... to be like a normal couple for once," she said, lowering her voice.

"What did you do that night?"

She thought about it. "Nothing special. We watched a film, streamed it online. We ordered a takeaway – an Indian – from the local place. It was a normal sort of evening but it was nice. He was pleasant company."

"And how did he seem, Gavin?"

She raised her eyebrows, open mouthed, answering as she briskly exhaled. "Normal." She smiled, shaking her head. "He was upbeat, funny. He had me in stitches at some points."

"But you weren't intending to stay over?"

"No, not at all," she said, firmly shaking her head. "That was never on the cards, unless Rod was away we could never do that. I think I only stayed over once or twice and not recently. I left around nine, I think." She lowered her head. "Rod was due home by ten and... I needed to shower first."

"How did you get there?" She looked at him, confused. "Did you drive, take a taxi?"

"I drove."

"Did Gavin drive? There is a car at his home registered in his name."

"Yes, of course he did. A big blue thing," her brow creased in thought, "Japanese, I think. Sorry, cars aren't my thing."

"And what were his plans for after you left that night?"

"I don't understand," she said, her eyes narrowing. "What do you mean?"

"Did he say what his plans were, whether he was going out anywhere or meeting someone perhaps?"

"No. I didn't think he had any plans. Why?"

"Because he ordered a taxi to collect him from his home shortly after you left his place. Why might he do that do you think? Had he been drinking?"

"Dear Lord, no!" she said shaking her head. "Gavin didn't drink."

Tom was surprised by the ferocity with which she delivered the comment. Leigh noticed.

"I know he used to be a drinker, Inspector. Heaven knows I listened to Jane lamenting his drinking habits often enough. They used to argue furiously about it... but..." she stammered and Tom encouraged her to continue. "Gavin had put a great deal of effort into... into his problems." She nodded briskly. "And he was winning, making real progress. He knew he had addiction issues and was getting help."

"Professional help?"

"He attended AA regularly, had a support network and a sponsor," she said, eager to praise her lover. "He'd been on the programme long before the two of us were together. I remember he was struggling with the whole religious side of things, though."

"Is Alcoholics Anonymous religious?" Tom asked.

"Well, no... but Gavin used to speak of it like he was part of some type of spiritual club. Attendees had to accept their lives had become unmanageable and needed to look to a higher power, be that God or whatever supreme power they believed in, and hand their lives over to it. As a committed atheist, I think he struggled with that aspect."

"But he was successful in the programme?"

"I think so, yes," she nodded, smiling. "I know he wasn't keen on *Step Five* but he didn't elaborate on why and, in any event, he hadn't got there yet."

"What is Step Five?"

"Confessions. Of your sins," she looked up at the ceiling, rocking slowly in her seat, "to someone else rather than just to yourself which is Step Four."

"I see. What about his work, did he ever discuss what he was working on with you?"

She shook her head. "He said he gave enough of his head space over to work as it was and we didn't see each other much – our time together being precious – and so while he was with me, he'd stay out of the office." She looked apologetic. "I'm so sorry. I'm not much help, am I?"

"And your husband?"

"Please! It would devastate him to find out like this."

Tom frowned. "I'm sorry, but I'm not a priest, Mrs Masters."

"But he is a lovely man," she said, reaching out with a hand as if she could touch Tom, somehow implore him to keep the secret. "And he has nothing to do with this! He wouldn't harm anyone. He's a gentle giant, and he arrived home early – at a quarter to ten – and was with me for the rest of the night. He knows nothing of all this. Please, I beg y—"

The door to the room opened and Rod Masters strode in, stopping before them with hands on hips, looking flustered. Leigh visibly retreated into herself under her husband's fierce gaze. Tom wasn't sure if he could have heard the tail end of their conversation or not. His body language implied it was possible.

"I think you've had more than enough time alone with my wife, Inspector." He was red-faced and agitated. "You've turned up here unannounced, turfed me out of my living room and deliberately kept me in the dark in my own home... my own marriage, no less! Now, what's this all about? I *demand* to know."

Tom looked at Leigh and she appeared to be on the verge of panic, ashen faced. He looked up at Rod Masters, rising purposefully from his seat.

"I think that's enough for now, Mrs Masters," he said, smiling at Leigh. "But if I need to speak with you again then I'll be in touch. Is that okay?"

She looked up, nodding and forcing another artificial smile. Tom turned to her husband, who was still bristling. "Perhaps you can see me out, Mr Masters?"

Rod Masters wore an expression like thunder while escorting Tom to the front door. He opened it forcefully and stepped aside, glaring at Tom as he passed by. Tom stopped on the porch, looking back at him.

"Thank you for your time, Mr Masters." He fixed him with a stern look. "Take a deep breath after I've gone, won't you?"

Masters said nothing and Tom walked to his car. He heard steady footfalls on the gravel behind him and turned, partially minded to adopt a defensive stance but it wasn't necessary. Rod Masters' anger had already dissipated, his expression now looked strained, almost pitiful. Tom realised. The bravado and indignation were all for show. Rod Masters' lower lip trembled as he tried to form the right words.

"Y–You know, don't you?" he all but whispered, his lips remaining slightly parted.

Tom inclined his head, toying with the key fob in his hands. "What's that?"

Masters met his eye. "About Leigh... and Gavin." Tom didn't speak, pursing his lips. "For crying out loud, man," Rod said, looking skyward, choking back the emotion. "Don't make me say it."

Tom nodded, catching sight of Leigh standing in the bay window watching them, arms folded across her chest. "How long have you known?"

Rod scoffed at the question, hanging his head and drawing a deep breath. He looked at Tom with a haunted expression. "Are you married, Inspector Janssen?"

Tom didn't answer.

"Well," he looked over his shoulder at his wife, his sixth sense seemingly telling him she was there, "if you ever do get married, and stay married as long as we have, then you'll understand how you get to know someone inside and out. Sometimes, you know them better than they know themselves... and they, you." He sniffed hard, biting his lower lip. "And you'll know... you'll know when something's changed. You might not know what at first, but you will know because you can feel it," he raised a closed fist to the centre of his chest, tapping it firmly, "in here. I love my wife, Inspector." He glanced at the window, Tom following his gaze but Leigh was no longer visible. "You see, I know how the mind works... when you feel trapped, stuck in a rut." He looked around. "We have our nice house, a comfortable life. Leigh has her admin job at the local primary school and I have had a pretty successful career... but it is exactly that – comfortable. It's not exciting and doesn't light the fires of passion anymore. It's normal. So, I can see why her head was turned. Everyone wants to feel wanted, special... and I'll forgive her almost anything."

"And what about Gavin Felgate? Could you forgive him?"

Rod Masters held Tom's eye for a moment longer before turning on his heel and striding back into the house. The door slammed and Tom took one more look at the bay window, still empty, before walking to the car. Leigh Masters described her husband as a gentle giant and crucially, also provided him with an alibi. However, an alibi from a spouse, particularly one having a long-term affair with a mutual friend was worth very little in a murder case. There was an edge to Rhodri Masters that Tom didn't care for. Not at all.

CHAPTER TWENTY-THREE

THE ACCESS ROAD to the rear of the seafront houses ran parallel to the promenade, albeit at sea level blocking a view of the sea. To Eric's right was a large car park that tourists would use a short walk from the beach. Right now, it was empty as were the extensive caravan parks beyond. They looked sad to Eric without families milling around. He spotted the liveried police car outside one of the newer buildings. Each plot was fairly extensive with access for multiple cars. Several had outbuildings or storerooms beneath the living space for garaging or storage of water-sports equipment and anything else that was only of use when at the coast. It saved people from having to cart things back and forth, although Eric knew it wouldn't be desirable to leave much of value here in the off season.

Many of the houses had stood in the same place since Eric was a child. His parents once owned a caravan nearby and they'd spent many weeks over the school holidays there over the years. Looking back, it seemed odd to him, his parents owning a caravan on the Norfolk coast when they only lived a short drive away from the beach the rest of the year, but at the time he'd loved the trip away and it seemed somehow exotic to be going to stay by the sea for a while. His father had never been one for foreign travel – the definition of which, Eric concluded, also encompassed much of the United Kingdom as well. His father was one to describe himself as *proper Norfolk*.

Eric passed through the open gate, parking the car between a chain-link fence and a double garage. He cast an eye over the house, raised on stilts and clad in silver-grey fibre cement weather boarding, increasingly popular due to its resistance to the rotting capabilities of the sea air and spray. Walking to the stairs he noticed the windows were aluminium and contemporary light fittings adorned the exterior walls. As he climbed the stairs running to the right-hand side of the property, he was greeted with a broad smile by PC Kerry Palmer, appearing from within, having heard his presence on the creaking stairs. The two of them had joined the police in the same intake and had remained friends ever since.

"I heard you were back at work this week, DC Collet."

"PC Palmer," Eric said, smiling. "No need for you to go to the trouble of producing a dead body just to say hello."

"Perish the thought," she said, stepping to the side and allowing Eric to pass through. "How are you?"

He recognised the concern in her tone, more so than just looking out for a colleague. He felt guilty then. She'd contacted him several times while he was convalescing after his stabbing but he'd never returned her calls. If he was honest, Becca didn't like him having female friends. Not that she'd ever said so, but he felt it was an unspoken view she held. He stopped at the threshold, looking back and smiling.

"I'm well. Really. Thank you for getting in touch. I'm sorry I didn't—"

"Detective Constable Collet!"

A booming voice came from within. Eric smiled at Kerry

once more and she returned it, her eyes dipping away from his gaze. He couldn't think why. Eric turned and headed inside. PC Marcus Weaver greeted him from where he stood in the kitchen. He was a bear of a man with a naturally intense stare that always aided him in gaining the upper hand in any given confrontation. He was the colleague everyone wanted by their side when policing the town on a Friday night, particularly when the pubs turned out.

"Hi Marcus, what do you have for me?"

Kerry Palmer remained at the door and Eric followed Marcus deeper into the house. The kitchen opened up into a vaulted living area, open up to the beams of the ceiling, with full-width glazing that opened out onto decking overlooking the beach. Eric's gaze was drawn to the horizon. They were in one of the few places in England where you could be standing in the east of the country watching the sun setting over the sea. The sun was beneath the cloud layer now and slowly slipping from sight. Eric was sure he would never tire of the view but Marcus wasn't facing the scenery. He had his back to it. Eric turned and stared.

The living room was double height but to the rear of the property was a mezzanine floor, by the look of it accommodating a bedroom – open to the room below via a glass balustrade – and from here a man was suspended, hanging from a length of bed sheet, Eric thought, tied around his neck and then looped over a newel post. The body gently swayed in the breeze caused by the draught from the open door through the kitchen. His feet were dangling at head height, the sound of what Eric realised was the weight of the body pulling the material tight and flexing the wood of the newel post, a low groan murmuring with each sway.

"You'd better come upstairs, get a closer look," Weaver said, gesturing to the staircase on the far side of the room.

He led the way and Eric followed, not taking his eyes from the body. The excitement of getting out of the office and back into the field had dissipated now. This was the reality of what the job was. The sheet had been doubled over and knotted to shorten it, the body hanging from the mezzanine but the man's head was only a foot or so below the top of the newel. The length was immaterial, though. Eric had attended suicides where the deceased had tied a belt to a wardrobe handle and achieved terminal asphyxiation; it was about angles and the tautness of the material above all else.

He leaned over the balustrade, eyeing the man's face. From the discolouration of the skin, Eric figured he'd probably been dead for a day at most, but no more than that. The smell of death was present but it wasn't that of a decomposing body, not yet at least. The house felt cold, as if the heating hadn't been on which slowed the process but, all the same, a dead body had a particularly distinctive odour to it. Either that or it was Eric's imagination. He never knew and hadn't ever asked anyone else if they felt the same.

"Do you see the neck abrasions?"

Eric focussed on the neckline where the sheet was tight against the skin. He immediately saw what Weaver was getting at. The material had been drawn across the skin before pulling tight under the man's weight leaving abrasions much as one might expect, red patches where it had forcibly scraped over the skin, but there was something about the angle of the injuries that looked wrong. Eric glanced at Weaver.

"You're thinking he was choked prior to the hanging, aren't you?"

Weaver smiled. "I always said you were smarter than most, Eric."

Eric felt his pride swell but he refrained from smiling. It didn't seem appropriate somehow. He looked over the body again. The man was early to mid-thirties and Eric noticed his tan before anything else. The tan didn't look bottled, and the crow's feet at the corners of his eyes were pronounced indicating he spent a lot of time under direct sun. Wherever he'd been recently, it wasn't wintery Norfolk. His hair was sandy brown, short at the back and sides but longer on top, flopping to each side in a mix of waves and curls. He was dressed in a loose-fitting polo shirt and jeans. Again, Eric was surprised due to the nature of their recent weather.

"Do we have a name?"

"The property is registered to Harry Empson," Weaver said, producing his pocketbook. "I can see his wallet in his back pocket but I thought it best to leave it where it is until you guys got here."

Eric nodded, looking around. The bedroom stretched to the back of the house, a window overlooked the parking area. There was a single door to an ensuite bathroom as well. The bed wasn't made and a rucksack lay atop it alongside a smaller sports holdall. Eric crossed to them. They were both fastened shut and he noted the airline baggage tags looped through the handles. They didn't look old, more likely recent which might explain the man's tan. Besides the barcodes, Eric noted the name *Empson* as well as the flight number which he recognised as a British Airways marker and an arrival point in the UK, Heathrow.

"I wonder where he's been?" Eric said to no one in particular. From his vantage point on the mezzanine, Eric noted the roller shutters along the top of the wall of glass opposite him overlooking the promenade. He gestured to them. "Were the shutters down when you got here?"

Weaver shook his head. "No, they were up. The old boy walking his dog stopped to pick up its mess and happened to glance inside. He got one hell of a shock; I can tell you. We haven't touched a thing."

Eric nodded, looking directly out at the path along the top of the sea defences. The glass was coated with something, no doubt to keep some of the summer heat out but also to cloud the interior and offer a measure of privacy from passers by. That was understandable seeing as the property boundary butted up against the promenade and only the deck separated the interior from the path.

"How did you gain entry?"

"The same way you did. The door was unlocked. Closed, but unlocked."

Eric rubbed at his chin, looking at the bags and the unmade bed before turning back to the dead man. He sighed.

"We'll get the FME over to confirm but I'd say he's been dead for less than a day. Do you agree?"

Weaver nodded. "No more than that."

"Bed's not made," Eric said. "Yet to unpack. I'll check his flight info but my guess is he got here some time yesterday, maybe last night."

"And died soon after," Weaver said.

"Ever hear of a suicide where the guy travels to another country just to top himself?"

"No... but people are strange."

Eric smiled. "True. I'd better get Scenes of Crime out here." He took out his mobile and switched it on, making his way back downstairs. There was a flurry of beeps as voicemail notifications and text messages came through. He was relieved to see they were predominantly from Cassie along with a text from Becca asking him if he needed collecting from work. Becca was less keen on him going back out into the field than Tom Janssen appeared to be, so he quickly typed out a reply to

say he'd get a lift home from one of the others. Then he called
Cassie.

"Cass—"

"Where have you been, Eric? I had something I needed you
to look into," Cassie said. "I've just got back to the station and
they tell me you're off out and I've been calling."

"Yeah, I can explain," he said, talking over her. "We've got
something that—"

"Eric, does Tom know where you are?"

He chewed on his lip. "No." He could sense her frustration
but she wasn't angry, more concerned. He was touched, until
she spoke again.

"He'll do his nut when he finds out you—"

"I'm okay, Cass. I promise." He felt guilty. "I'm already tired
of sitting behind a desk, you know?"

There was a pause.

"Okay, fair enough. Don't worry about Tom. He'll be fine, I
should imagine. Eventually. Where are you anyway?"

"Heacham. Suspicious death."

"And is it?"

"I'd say so," Eric said, glancing back at the body he
presumed was Harry Empson. "Crudely made to look like a
suicide if you ask me."

"Great. That's all we need. I'll have to do my own leg work
if you're tied up there." Her voice sounded lighter, relieved.

"Did you have any joy with David Fysh's other half?"

"No, he's gone off on business for a few days but she
doesn't know where. For what it's worth, I believe her. But she
has given me the name of an old school friend that he may
confide in, so that's worth following up. Some bloke called
Empson."

"Sorry, what?" Eric asked, staring up at the body. "Did you
say… *Empson*?"

"Yes, why?"

"Um... I think I know where to find him."

"You do? Great! Where?"

"I'm looking at him... but he's not going to have a lot to say for himself."

CHAPTER TWENTY-FOUR

THE FLASH of camera bulbs going off momentarily distracted Tom as he knelt alongside the body. The crime scene technicians had brought the body down, laying it on a gurney on the lower floor in the centre of the living area, having been photographed prior to his arrival. The body bag was yet to be closed, allowing Tom a chance to take in the dead man's appearance. He cast a glance up at the mezzanine and then looked out over the sea. Dr Fiona Williams tracked his gaze.

"I think Eric was spot on," she said. Tom looked back at her, offering her a half-smile. He saw Eric in his peripheral vision speaking to a forensic investigator at the top of the stairs. They hadn't caught up yet and Tom knew his detective constable was keeping his distance from him. Fiona Williams drew his focus back to the body. "You see the damage to the skin tissue from the sheet?"

He looked closer to where she was pointing and nodded.

"The width of the abrasion where the cotton was drawn tight against the skin is fifty millimetres, give or take, about what you'd expect from a sheet fashioned into a makeshift noose." She held a pen in her hand, moving the tip up and down to signify the start and end of the abrasion. "It moves in a V-shape, upwards from just above the larynx in an upward trajectory to the crown of the head."

"As one would expect with a suicide by hanging."

"Quite so," she said smiling. "Likewise, death was most likely by way of ligature strangulation. The petechiae we can see beneath the eyelids and at the corners of the mouth, as well as the bleeding within the mouth itself, are all indicative of constriction to the arterial flow of blood to the head. But here's the thing," she beckoned him closer still, pointing to a narrow channel in the skin of the neck moving width-ways across the neck, just above the larynx, "this line here was not caused by the sheet. It's too fine, too narrow, almost cuts into the tissue itself and moves horizontally."

"He was strangled prior to hanging," Tom said quietly.

"I'm absolutely certain of it," she concluded. "Whether he was dead prior to hanging or merely unconscious, I can't say. I should imagine he will have lost consciousness within a few minutes under the strain. You can also see these random marks to either side of the line."

"Scratch marks," Tom said. She nodded. "He was clawing at it."

"The attacker must have had some strength about him." She frowned, eyeing the body up and down. "He's in his early to mid-thirties, in physically good shape – besides being dead, obviously. You'd think he'd have managed to put up quite a struggle."

Tom looked around. There were no signs of a struggle which surprised him. "You're sure he pushed back? I don't see any facial wounds. What about his hands?"

She lifted one arm from where it lay at his side, examining the back of the hand and the fingertips.

"Well, there are no cuts or grazes to the knuckles

suggesting a physical confrontation, but I'd say that with the bruising to the tissue of the neck, he fought to free himself. There is some tissue under the nails but the lab analysis may determine it belongs to him. The scratching, as you said."

Tom scanned the interior again. "What do you think was used?"

Fiona screwed her nose up, thinking hard. "It won't be a length of wire, more likely a narrow cable. A length of electrical flex, perhaps? There are no patterns in the skin depressions, so that would make it smooth, so I think that's your best bet. But if I had to guess, I'd say he wasn't strangled here."

Tom offered her a quizzical look.

"I could do with some help," she said.

"Eric!" Tom called and the DC broke away from what he was doing and hurried down the stairs to them. He smiled nervously at Tom as he approached.

"If you could help me lever him up onto his side please, Detective Constable Collet," Fiona said. Between the two of them, they eased him up so Tom could see the man's back. "Do you see his backside?"

Tom bent and looked, noting some vegetation and detritus caught in the metal studs around the pocket of his jeans. There appeared to be sand or dried mud in the seams as well. Eric and Fiona lowered him back down.

"Eric, make sure forensics are searching the compound out back. He may have been attacked outside as he came home." Eric nodded and, as he turned to leave; Tom touched his forearm stopping him from moving off. "Good work, Eric."

Eric smiled and made his way over to speak to the head of the processing team.

"I've bagged samples for the lab."

Tom nodded his thanks to Fiona. "Time of death?"

She looked at the body. "Around midnight last night, I'd say."

Tom sighed. "Okay, thank you."

"One hell of a welcome home, isn't it?"

He agreed, stepping away. Cassie bounded over to him, notebook in hand.

"What have you got, Cassie?"

"Passport found in the side pocket of his holdall matches the driving licence in his wallet," she said, scanning her notes. "Harry Empson, thirty-three years of age. This is his registered address, although," she glanced around, "it doesn't look like he spends a great deal of time here. He's unmarried, no dependents and as far as I can tell he has no family living locally either. There is a sister, though, living in Manchester but the address isn't current, apparently. Local officers are trying to track her down."

"Right. Where's he been recently?"

"Flew into Heathrow yesterday afternoon on a British Airways flight out of Lagos, Nigeria. He landed at six. What time did Fiona give us as time of death?"

"Midnight."

Cassie frowned. "Doesn't leave a lot of time before coming here, does it?"

Tom shook his head. "Must have cleared customs and travelled. Does he have a car?"

She shook her head. "There was nothing here. I'll check with the DVLA to see if he has one registered to him and, if he has, it may have been stolen."

"Good thinking. Find out who has the airport shuttle contracts locally among the taxi firms as well, see if anyone had a collection booked for that flight yesterday."

"Will do."

"Any idea what Mr Empson did for a living?"

"He had this in his wallet," Cassie said, producing a plastic evidence bag and passing it to Tom. Inside the bag was a credit-card sized photographic ID with an issue date eight years ago. The picture was undoubtedly Empson, only he looked fresh-faced and was sporting a goatee beard. The logo was one Tom didn't recognise, with the abbreviation W.o.B. in the top right-hand corner. He held it aloft with a quizzical look towards Cassie. "*Without Borders*," she said, raising her eyebrows. "It's a non-governmental organisation working in various locations across Africa, prioritising the development of health infrastructure to remote communities. Fresh water, access to basic medicines and vaccinations, that type of thing according to their website. I ran a background check on him."

"Any hits?"

She shook her head. "Clean as a whistle. I ran this place," she waved her hand in the air in a circular motion, "and it belonged to his parents. Both of them are deceased; killed in a traffic accident a decade ago. The ownership transferred to him following the completion of probate."

"Check this out," Eric said, approaching them from the rear of the living room clutching something in his hand. Tom hadn't noticed he'd come back in from outside. Eric was excited, handing a book to Tom. It was a crime thriller. Tom opened it at Eric's insistence, finding a handwritten dedication at the foot of the title page.

To my fellow Musketeer,
    G.

Tom's lips parted slightly and he looked at Eric, closing the book and passing it to Cassie. She opened it and leafed through to the entry.

"What on earth is going on here?" she asked. Tom raised his eyebrows. Cassie quickly flicked further through the book with her thumb, and a slip of paper fell out onto the floor. She knelt, picking it up. It was a picture. Before rising she cursed under her breath.

"What is it?" Tom asked.

She stood up, reversing the photograph so Tom could see. He squinted at the faded image. It was tatty and dog-eared. He didn't understand the significance. Cassie smiled wryly.

"I've seen this picture before." Tom and Eric exchanged a glance. Eric was in the dark too. "Gavin Felgate had this picture set as the background on his laptop."

"Who are they?" he asked, taking it from her and examining it closely. Three boys were sitting side by side, smiling at the camera. Tom guessed they were teenagers. They were all wearing shorts and T-shirts, so he figured it was summer. Their clothing was nondescript but modern, as were their haircuts. Nothing was distinctive enough to identify the era or any particular location, but it did seem as if they were in someone's back garden; a wooden fence was in the background and a bicycle wheel had crept into the shot lying across a concrete path, the likes of which were commonly found in housing estates built in the twentieth century.

"I didn't think much about it when I was going through Felgate's files, it was just a background." Cassie shrugged. "I figured they were nephews, his kid and friends or something."

Tom clicked his tongue against the roof of his mouth. "We need to know who they are."

Eric reached for the picture and Tom handed it to him. Eric smiled, appearing thoughtful.

"What is it?" Tom asked.

"What if," Eric said, flipping the photo and holding it up, "these are our Musketeers?"

Tom inhaled deeply. "Empson, Beaty, Fysh… makes three."

"And whoever is holding the camera makes four," Cassie said.

Tom nodded, looking to his left as Empson's body bag was zipped up ready for transportation to the Home Office pathologist. "You're asking the right question, Cass, what on earth is going on here?"

"This is too weird," Eric said, shaking his head.

"We need to find David Fysh," Tom said, looking at both of them.

"Yeah. I hope he's still alive?" Cassie replied.

Tom sighed. "Fysh, Empson and Beaty are linked. The only one we have access to," he looked at the gurney currently being removed from the beach house, "is Beaty, so let's start there. He knows more than he's letting on. He has to. Eric, you're with me. Cassie, I want you to follow up on Empson, how did he get home, who, if anyone, saw him and put a call into his employers. See if you can find out why he might have been travelling back here yesterday? Is it a holiday, planned… anything you can find out."

Cassie looked at her watch. "Any idea what time it is in Nigeria right now? Mind you, we don't even know if that's where he was based."

Tom nodded. "Tonight, is looking like a late one, so make your calls to loved ones," he said, taking out his phone and walking away from the others to call Alice.

Eric grimaced. "Becca's not going to be happy with me."

"Shouldn't worry, Eric. You've been off sick for months, so she'll probably be glad to be rid for a couple of hours!"

She was being tongue in cheek and Eric knew it. He laughed.

CHAPTER TWENTY-FIVE

IT WAS NEARING nine o'clock when Tom and Eric pulled the car into the kerb on Cliff Parade in Hunstanton. The wind was whipping in off the sea, buffeting them so hard as they got out that Tom had to use his strength to brace the door, stopping it from slamming against him. The cloud cover was such that nothing of the sea was visible to the naked eye, aside from pinpricks of light dotting along the horizon, passing ships seeking calmer water by hugging the coast as they tracked north.

Greg Beaty's house was in darkness. There was no traffic about, a few of the neighbours' homes had lights on but everything was quiet apart from the roar of the sea hammering against the cliffs barely a hundred feet away and below them.

"Do you think he's in?" Eric asked.

"Let's find out," Tom said, imagining he would be. On his first visit he didn't leave with the impression that Greg Beaty had much of a social life. Even if he chose to venture out, with his condition, he'd find it tricky. They made their way up the drive and Tom rang the doorbell several times. With the interior lights off, it was quite possible Beaty would be asleep. He spoke of how his daily pattern didn't really correspond with what most people would consider a normal life; his routine largely determined by his physical health.

Tom was about to ring again when the veranda lights flickered on and a face appeared behind the obscured glass of the front door.

"Who is it?"

"Police, Mr Beaty. DI Janssen."

He heard the door unlock. It cracked open. A bleary-eyed Greg Beaty peered through the gap, his eye line slightly above the security chain. The look of recognition crossed his expression and the door closed again, the chain sliding clear. He smiled weakly at Tom as the door opened.

"Sorry, I'm a little… out of sorts." Beaty ran a hand through his hair, as lank and greasy as it had been on Tom's first visit.

"No problem," Tom said. "I appreciate it's an odd hour for a visit."

"What time is it anyway?" Beaty asked, backing up to allow Tom and Eric space to enter. Tom noticed he was only on one crutch tonight. Eric closed the door, the sound echoing in the hall with its wooden floors and blank walls, where there was nothing to dampen the noise.

"Nine-ish," Tom said. "How have you been?"

"Ah… same old, same old. Sick of my own whinge, so I won't bore you with it," Beaty said, turning and heading towards the living room. He flicked on a couple of lights as he entered before heading to his customary seat by the window. He stopped, looking over forlornly at the wood burner and its fading orange glow, the embers were dying out. Eric entered the room and saw the wood burner, looking at the basket of woods alongside it.

"I could get that going again for you, if you like?"

"I'd appreciate that, thanks," Beaty replied. "I feel the cold terribly these days. What with all the pills I throw down my throat and all my muscle spasms... I really feel it."

"No problem," Eric said, moving over to reignite the flames.

Beaty looked at Tom, hesitating. "Do either of you want a drink? A cup of tea, beer or something."

"No, thank you," Tom said. Eric glanced back over his shoulder, shaking his head and Beaty nodded, dropping himself into his armchair. Leaning his crutch against the small nest of tables next to his seat, he reached forward to a case of beer cans at his feet, withdrawing one and popping the ring pull as he righted himself and sinking back into his seat with a forceful exhale.

"What brings you here so late?" Beaty said, wiping his mouth with the back of his hand. In the soft light of the lamps, Beaty cut a pained figure, easily looking far older than his years. Tom couldn't help but think the alcohol on top of the cocktail of medications he seemed to be on couldn't be very good for him. There was also a faint odour lingering in the room that was unmistakably cannabis.

"We wanted to ask you about your associations past and present."

"At this time of the night?" Beaty took a swig from his can. "Must be serious," he said with an easy smile. It looked artificial.

"You've lived here a long time, haven't you?"

Beaty rocked his head from side to side. "Pretty much all my life, on and off, in and around this area, yeah. I mean, I lived with my dad in London for a year or so when I was young and I've moved around a fair bit with work and stuff but the Norfolk coast has always been where I call home. I thought we'd already discussed that?"

"Must have a lot of friends?"

"One or two, yes." Beaty grinned, looking slightly perplexed. "Doesn't everyone? Why do you ask?"

"Harry Empson?"

Greg Beaty's eyes narrowed and he formed an O with his lips, slowly drawing air through them. Eric handed Tom the evidence bag with the book inside. Beaty's eyes followed the exchange.

"Yeah, I know Harry. We were at school together."

"Close?"

"Have been..." Beaty said coolly. "On and off, you know?"

Tom held up the bag so Beaty could see the contents, not that he thought they were in doubt. Tom could tell Beaty recognised his own book.

"When was this published?"

"Last spring. Where did you get that copy?"

Tom ignored the question, putting the bag down on the sofa next to him. "And when did you last see Harry?"

Beaty shrugged, looking out of the window with a focussed expression. He sniffed, looking back to meet Tom's eye. "Probably around then or later, summer maybe? I'm not sure. Harry isn't around much these days. He works abroad."

"Right. What does he do?" Tom asked, feigning total ignorance.

"He works for a charity. In Africa. Helping rural communities do... stuff," he said, waving a hand in the air and then lifting his beer with the other. He took a long swig, but his eyes never left Tom's. "Why do you ask?"

"I'm afraid I have some bad news, Mr Beaty. A body was found this evening at an address in Heacham. We believe it is that of Harry Empson."

Beaty's mouth fell open but other than that, he remained rock still.

"It looks like a suicide."

Beaty shook his head, his forehead creasing. "Not Harry. I don't... I mean, he wouldn't. What's he doing back here? I didn't think he was due back—" He stopped short of finishing the sentence, instead drinking more from his can. "Are you... sure?"

Tom nodded. "We believe so." He turned and picked up the book. "This copy has a handwritten dedication. We found it at Harry's house on the seafront."

"I gave it to him," Beaty said, nodding and looking straight ahead, cupping his beer can with both hands in his lap. "Last year. I hadn't seen him for some time and then he got in touch."

"When was this?"

Beaty took a breath, raising his eyes to the ceiling. "Um... September, October, I think. Yeah, around then."

"So, you saw him after spring or summer then, didn't you?" Tom said, fixing him with a stern look. Beaty held it for a moment and dipped his head in acknowledgement of the contradiction.

"I'm sorry, Inspector. I–I get confused sometimes. It's my medication."

"Easily done, Mr Beaty, but perhaps you need to think before answering further—"

"Am I being accused of something here? Because, if so—"

"We have reason to believe that Harry's death was not self-inflicted, so I think you should bear that in mind."

Beaty's shoulders sagged, his lips parting. "You think... someone... killed him?"

"Can you think of a reason someone, anyone, might want to do harm to your friend, Harry?"

He shook his head emphatically. "No. Harry was a great guy. He's dedicated his adult life to helping people, helping them to improve their own lives. He hasn't got an enemy in the world as far as I know." He brought a closed fist up to his mouth, his eyes watering. "Dear God, poor Harry."

Tom took the photo that Cassie found in the book and reached over, handing it to Beaty. The man put his beer down on the table, wiping his nose with the back of his hand and held the image up and away from him.

"Sorry, I don't have my glasses on."

He scanned the image, his eyes lingering on it for a few seconds as he bit his lower lip. He slowly lowered it into his lap, keeping his eyes on it the whole time as he took a deep breath.

"That's from a long time ago," he said quietly. "Man, they look young in this."

"Can you tell us who is in the picture?" Tom asked.

"Erm... yeah, sure. Harry is on the right," he said, holding the picture up and pointing to the boy on the right with wavy hair hanging past his ears with a central parting. "And the one in the middle is Davy—"

"David Fysh?"

Beaty nodded. "Yeah, that's him."

"You're friends?"

"Not so much now, no." Beaty tapped the image gently on his thigh, lifting his eyes to Tom. "We were tight at school for a while but, well... you move on in life, don't you? I went to college, photography took over my life and I was never really about anymore. Same with Harry, really."

"How old were they in this picture, would you say?"

Beaty pursed his lips. "I'd say fourteen, fifteen... maybe."

"And the other boy in the picture, who is he?"

Beaty raised the photo again, staring at it intently for a few seconds. Lowering it, he handed it back to Tom.

"Sorry, I can't place him."

Tom nodded, accepting the image back. "Right, thanks." He

looked at it himself briefly, then peered over it to see Beaty watching him warily. "You see, they all look pretty friendly, don't they?" Beaty shrugged. "And it's a small place where you all grew up. We checked your childhood addresses." Tom glanced at Eric.

"The three of you," Eric said, flicking back a page in his notebook, "David Fysh, Harry Empson and yourself, all lived within a mile radius of each other when you were teenagers."

Beaty nodded. "Sounds about right, yes. So what?"

"I grew up in Sheringham," Tom said, smiling. "It's a nice place to bring up kids – not that I thought so when I was growing up. We were bored as hell, me and my friends. Our parents would turf us out and we'd be off out on our bikes heading all over the place, only coming home when we were hungry."

"Or when it got dark," Beaty said, grinning.

Tom nodded. "The dedication in the book was made out to *My fellow Musketeer*."

"Yes, we gave ourselves that nickname," Beaty said, smiling.

"And how many Musketeers were there?"

Beaty was about to speak but Tom held up his hand and continued, "And bear in mind we'll be talking to David Fysh later as well."

It was a gamble on Tom's part. Either Beaty would be rattled at potentially having someone else contradict what he was about to say or Greg Beaty was in touch with his child-hood friend, in which case he would know he'd dropped off the radar and might give that away.

Beaty laughed nervously, speaking quietly. "It was just a nickname."

"But here's the thing, Greg," Tom said. "When I was a kid,

running with my friends in a small town, we knew everyone around us who was a similar age, or a year or two either side."

"I'm sorry, Inspector," Beaty said, his shoulders flinching upwards as he shook his head, smiling apologetically. "I don't know the kid. Or if I did, then I've forgotten. It was all a life-time ago."

"Sadly, your friend's life is over." Tom fixed his gaze on Beaty, who looked decidedly awkward under Tom's scrutiny. "So, we would appreciate your help."

"I–I'd be delighted to help," he said, "and if I knew, I would say but… I'm really very sorry, b–but I can't help you."

Beaty picked up his beer can – realising it was empty – he swore softly before putting it back down and reaching for another.

"Perhaps you might want to go easy."

Beaty laughed. It was a bitter sound without genuine humour. "Yeah. I've heard that a lot in the past!" He pulled the ring and was sprayed with beer which he ignored, shaking the residue from his hand and taking a large swig, then licking his lips. He stared at Tom.

"Tell me," Tom said, "in all the conversations you had with Gavin Felgate, did he ever speak to you about your friendship with David Fysh?"

Beaty held Tom's gaze, shaking his head. "No, not at all. Why would he? And Davy and me… we're not really close anymore anyway. Why would he?"

"You know Gavin Felgate was running a story on David's business dealings."

"Successful bloke, Davy."

"And not necessarily achieved legally," Tom said. Beaty looked at him sternly. "At least, that was the angle we believe Felgate was coming at it from."

Beaty smiled, shaking his head. "Doesn't sound like the Davy I know."

"But you're not friendly with him anymore, though, right?"

"Yeah, that's right. I'm not." Beaty looked away. "I guess people change, don't they?"

"Yes," Tom said. "In my line of work, I find people are full of surprises."

CHAPTER TWENTY-SIX

GREG BEATY CLOSED the door on the detectives, locked it and slid the security chain into place before they'd set foot off the veranda. He switched the exterior lights out and hobbled back into the living room and the warmth of the fire. Entering the room, he switched off the lights, leaving the orange and yellow flickering light from the wood burner. It was the only light source aside from the glow from the streetlights on Cliff Parade.

Grimacing with every step, he hurried over to the picture window – as hurried as he could be – to observe the policemen departing. He was there in time to see them get into their car; the taller of the two, Detective Inspector Janssen, paused to look up at the house. Confident that he was only visible in silhouette form, Greg remained where he was. Moments later, DI Janssen got into the car.

That nagging sensation of fear – the familiar knot in his chest – was back, his breathing short and ragged. A few years ago, it was the unknown that spurred him on, that created the drive to take the risks and fuelled the adrenalin that he loved to experience. These days it was different. What was it that bothered him? When he was abroad there was a sense of lawlessness in the environment, a feeling that the here and now was all that mattered. Long-term vision was something the people around him didn't consider; it wasn't their role. They didn't need to.

Back home everything was different. He was different.

The policemen drove away and he felt relief. But they would be back. When, he didn't know but they would be back. Picking up his mobile phone he scrolled through the contacts and selected one. He leaned against the wall, listening to the ringing phone. His eye was drawn to the passing ships on the horizon, their lights blinking as their position shifted on the rise and fall of the waves. It must be rough out there tonight. The call transferred to voicemail and he swore softly, waiting for the automated message to finish. The beep sounded.

"Hey, it's Greg. Listen, things are really starting to get out of hand… the police have just left my place and… and they're saying Harry… Harry's dead, man! I didn't even know he was back in the country, did you? They're telling me it looks like a suicide but that it isn't. First, that journalist is sniffing around and… then he's dead. Now Harry…" He paused, realising he was starting to ramble which he was prone to do when he felt overwhelmed – another recent change in him he didn't care for – and in any event, the less he said on the telephone the better under the circumstances. "Look, you need to call me when you get this message or come over to the house. I know you didn't want to before b–but I'm not mobile. I'm stuck here." He stood in silence, half expecting, half hoping he'd hear another voice on the end of the line. "Look, just call me, yeah?" He took a deep breath. "Please," he said, hanging up.

Greg touched the mobile to his lips and shut his eyes, attempting to get a handle on his breathing. Tossing the mobile to his armchair, he made his way over to a sideboard beneath the window and with great effort, lowered himself down onto his knees, an action that sent shooting pains and muscle spasms from his left foot up through his body culminating in a surge of pain in his forehead. He winced, tears coming to his eyes. Bracing himself against the sideboard, he took controlled breaths until the moment passed, reassuring himself that it would do so soon enough.

Opening his eyes, he reached into the right-hand cupboard in front of him and came away with an old shoe box. Holding it between his arm and chest he lifted himself up and limped over to the fireplace where he sank down on the rug before the wood burner, the shoe box spilling to the floor and emptying its contents onto the rug. Cursing, he began gathering the pictures together, old photographs he'd kept for some unknown reason for all these years. Photographs he never intended to look at. For the first time in years, he allowed himself to look, thumbing through them slowly and smiling at the happy faces; young teenagers without a care in the world, their whole lives in front of them. He stopped on one in particular, holding it up to see the detail better in the dancing firelight.

"Maybe you deserved it, Harry."

His gaze lingered on the photograph and he felt his eyes water. Hurriedly gathering the remaining pictures together into a small pile, he leaned forward and opened the door to the wood burner. The increase in oxygen to the fire saw it surge, the burning log crackling. He carefully placed the photographs inside and closed the door. The pictures caught alight, shrinking from the outside in. The image facing him was one of three boys, smiling at the camera.

"Maybe you're not the only one."

Tears came unbidden, rapidly turning to sobs as his lower lip trembled.

"I'm so sorry," he whispered as the last of the image was consumed by the heat, the wide eyes of an innocent face still smiling as the image shrank and then it was gone.

Greg Beaty wept. His physical pain momentarily forgotten as years of repressed feelings overwhelmed him.

"I'm so, so sorry."

CHAPTER TWENTY-SEVEN

TAMARA GREAVE ADDED the fresh coriander to the diced tomato, garlic and jalapeno peppers tossing them together, hearing the rice cooker click at the same time as her mother tutted. She ignored it, spooning out some of the mixture onto a plate and setting the remainder aside to go in the fridge for tomorrow. Not wishing to keep her counsel, Francesca Greave tutted again, only this time louder. Tamara, her back to her mother, cast her eyes heavenward and glanced over her shoulder.

"Have I missed something?"

"No, not that I'm aware of, Tammy." Her mother smiled in that artificial way she did when she had something to say but needed encouragement to say it. Tamara didn't offer it. Undeterred, her mum said it anyway. "It seems like a bit of a faff, if you ask me?"

Tamara smiled, lifting the bowl from the rice cooker by its edge with a tea towel, moving back to the island, and ladling out a portion of rice next to the salsa.

"I didn't think I had," she said under her breath.

"What was that dear?"

222 J M DALGLIESH

"Nothing, Mum. Just thinking out loud."

She finished laying out her meal by adding the lentil dahl on top of the rice and picking up a packet of corn tortillas, she crossed to the dining table and sat down opposite her mother, already halfway through her own meal. The two of them sharing the same space to prepare different meals at the same time, in order to eat together, made for a challenging experience. Tamara offered to cook for her house guest, repeatedly, only to be knocked back.

"It takes a while doesn't it?" Francesca said, cutting into her pork chop.

"What's that?"

"Preparing vegetarian food."

"Vegan."

"Same thing," Francesca said, hesitating as she raised her fork to her mouth.

Tamara sighed internally. This was only the third or fourth time the subject had arisen in as many days. "How's your flesh?"

"Oh, really, Tammy. But must you be so churlish? And it is lovely, thank you."

Francesca frowned at her, but Tamara knew she wasn't genuinely offended. This was how they conversed with one another much of the time, always had done. They were too similar in character. At least that was what her father had always said. Tamara didn't see it, but such was the way with these things, he was probably right. The thought of her father coming to mind sparked her into bringing him up. She'd wanted to do so for two days now but openness was not something the Greave women did particularly well.

"So, I spoke to Dad," Tamara said casually between mouthfuls, picking up her glass of water and sipping from it. Her mother continued eating as if nothing had been said. She might not have heard, but Tamara doubted it. "He's finding things difficult." Still, there was no reaction. "Mum—"

"Yes, I heard you," Francesca replied. "The first and the second time. I'm not deaf."

Stubborn and obstinate though.

"I think he'd appreciate it if you called him."

"Would he?"

"Yes, I think so. Even if it's just to let him know you're okay."

"Didn't you tell him?"

Tamara took a breath. Her mother was a guarded individual, contrary to the image she always sought to project to those around her. That was a trait Tamara could relate to. Usually, it was hard to get a steer on what she was really thinking, but on occasion, much like now, the barriers she erected gave her away.

"He misses you, Mum." Francesca inclined her head at hearing the comment, but she only had eyes for the plate in front of her, pushing the food around it in a culinary dance between knife and fork. "And I think you miss him too."

"Have you ever thought, dear, that it's your veganism that's stopping you from getting a man?"

That was also a typical Greave response when pushed into a subject you were desperate to avoid – go on the offensive and cut as close to the quick as possible.

"I'm hardly unable to *get a man*, Mum."

"Well," Francesca said, raising her head and looking around as if searching for something in the kitchen, "I don't see them knocking at your door, darling. And let's face it, you're not getting any younger, are you?"

Tamara sighed. "Nice attempt at deflection, Mum, but it's not going to work," she said pointedly, smiling.

Francesca returned the smile, raising her eyebrows. "I'm

sorry if you think it's trivial, Tammy, but I would like to see some grandchildren before I'm too old to enjoy them."

"Mother, you have four grandchildren already, three girls and a boy. A fact you know only too well."

"Yes, but not from you, dear," Francesca said, smiling weakly.

"Children aren't for everyone, Mum." She raised her eyebrows, casting a stern look at her mother. "You might just have to make do with what you have."

"What about that nice detective inspector who works for you?"

"Tom?" Tamara heard the change in tone as she said his name. This wasn't somewhere she wanted to go with her mother. "We're colleagues."

"Yes, but you're his boss." Francesca winked. "Can't you – what would you say – pull rank or something?"

"Mother!"

Francesca chuckled and Tamara found herself smiling as well, shaking her head as she returned to her dinner.

"Unless, of course, you are more inclined towards your detective sergeant."

"Now you're just stirring, Mum."

"Well, it's not natural is it? A woman of your age should at least be down the aisle by now and thinking about children."

"Are you going to call Dad?"

The doorbell rang. Francesca eased herself out of her chair. "I'll go, dear. You finish your rice. Brown rice doesn't have a lot of flavour to it, does it, dear? A nice jasmine rice will go a little better if you ask me."

Tamara rolled her eyes as her mother hurried from the kitchen. It was galling. Tamara spent the first part of the week avoiding a conversation and now her mother had explained the reason for the impromptu visit, she was the one trying to avoid the discussion. She heard an exchange of greetings, her mother fussing around the newcomer in that overtly artificial, over-the-top manner that she was prone to. They returned to the kitchen, Francesca taking the lead.

"Look who it is, Tammy darling," she said, smiling broadly. "Speak of the devil and he shall appear!"

"All positive, I hope," Tom said, loosening his coat in the warmth of the house. He spied Tamara's dinner, frowning. "Ah, sorry. Bad timing."

"No, no, it's fine, Tom," Francesca said. "Take a seat here, next to me."

"Or maybe – seeing as it's work related – it would be better if you left us to it, Mum?"

Tom looked awkward. Tamara met her mother's eye and Francesca smiled warmly.

"Of course, dear. It's probably for the best if the two of you have some time alone together."

The tone of the comment didn't pass Tamara by and the accompanying expression left her in no doubt as to what her mum meant. By the look on Tom's face, he hadn't needed to be present earlier to grasp the not-so-hidden meaning behind it either.

"Thank you, Mum."

Francesca smiled, picking up her plate to carry it into the kitchen, gently placing a comforting hand on Tom's shoulder as she passed. Having put the plate next to the dishwasher, she left them to it. Tamara felt her face redden.

"Sorry about that. Mum's just stirring… the embarrassment of having a spinster daughter is a matter very close to her heart."

"Really?" Tom looked over his shoulder to the place where Francesca had been, looking back and raising his eyebrows.

"What brings you out here at this time?"

"Harry Empson."

"Murder dressed as suicide?" Tamara said, loading her fork but pausing before raising it to her mouth. Tom nodded. "Run him past me again."

"Anna Fysh states Harry and her husband are pretty close. She had him down as the one he would likely turn to if he needed help in some way."

"And did he?"

Tom's brow creased. "We're trying to ascertain if there's been any recent contact. Cassie is trying to locate mobile phone records for Empson but – because he lives and works out of the country – we've no idea who his network provider is."

"No mobile at the scene?"

Tom shook his head. "The airline confirmed Empson's travel plans and that he checked in online through his mobile app, so he had a phone."

"Robbery?"

"Wallet was still in his pocket, travel bags placed neatly on his bed and unopened. His place was immaculate. Forensics reckon he was most likely attacked outside due to traces of vegetation found in his clothing, probably as soon as he arrived home. I imagine he was either incapacitated or subdued and taken inside, no evidence of a struggle indoors, so I think he was unconscious before being hanged."

"Waiting for him?"

"Unlikely," Tom said, sitting back and stifling a yawn. "Sorry, late one today. Those beach front homes are all empty at this time of the year. No one is going to be lying in wait for a man to turn up. They could be waiting there until spring. Empson would have to be the unluckiest man alive or—"

"They knew he was coming," Tamara said.

Tom nodded. "My thoughts exactly. So, who would know he was coming home?"

"His closest hometown friend might," Tamara said, inclining her head. "Where are we with locating David Fysh?"

Tom sighed. "We're struggling there. His mobile phone is off and hasn't pinged on the network since he texted his wife to say he was going away on business for a few days. There have been no hits on his bank account and no transactions recorded on any of his credit cards. Eric checked with the Border Force and we have no recorded data to suggest he's left the country but..."

"But?" Tamara asked, swallowing the last mouthful of her dinner.

"He does own a yacht. It's moored at Wells."

"Still there?"

"We'll check in the morning."

Tamara put her knife and fork together on her plate, loosening a bit of food stuck between her teeth with the end of her tongue. "What are you thinking?"

Tom frowned. "At first, I thought Fysh had gone to ground. We're sniffing around his business and judging from the footage Gavin Felgate recorded, it would appear as if Fysh has been up to no good in his business: at one end of the scale cutting corners on quality or at the other end selling food not fit for human consumption. If it's true, he has a lot to lose—"

"There's a motive to kill for, right there," Tamara said. Tom agreed. "But now you're thinking differently?"

"Yes, it just doesn't fit everything else though, does it? Where does Empson fit in? Or the Haverson suicide for that matter. Gavin Felgate rigged the noose on Roydon Common... why?"

Tamara exhaled. "You were talking about a photograph earlier on the phone."

"Right," Tom said, producing the folded evidence bag with the picture inside they'd discovered at Empson's house and later shown to Greg Beaty. He handed it to her. She unfolded the bag and focussed on the image.

"And what did Greg Beaty have to say about this?"

Tom shook his head. "Not a lot, to be honest. He picked out Fysh and Empson but not the other lad, the one with the glasses."

"So, what we really want to know is what did Gavin Felgate uncover?"

Tom bit his lower lip, apparently thinking hard as she spoke.

"If we knew that, it might help us understand where David Fysh has gone."

"Unless he's just trying to stay off the radar for a bit," Tamara said, "leave no digital footprint while he..." she shook her head, puzzled "...what... cleans up?"

"I had another thought regarding Fysh."

"Go on."

"Maybe it's not by choice that he hasn't shown up. Particularly in light of what happened to Harry Empson."

Tamara scratched at her forehead, closing her eyes and concentrating. The complexities of their prospective theories were making her head hurt. They weren't there yet and needed more, but she could sense they were close. "I know what you mean but we have too many variables at play here. We need to go back to the beginning. The answers are there, I'm sure of it. In the meantime, we keep looking for David Fysh. If he has come a cropper, then we've no reason to believe his body would be concealed. Felgate and Empson weren't disposed of."

"Felgate could've been a spur of the moment killing, though – for a reason as yet unknown – whereas Empson's looked calculated. They tried to disguise what happened to him. Very amateurish when you scratch the surface but still it was a considered occurrence."

Tamara had to admit that was true. "Okay, but we still need to locate Fysh and determine one way or the other whether he's a victim or a suspect. Square one – tie those three boys to Ciaran Haverson, even if it's just by association, and then we can put the squeeze on Greg Beaty, seeing as he is the only one of the three still available to us at present. Do you think he could be the one?"

"To kill Felgate and Empson?" Tom asked, immediately shaking his head. "Not physically capable. Not by himself anyway."

"Has he had contact with Fysh?"

Tom shook his head. "Says not… but he's holding back. We could bring him in, press him harder."

"Not yet," Tamara said. "Go back and speak to people around David Fysh. Find out whether there's anything we missed about him that might indicate something else is going on in his life at the moment or where he's gone to. People talk to one another; friends, employees, neighbours… whoever. They might not have been willing to speak up before but now… with everything that's going on, they might be more open, even if it's loose talk. You never know, there might be something we can use."

"He's been spending the bulk of his time at the new restaurant in Hunstanton, so I'll head over there tomorrow."

"The same goes for Empson," she said. "We need to know why he came back unannounced, his associations, back story… everything? It's a strange time to come home."

"Cassie's already on it," Tom said, yawning.

"Gavin Felgate was taking an interest in Fysh's business and also interviewed Greg Beaty. Is it a coincidence that they are both friendly with Harry Empson, who turns up out of the blue and winds up dead for his troubles?"

Tom drummed his fingers on the table, rolling his tongue

across the inside of his left cheek. "I wonder if Felgate had looked into Empson as well? Worth checking with his editor... and revisiting the files on his laptop while we're at it."

"What did you make of this woman Gavin Felgate was seeing, Leigh...?"

"Leigh Masters," Tom said. "Genuinely upset at Felgate's passing. She confirmed she was with him on the night he died but she left before he did."

"And didn't know where he was going?"

Tom shook his head. "Says not, and I believe her. She also claimed her husband is unaware of the affair – he is aware, by the way – and gave him an alibi for the time of death as well."

"And you met him?"

"Yes. He's angry... upset, and I think he's known for a while that she was playing away."

"Angry enough to kill?"

"Maybe," Tom said. "But he doesn't fit into David Fysh's vanishing act or Empson's faked suicide, so I don't know where to go with that. Unless they're not connected."

"But they are. It's all too coincidental otherwise. First things first," Tamara said. "Go home and get some sleep. We'll pick it up again in the morning."

"Right," Tom said, pushing his chair back and standing up to put on his coat. The legs of his chair scraped on the tiled floor, echoing loudly. Francesca appeared as if it had been a call to summon her.

"You're not leaving already are you, Tom?"

He smiled. "I'm afraid so. I've missed Saffy's bedtime but it wouldn't serve me well to miss Alice's as well."

"Oh yes, of course. Alice and Saffy. Quite sweet, both of them. You'd better run along," she said, looking at Tamara. "Not much to keep you here, anyway, is there?"

Tamara shot daggers at her mother but Tom didn't appear to notice. He said goodnight and headed for the hall.

"See you in the morning, Tom," Tamara said and he waved his hand over his shoulder without looking around.

Francesca took the seat he'd just vacated, resting her elbows on the table and crossing her arms. "Honestly, if you'd told me all the men in Norfolk were this handsome, I'd have come across—"

"Mum!" Tamara said, putting her head in her hands. "For the final time, *why on earth did you choose to come here*?"

"Why shouldn't I come to stay with my daughter?"

"Mum, why me? I have two sisters... and let's not beat around the bush, you prefer spending time with both of them far more than you do me." Francesca made to argue but Tamara raised a hand to halt the protest before the words escaped her mouth. "I'm not looking to beat you up about it, Mum. It's just the way it is. I know that you care for me – love me even – when you're not really irritated by my life choices, but why did you bring this to me?"

Francesca's lips parted and Tamara read something in her expression, was it sadness, vulnerability... or something else entirely? She couldn't recall ever seeing it in her mother before. Francesca hesitated, appearing nervous.

"I had to come to you, Tammy," she said quietly. Tamara really hated that nickname.. "You're the only one who I thought would understand."

Tamara frowned, exhaling hard. "Why *on earth* do you think I would understand what this is all about?"

Francesca reached across the table taking one of Tamara's hands in both of her own, squeezing it. "Because of Richard."

"Richard? What are you talking about?" Tamara couldn't understand what her ex-fiancé had to do with any of this.

"You left Richard before you got married... it was all arranged and—"

"Yes, I did. I couldn't see myself spending the rest of my life with a man whom I wasn't committed to. We were on different paths," she shook her head, "and we could have wasted years before we worked out we should never have been together in the first place!" She met her mother's eye and saw the pain in her expression. Then she realised. "Oh, Mum…"

Francesca nodded, smiling weakly and clearly emotional. "You see, Tamara… I married my Richard."

CHAPTER TWENTY-EIGHT

HUNSTANTON HIGH STREET still had a few parking spaces along the one-way system and Tom pulled in outside the restaurant. He peered through the window and could see the place was already filling up. It wasn't large, perhaps a dozen tables at most but at this time of the day he was surprised.

"Word must be spreading," Cassie said, following his eye line. The restaurant had only just opened and the locals certainly seemed to be taking a keen interest. "What do you want to do?"

Tom glanced sideways at her, then outside at the line of shops opposite. "Take a walk around the neighbouring businesses, see if anything out of the ordinary caught their eye in the last week. Especially if it comes to David Fysh and Gavin Felgate. Felgate's picture has been all over the press this past week, so it may have jogged a few memories but they might not realise the significance."

Cassie nodded, cracking her door open.

"How did you get on with tracing Harry Empson's movements with his employer?"

She shook her head, still holding onto the door handle. "I

couldn't get hold of anyone of any note last night, even at their registered offices here in the UK, just an automated answering service. I had a call back first thing and my request has been forwarded to HR."

"Sounds about right. Any organisation goes through their corporate procedure when the police call."

"Right. I'll chase them up as soon as we're done here."

"And Eric?" Tom asked. He hadn't seen the detective constable before they left.

"He put in a request to the Home Office pathologist to expedite Empson's autopsy. Luckily, *Dr Death* is keen, so he's headed straight over there this morning."

They both got out, Cassie crossing the road in between passing cars while Tom walked into the restaurant. The manager, Sally, spied his arrival before the door closed behind him and he saw her roll her eyes. He made his way through the tables to the bar where she was standing, seeing only four tables unoccupied.

"Good morning," he said, smiling.

"Morning, Inspector. What can I do for you today?"

A patron waved at her, attempting to get her attention and she smiled to indicate she was aware before turning back to Tom.

"As you can see; we're rather busy, so I hope you're not here to turn everything upside down like last time? I don't think an environmental health inspector could have cleared this place faster than your lot managed to do the other day."

Tom smiled, looking around. "It doesn't seem to have done trade any harm."

Sally couldn't stop herself from grinning. "True. It seems we are popular." She lowered her voice so only the two of them could hear. "I think we're the most exciting thing to happen to the town in ages. The brunch menu seems to have gone down well. We're booked up until the weekend! I just wish..."

"Wish what?"

The joyous expression on her face faded. "That the staff could be as reliable as the clientele."

Tom offered her a puzzled look but then he heard a shout from the kitchens and the sound of something crashing, an accident of sorts. Sally sent a withering look in the direction of the kitchen as if she could see through the closed service doors. Another shout, only this time it was someone else. Several patrons looked towards the kitchen and Sally nervously smiled, a vain attempt to portray everything as normal.

"Miss, we've been waiting—"

"Yes, yes," Sally said, inclining her head towards the gentleman who had spoken, "I'm terribly sorry. Teething problems in the kitchen. I'll have your order out to you soon."

The man didn't appreciate her reply, grumbling something to the woman sitting opposite him. Sally looked at Tom, exasperated.

"I can see you're having problems today," Tom said.

"We're two down today," she said, "if you include David."

"He's still not reappeared then?" She shook her head. "Are you worried?"

Another shout came from the kitchen and Sally headed towards it, Tom falling into step. She pushed open the swing door to the kitchen and passed through. Tom followed. The kitchen was in chaos. Two male members of staff appeared to be on the verge of coming to blows, the heated situation calming only when they caught sight of Sally's entrance. Another woman, in her early twenties, was standing off to the right dressed in a white blouse and black skirt. Tom guessed she was front-of-house serving staff. The two men, in chef's garb of white tunics and checked trousers separated. One of them returned to his station at the grill while the other knelt to gather up a tray and whatever ingredients were once upon it. Tom guessed that was the source of the crash. Sally glanced sideways at Tom.

"Whatever it is you need, Inspector, please can you make it fast before this place grinds to a complete halt!"

The waitress picked up three plates and eased herself past them and out into the restaurant, smiling at Tom as she passed.

"It's just a revisit really, although there's nothing new," Tom said. "I'm hoping someone will remember something about Gavin Felgate's interview that they'd previously not mentioned." He looked around for James Cook, the chef he'd spoken to before but couldn't see him. "James not in?"

Sally shook her head. "No! And he damn well better have a decent excuse too." Tom looked at her quizzically. "He called in sick yesterday but hasn't turned up today. He said he felt rough but would be back in today." He could hear the stress in her voice. "Most of the team are new hires – inexperienced – and without David around I'm relying on James to get me through."

"Right," Tom said, feeling for her. "That's a shame. I was hoping to speak to him as he was the only one Felgate interviewed."

"What about Mikey?"

"Mikey?"

Sally pointed to the man who'd just finished clearing up the mess and was now washing his hands, offering the other chef the evil eye. "Felgate interviewed him as well. By the look on his face, he could use a break." She pointed to a door on the other side of the kitchen. "That goes into the yard at the rear. If you take him out there for five minutes," she saw the other chef glare back at Mikey as he returned to his station, "you'll probably be doing me a favour. I don't need these two kicking ten bells out of each other before half past ten."

CASSIE STEPPED out of the coffee shop. The third business she'd been into in the last twenty minutes and no one had anything insightful to say. The restaurant was a talking point, a welcome addition to the town by all accounts and everyone had been watching with keen interest as the place took shape. David Fysh was recognised by his description but he hadn't made much of an impact in terms of being noticed. The tradesmen working in the set-up phase had been in for snacks and drinks but there was nothing of note to report. Walking a little further, she passed a fabric shop which she thought unusual for a high-street enterprise these days. The signage above the window had seen better days, looking tatty, the colour having faded long ago. The lights were off and the sign on the door said it was closed. Cassie was about to walk by to a small bakery that had a queue almost to the door when she saw movement within.

The front door was recessed from the pavement and Cassie knocked on the glass. A head appeared from behind a rack of material samples, peering out to see who was knocking on the door. Cassie held up her warrant card and pressed it against the glass. The woman walked over, gave her ID a cursory inspection and unlocked the door. She was in her sixties, closer to seventy when bathed in the natural light streaming through the glass of the door as she opened it, smiling.

Cassie indicated the restaurant across the road. "Have you met the new neighbours yet?"

The woman snorted. "I'll be steering clear of them. So should everyone else if you ask me?"

Cassie was intrigued by the strength of the venom in her tone, especially coming from such a sweet-looking lady. "Oh, really? Why's that then?"

"I don't care for the attitude."

Cassie raised her eyebrows. "Whose?"

"Well, the owner for a start. The spiv who wears the fancy suits."

"David Fysh?"

"Yes, that's his name, I think. Never trust a man who treats his friends the way he does. Whatever would he do to his enemies?"

"Sorry, you've lost me," Cassie said. "What have you seen."

"The spiv, David, having a stand-up argument with another man right outside the restaurant," she said, pointing across the road. "Right there."

Cassie looked over and back again. "Between who, do you know?"

"One of his friends, I think."

Cassie took out a picture of Gavin Felgate, passing it to her. "This man?"

She held it up before her, lifting her glasses away from her eyes so she could see better and shook her head. "No, not him... another man."

"Can you describe him to me, this other man?"

"Similar age... but a bit taller. I've seen them together before leaving the restaurant at the end of the day. Like I said, friends."

"And they had a falling out?"

"Oh, yes. I thought it was all going to turn nasty for a minute. There was a bit of pushing and shoving."

"Okay, did you hear what was said?"

"No, I'd closed up. I was just here doing a bit of cleaning up after a busy weekend, but it was definitely a heated exchange."

"When was this, please?" Cassie asked, taking out her notebook.

"Let me see... after the weekend just gone. I had a rush order come in on the Saturday and I worked Sunday – I never work Sunday – and the customer collected it late on Monday, so it would have been then."

"Monday evening?"

The woman nodded. "Absolutely."

"And how did it end?"

"They parted and both stormed off in separate directions."

"Okay," Cassie said. "And you'd recognise the other man, not David, if you were to see him again?"

"Yes, I see him every day coming into work. He's one of the chefs."

MIKEY TOOK a deep draw on his cigarette, leaning against the brick wall at the rear of the restaurant, then exhaled deeply, blowing the smoke upwards and away from them.

"So, what did you make of the interview with Gavin Felgate?" Tom asked.

Mikey shrugged. "Not very exciting for either of us, to be fair. Felgate was asking the questions but his heart wasn't in it."

"How so?"

"Well, he was as bored as I was. Fysh was lurking in the background trying to make sure I didn't say anything that'd make him or his precious empire look bad."

"And could you?" Tom asked. "Make it look bad?"

Mikey chuckled. "It's a decent job I've got here, Inspector."

"And I'm not looking to make trouble for you."

Mikey tilted his head to one side, his eye fixed on Tom as

he took another drag. Exhaling, he sniffed and broke eye contact. "Dare say I could have dropped a couple of grenades if I'd chosen to. Not that I did, mind you."

"For example?"

Mikey pursed his lips, reticent. Tom stared at him hard, letting him know he wasn't going away.

"You know how Fysh hires most of his staff, don't you?"

"People who need a second chance, yes."

"That's the corporate line, yeah," Mikey said, laughing. He shook his head. "Fysh likes having us around for the good PR but," he smiled, "he likes our expertise as well."

"Expertise?"

"We have skills that most don't, Inspector." He looked away, tossing his cigarette butt to the floor and pressing it into the stones with the ball of his foot to extinguish it. "Ex-offenders and addicts know how to get things done. The need... the desire, the ability to go against what we're supposed to do is useful to a man like Fysh."

"It doesn't sound like he's someone you're particularly enamoured with."

Mikey shook his head. "Gave me a job when I needed one... and I bought into his rehabilitation crap but that's all it is, crap."

"You know what he was up to with dodgy ingredients?"

Mikey looked away, shaking his head. "I don't know anything, Inspector."

They both knew he was lying but Tom understood. Mikey didn't want to incriminate himself as a participant or by association.

"And how does everyone get along with David Fysh?"

He scoffed. "He's proper Marmite to most people. If you're young enough, and pretty enough, for him to want to get into your pants, then you'll probably find him a courteous and generous guy but..."

"But?"

"Once you see him for what he is... then you don't turn your back."

"Everyone feel that way?"

"Except Sally and James, yeah, I'd say so."

"Why do you single out those two?"

Mikey checked the door to the rear, currently wedged open so as not to lock them out. He didn't want them to be overheard.

"Sally's father lent David some of the money to set this place up. That's why she's so stressed about it going well. What with Fysh doing a Houdini act this week, any other manager would've walked by now but she's hanging in there."

"And James?"

Mikey shook his head. "They go way back. They've been friends for years as far as I can tell. James was always defending Fysh, so you had to be careful what you said in front of him or it'd get back, you know?"

"You said *was*."

"Sorry?"

"James *was* always defending him. Why the past tense?"

Mikey waved away the comment. "Fell out, big time. Come to think about it, it was around the time that Felgate guy was asking all the questions. He was just as interested in James as he was with Fysh. It was a bit weird, thinking about it."

"Asking what type of questions?"

"Like... how they got on with each other. I figured he thought they might be in a relationship or something."

"Why would you think that?"

"Well, I didn't... I mean, I always knew they were great friends and all that. They used to hang out all the time after work and stuff, go out drinking but not as often once Fysh married and even less once they had the children." Mikey raised his eyebrows in a knowing expression.

"They were that close, James and David?"

"Oh yeah, you'd better believe it," Mikey said, lighting another cigarette. "And when Felgate was asking about the two of them – after Fysh had got bored and cleared off – I guessed there might have been some angle like that he was exploring, otherwise why ask?"

"Why indeed?" Tom thought about it, Mikey enjoying his break from the stressful work environment in the morning sunshine. "And this falling out, what was it about?"

He shook his head. "No idea... but the two of them stopped talking and they were frosty with each other after that."

"When was this?"

Mikey thought about it. "Early last week sometime. Maybe on Monday. Yeah," he said, his brow creasing as he nodded, "Monday, as we were locking up. They were sniping at each other. I just left them to it."

"And you've no idea why?"

He shook his head. "Nope... and I didn't ask!"

Sally appeared at the doorway, glaring at Mikey who looked at Tom.

"Yes, we're done," Tom said. "Thanks."

"Any time."

Mikey exhaled his last draw of the cigarette, tossing it aside and re-entering the kitchen. Tom smiled his thanks at Sally who nodded and retreated from view. Moments later, Cassie appeared from within. Looking over her shoulder to check they were alone, she grinned.

"You'll never guess what I just heard from a lady running a business over the road," she said, leaning against the wall. "Last Monday."

"David Fysh had a stand-up argument with his head chef, James Cook?"

Cassie's smile faded. "Damn, is there anything that you don't get to hear first?"

Tom laughed.

CHAPTER TWENTY-NINE

"DETECTIVE CONSTABLE COLLET," Dr Paxton said, peering over his spectacles as Eric entered the pathology lab. Eric smiled. "Have I been demoted in status?"

Eric frowned, unsure if that was an attempt at humour or the pathologist was actually annoyed. He decided to err on the side of caution. "Tom said it was about time I got back out into the field."

Paxton looked him up and down with an expert eye.

"Well, I can't see any adverse reaction to your recent experience. How are you finding manoeuvrability?"

Eric stretched out his right arm. "Feels better every day."

"Good, good. You'll need all of your strength when the baby makes an appearance. When is that by the way?"

Eric was surprised. Dr Paxton always seemed so aloof and disinterested in the team, and Eric couldn't remember interacting with the man on a personal level.

"Due in six weeks, give or take."

"Excellent." Paxton led them over to his autopsy table where the clear form of a body lay under a sheet. "I spend so much time around the dead, DC Collet, that it's nice to pay attention to the living every once in a while."

Eric nodded, eyeing the covered body and finding the conversation a little odd bearing in mind where they were. He could see why Cassie found the man quite odd. Dr Paxton didn't appear ready to talk business and Eric found himself mentally scrabbling around for suitable small talk, tricky considering he barely knew the man.

"Um… do you have children yourself?"

"Me? Certainly not. Very impractical little things… fiddly," Paxton said holding up his hand and squeezing thumb and forefinger together momentarily.

"Right, yes of course." Eric pursed his lips. He was spent. "Harry Empson?"

"Mr Empson, absolutely," Paxton said, grasping the sheet and gently drawing it away from the head and revealing the upper torso down to the waist. "As you guessed at the scene, it was a rather amateur attempt at staging the scene and attempting to pass it off as a suicide. You're either dealing with inexperience or basic incompetence. This would never get past even a cursory examination by a professional."

"What can you tell me that I didn't already know?"

"Patience, young man. Please don't steal my moment," Paxton said. "I live for these days; they validate my years of academic study."

He crossed to retrieve his notes from his desk off to one side, returning and reading through them as Eric cast an eye over Harry Empson.

"I can confirm that it was not a death by suicidal strangulation. In a hanging the signs of venous congestion are very well developed above the ligature and are also especially prominent at the root of the tongue, most likely due to the slow tightening of the ligature as well as the fact it remains in place after death – until you arrive or some poor soul who discovers them. Now, if you'll look here," he encouraged Eric to look at the neck, pointing to the abrasions clearly visible, "you can see this yellowing of the skin but there are no signs of vital reaction." He read Eric's expression, sighing. "It means he was already dead before this particular ligature was applied. You can also see these other marks here and here," he pointed to them with the tip of his finger, "where there are more than one ligature mark demonstrating he was attempting to free himself from his assailant or his attacker was attempting to tighten the ligature. Neither of those marks come close to fully encircling the neck and they are mostly prominent at the front of the neck which is indicative of the main force of the pulling coming from behind. This would also explain the lack of defensive wounds."

Eric met his eye. "He was jumped from behind."

Paxton nodded. "I did find trauma to the abdomen, tissue damage that didn't have time to bruise seeing as he was dead shortly after."

"So, he was in a fight?"

Paxton nodded. "Oh, I would say so, yes. I think he was fighting for his life and he knew it but, sadly, which is the way with these things, he wouldn't have had a great deal of time to react. One can slip into unconsciousness rather quickly once a cord is around the throat. I found macroscopic bleeding of the laryngeal muscles which is seldom found in suicides."

"Why is that?" Eric asked, doing his best to remember his biology classes at school and the layout of muscles in the throat.

"As is often the case, the murderer applies a little too much overkill. In their desire to finish the victim off, they deploy far more force than is required for the kill, often as a result of blood lust or adrenalin as the thrill of the kill takes over. I noted there were also two hairline fractures to both his second and third ribs on the right side of the cage to the front, which back up the evidence of there being a struggle."

"But no defensive wounds to his hands that I could see," Eric said, looking down at the body.

Dr Paxton put his folder down and lifted the right hand, splaying the fingers wide and encouraging Eric to look closer. "No scratches, you're quite right. But you see here," he held the index finger, "the fingernail is split and that was most certainly recent as it hadn't hardened or discoloured. I also removed detritus from beneath several fingernails. I've sent the samples off to be tested but I would expect a healthy DNA sample to come back to aid you in narrowing down his attackers."

"That's great."

"Don't be too excited, young man. There's every possibility it was his own skin deposited there as he clawed at the cord around his neck, but you never know."

"Why did you say plural just then?"

Paxton shot Eric a look as if it was the most obvious statement he could have made. "Logical, I think you'll find, Constable. How tall would you say Mr Empson is?"

Eric looked him up and down. "Five ten—"

"Very good, that's almost spot on. You have a keen eye. Weight?"

"One hundred and eighty to ninety pounds?"

"Close. Two hundred and five pounds, to be precise." Paxton produced copies of photographs taken at the beach house with Empson still hanging from the mezzanine. "My conclusion is that the man was dead prior to his suspension. If you look at the photos you can see where he was hanging. In order to lever a man of this size over the edge while he was unconscious would take an incredible amount of strength. The dead weight, if you'll pardon the expression, of a man this size may as well be three or four times his actual weight when you consider getting him up the stairs and into position. Now, remember the yellow skin around the ligature caused by his post-mortem hanging, there is no movement in the positioning of that ligature. Do you see?"

Eric smiled, nodding along but he didn't see it at all. He felt a little embarrassed to ask. Fortunately, Dr Paxton realised and waved away Eric's blank expression.

"I suspect they were worried about the makeshift noose holding and carefully lowered him over the edge. Maybe they thought his weight alone might pull the newel post down with him or yank his head clean."

"Yes, thank you," Eric said, holding up a hand. He could already feel his breakfast churning in his stomach and didn't need further detail to colour his imagination even more.

"Well, anyway, I think he was lowered over the balustrade just in case it didn't hold. Otherwise, I would expect to find a more deviated pattern as he swung back and forth."

Eric gagged, grimacing.

"Are you all right, Detective Constable? You're looking a little green."

"I'll be fine," Eric said. "And I get the picture. There must have been more than one. But are you sure one man couldn't do it?"

Paxton's brow creased in concentration. "I suppose if your killer has superhuman strength... no, that's not fair, if he works a physical job or spends a lot of time lifting weights in the gym, then it is plausible that he could have acted alone but I would be impressed."

"Impressed?"

Paxton smiled. "Poor choice of phrase." He inclined his head. "Sorry."

"And what do you think was used? The FME thought it

might be an electrical flex of some kind, smooth, rather than a rope."

"Yes, I should say so. There is a consistent groove pattern in the skin, too thick to be a wire and seeing as it left no pattern it is unlikely to have been a rope. Electrical flex would do the trick, right enough."

CHAPTER THIRTY

"SO, WHAT ARE YOU THINKING?" Tamara asked Tom, standing in front of the information boards in ops, scanning the photographs.

"From what Mikey, the sous-chef I spoke to this morning, says, David Fysh and James Cook go way back." His forehead furrowed as he tried to see the link that remained tantalisingly out of reach. "But, according to Cook himself, he was just an employee and they barely knew one another. Cook also told us that Gavin Felgate only spoke to him and Fysh in relation to the article he was supposed to be writing but Mikey was also interviewed at the time."

Tamara sighed. "He may not have realised... or he plain forgot." Tom glanced sideways at her, completely failing to mask his dismissal of the suggestion. She smiled. "I know, I know, but it's the first thing a decent solicitor would throw at us. Admittedly, I think it unlikely. He was lying to us. The question is why? What do we know about James Cook?"

Tom shook his head. "Nothing yet. He isn't in the system but Cassie is looking into it." He looked over to her sitting at her desk, phone clamped to her ear by her shoulder and scribbling away in her notebook and apparently surfing the internet at the same time.

"How can that be? Fysh employs ex-offenders and didn't Cook himself say he'd most likely be in jail if it wasn't for Fysh giving him a chance?"

Tom nodded. "Yes. So, you're right, he should be in the system, even if it was just a caution."

"Unless it was a juvenile conviction that has already been expunged from the record?"

"You don't understand," Tom said, shaking his head, "there's no mention of James Cook at all in the system, prior to four years ago anyway."

Tamara looked at him, perplexed.

"Exactly," Tom said, his frown deepening further. "James Cook appears on the electoral register four years ago and that's the first official reference we have for him so far. We looked into social media accounts and he's there, sharing pictures and jokes but—"

"Only going back four years?"

Tom nodded. "Now, it's possible he was inside and after release landed the job locally which would explain it to some degree but we'd still expect to find his record."

"And if they go way back that would suggest they knew each other for more than just the last four years."

"Agreed," Tom said, indicating the photo of the three boys they'd recently found to be of significance. "What if he's this one here," he said, pointing to the boy Greg Beaty failed to identify. Tamara moved closer, examining the picture.

"Ciaran Haverson."

"What?" Tom asked.

"That's Ciaran Haverson," Tamara said, pointing to the boy

in question and tapping the picture with her forefinger. Tom leaned over, his gaze narrowing. "That's the third boy. I'm almost certain."

"Really?" he asked, looking closer. Imagining the boy without the glasses, he could see the resemblance. Although, his hair looked lighter than it had in the crime scene photographs of the day.

"But the hair..."

"Summer's day, lots of sun... take it from me, your hair can be bleached and look totally different at the end of the season," Tamara said, her eyes flitting to Tom's hair. "It's not something you'd understand being so fair already. If yours lightened further, we'd think you were turning white!"

"Thanks very much. Why didn't I see that?" He was irritated.

"That's why I'm in charge, Thomas."

Tom offered her a sideways smile, still peering over the picture. The revelation, however, did little to help him understand the relationship with James Cook.

"So, does Cook have a hold over Fysh?" he asked.

"What sort of hold?"

"I don't know. I'm just thinking out loud."

Cassie said her goodbyes, drawing their attention as she thanked the caller and hung up. Spinning her chair to face them, her face split into a broad grin.

"Now that was illuminating," she said.

"Well don't keep us in the dark, Cassandra," Tamara said.

"That was our human resources contact for the NGO Harry Empson works for in Africa." She looked at Tom. "Scrub what I said earlier about corporate interests slowing stuff down, she was the complete opposite. Harry Empson has been working for them in Benin, West Africa, fairly close to *Massè* which is close to the border with Nigeria."

"Which explains why he flew out of Lagos," Tom said.

Cassie smiled. "You know your African geography."

"I got good grades at high school, it's true."

"Where it gets interesting is Empson is at the heart of a project improving schooling which is of little interest to our case, but he was due to head up a presentation to several high-profile visitors in the coming days but requested compassionate leave to return home." Tamara exchanged a look with Tom. "Apparently, Empson's father has been taken gravely ill and Harry had to return. The thing is, I checked and both of Harry Empson's parents have been dead for years. The only living relative we know of is his sister."

"And they are sure?"

"Absolutely positive. Harry Empson wasn't due to return to the UK until January. In fact, she confirmed the last time she knew of him leaving his post to come back to the UK was over two years ago. So why now?"

"That is the repeating question at the moment, isn't it?" Tom said. "Did they give us anything else?"

"He has a company mobile that they pay for and she's going to get me all his records relating to it. It is part of their policy to monitor usage as well as tracking where it goes via third party software."

"That's a little 1984, isn't it?" Tamara asked.

Cassie shrugged. "Following those cases a couple of years ago where aid workers were caught exchanging food and supplies for sexual favours, they seem to have taken things more seriously. We should have his phone records by the close of play today."

"Good work, Cass," Tom said. "Now can you find me James Cook?"

"I'm on it," she said, turning back to her desk.

Eric bounded into the room.

"Dr Dea—"

Tom and Tamara looked in his direction.

"Dr Paxton had an interesting take on Empson. He confirmed much of what we already suspected, a murder crudely disguised as a suicide, but he believes there to be more than one assailant. At least, he thinks it would have taken two people to hang him in the way he was found. Paxton says death likely occurred prior to his hanging by way of manual strangulation but, and this is interesting, he says Empson put up a fight. His body showed signs of trauma, a couple of cracked ribs and so forth that were so fresh that bruising hadn't been able to form. Most likely in the struggle. He says it would have been over fairly quickly, Empson losing consciousness rapidly, because the doctor thinks he was jumped from behind. Had the attack been from the front, he'd have seen it coming and therefore his injuries would be greater to reflect the longer struggle."

"Did he give us anything to work with?" Tom asked.

"Trace evidence beneath the fingernails that is being processed that will give us a DNA sample, but with the caveat that it could be Empson's own, left while he clawed in vain at his own neck, trying to free himself. But two attackers suggests a conspiracy of sorts, doesn't it?"

"If you have more than one person, then by definition, you have a conspiracy," Tamara said.

Tamara turned back to the board, looking at the same picture as before. "Something tells me the answer lies with these boys."

Eric came alongside them. "I've been thinking about that since we left Beaty's place last night," he said, looking at Tom. "Beaty said he was given his first camera when he was a little boy, didn't he?"

Tom nodded. "Yes, around nine years old, I think. He said it ignited his interest in photography and he carried a camera everywhere since."

"Then it's quite possible he took this picture, right?"

"If they were all friends, then it stands to reason that's plausible, yes," Tom said.

"And Ciaran's dad, Ian, talked about how his son just wanted to fit in with the other kids at school." Eric was working up to something and couldn't seem to stand still. "And that he was unhappy, possibly even suicidal, because he couldn't do it."

"Yes, that's right. He said they bullied Ciaran," Tom said, pointing at the picture, "and we think the unidentified boy is Ciaran."

"Of course," Eric said. "Beaty, Fysh and Empson... old school friends. What's the betting if we check their year group, we'll also find Ciaran Haverson was there at the same time? Maybe some others, who knows?"

Tom ran his hands through his hair to each side of his head, interlocking his fingers when they met at the rear. He exhaled softly. "Do some digging, Eric."

Eric grinned, hurrying over to his desk and turning on his computer.

"So, what are they hiding?" Tamara asked. "And whatever it is, if we're right, Gavin Felgate found out about it and everything that's followed has been about keeping it quiet. Do we know if Felgate sought to interview Empson as well?"

"No," Eric said, over his shoulder. "I checked with his editor and Harry Empson's name didn't come up at all."

Tom inclined his head to one side. "Although it is fair to say Felgate was playing this very close to his chest. He didn't tell his boss or his girlfriend."

"I wonder if the interviewees cottoned on to it, though?" Tamara asked. "If they were keeping a secret and someone randomly starts asking you questions relating to it, then they might have put it together without him realising."

"They got to him before he could run the story and expose them?"

Tom perched himself on the edge of the nearest desk, his face a picture of concentration.

"What is it?"

"Empson," Tom said, "working this through logically, I see Felgate." He wagged a finger at the journalist's picture. "He uncovers something and, I know it's an assumption but let's run with it for a minute, it's related to Ciaran Haverson's death. Let's not get carried away and start calling it anything other than an unexplained death at this point." Tamara nodded. "But it's something these guys don't want in the public domain because they each have something to lose, so one or more of them take it upon themselves to silence Felgate. We'll have to put aside Felgate's apparent motivations for stringing the noose up on the common like he did, for now."

"Right," Tamara said. "Even if it's just one of them, the others are committed to silence by association and have to go along with it or everything comes out."

"So, David Fysh falls out with James Cook about something, we don't know what, and Cook then denies being friends with Fysh—"

"Who subsequently disappears himself," Tamara added, "followed closely by Cook."

"So where does Empson fit in?" Tom asked. "He comes back on short notice with some cock and bull story about a sick relative, only to be killed as soon as he gets here. Why come back at all?"

"Who knew?"

"Say again?" Tom asked.

"Who knew Empson was coming home?" Tamara said. "He wasn't expected back and is killed before he can even unpack his bags. He's either the unluckiest man in the world or someone knew he would be there."

"He didn't drive himself back to Heacham. At least there's no car at his place and there was no evidence of a rental car in his name at the airport."

"Then someone picked him up from the airport," Tamara said, "or from the nearest train station, whatever. And whoever it was, Empson was relaxed enough in their company to let his guard down."

"Like when among friends?" Tom asked. Tamara nodded. "Stands to reason. Eric, any joy with the school?"

"I went to Greg Beaty's website and checked his *About* page to find a starting point of where he grew up," Eric said without moving his eyes from the screen in front of him. "I've cross referenced that with electoral roll and census data with Empson, Fysh and the Haversons. I think there are only four schools that all of them could have attended at the same time, one secondary and three primaries."

"Stick to the secondary," Tom said. "Ciaran was fifteen when he died."

"I'm just in the Local Education Authority database now," Eric said, his fingers a blur on the keyboard. "Yes, here we are." Tom and Tamara came to stand at his shoulder, scanning a list of names. Eric glanced up at both of them in turn. "All four went to the same high school, in the same year group."

"Damn. I don't see James Cook in this, do you?" Tom asked.

"No, I don't either," Tamara said. "But we've linked them to Haverson. They'd have known him and Gavin Felgate recreated the scene of Ciaran's death. It's all revolving around that.

Maybe he was in a different year group? Eric, can you go one year either side?"

"No need," Cassie called. They looked at her. "You won't find James Cook listed at their school. Or any other for that matter."

Something in her tone made Tom think it wasn't quite the dead end that it first sounded.

CHAPTER THIRTY-ONE

HE WOKE WITH A START. This was normal and happened frequently. For once though, it wasn't a shooting pain or an immediate sense that he was about to throw up which made a change. Greg Beaty remained where he was, lying on top of the covers on his bed, still fully clothed. He looked at his clock-radio on the bedside table but the display was blank. He had no idea what time it was, not that it mattered. The wind was strong, buffeting the windows of his bedroom and every now and again the force caused the exterior cladding to vibrate, reverberating as if it was about to be torn from the battens holding it to the wall. It wouldn't. At least, it hadn't done so before and the sound was nothing new. In the past he would've been able to secure the fixings, tighten the boards but not now. Now all he could do was lie there and listen to it.

A car passed by outside followed shortly by another, their headlights flashing the interior as they rounded the bend in the road. It couldn't be very late. This end of town was almost silent after eleven o'clock, earlier in winter like now. The brief respite he felt was passing, that familiar gnawing pain rising in his leg. Soon it would progress further and he wouldn't get any more sleep tonight unless he acted. Gritting his teeth, and with a lot of effort, he hauled his legs to one side of the bed and levered himself up into a sitting position ignoring the nausea that followed. Reaching for the blister packs of pills lying next to the alarm clock, he rifled through them discarding one and popping two tablets from one strip along with one from another before lifting the beer can from the bedside table and finding it empty. He cursed softly. His throat was dry, his teeth felt furry.

An orange glow from the streetlights streamed through the slats of the window shutters illuminating the bedroom. He flicked the switch on the bedside lamp but it didn't come on. That was odd. Something must have tripped. Two of the tablets had a smooth coating and he put them in his mouth, endeavouring to swallow them with whatever saliva he could generate. The other he put into his pocket and reached for his crutches, wedged between the bedside table and the mattress. He grasped them, braced himself, and stood up, releasing a whimper as he put his weight on to his right leg. Closing his eyes, he steadied himself and hobbled into the nearby ensuite shower room. Pulling the cord, he confirmed what he'd already guessed, the power was out.

Holding the rim of the basin for stability, he slipped the remaining pill into his mouth before leaning over and taking a mouthful of cold water from the tap. Righting himself, he almost stumbled as he swallowed the painkiller, water running from his chin and onto his shirt but he didn't care. Catching sight of his reflection in the mirror, he stopped to stare at himself seeing the haunted ghost that he'd become.

Turning away, he went back into the bedroom and out onto the landing. Hesitating at the top of the stairs, as he always did, he realised the futility in his obstinance. The reason he slept most nights in his armchair was because of his difficulty in managing the stairs but somehow having to make that effort, something most people took for granted – the trek upstairs to bed – made him feel normal, like a regular person.

Casting the thought aside, he started down the stairs. Around halfway he heard something or thought he did. He stopped, listening intently. Had he left something outside on the veranda? With the strength of the wind coming in off the sea, along with the elevated position of his home on Cliff Parade, anything not securely fastened down was prone to be lifted and often carried some distance if the conditions were right; but he had, he was sure. And the sound wasn't familiar, a repetitive dull thudding. He continued on, reaching the foot of the stairs and turning to his left. The consumer unit was in the pantry off the kitchen, rehoused from the cupboard beneath the stairs when the house was renovated. That seemed sensible at the time but Greg dreaded having to check the switches. He couldn't reach them without first climbing onto the worktop below or by using a chair to stand on. Hunching to access a half-height cupboard would be preferable these days. If he was lucky, he could flick a single switch with the end of his crutch, otherwise he'd have to wait until his carers came around in the morning.

There was that noise again… only louder.

Greg froze in the hallway, the instincts that he'd honed, in conflict zones around the world, screamed at him silently in his mind. The exterior door to the kitchen burst open and a figure staggered into view. Greg reacted, made to turn and head back the way he'd come, only his mind was too fast for his body and he stumbled losing his grip on the crutch in his right hand and his momentum carried him into the living room. He bounced off the open door just as he heard an excited shout from behind him, two voices coming almost on top of one another.

Eyeing his mobile on the arm of his chair across the room, he hurried towards it, feeling the strain in every muscle of his arms and legs. He heard them approach, turning in the room. Two dark figures, dressed in hoodies with masks covering their faces, rounded on him from the hallway almost scrabbling to get past one another to reach him first. Greg stooped and reached into the crate of beers he'd left on the chair earlier, hurling the first unopened can at his would-be assailants, and not stopping to see if it registered before grasping the next but he heard a shout of protest so assumed it had landed. How many he threw he didn't know but their advance slowed, punctuated with obscenities, but advance they did.

Turning his one remaining crutch, Greg held it at the base and swung it like a club. The first pass didn't connect, but the second, a reverse sweep, caught one man on the side of the head and he howled in pain, raising a gloved hand to the side of his face and stumbling to his left and obstructing the other man's approach. Greg felt a surge of hope, a belief that he might win out and swung his crutch again with all the strength he could muster. This time he struck the other man but instead of falling or backing off, he merely uttered a guttural growl of intent and lunged forward, brushing the makeshift weapon aside with consummate ease. Greg yelped in panic, off balance and with nowhere to go he let out a scream in frustration and denial before throwing himself forward at his assailant.

The two men came together and despite the obvious mismatch, the attacker being taller and more agile, they locked into a physical embrace. Greg was forced back and they quickly gathered pace before he was slammed into the wall, air rapidly escaping his lungs. Pinned to the wall, his opponent with the upper hand, Greg felt a rush of panic. The man's head was pressed into Greg's chest, his entire bodyweight ensuring there was no way out. Managing to drag his arms free, Greg clasped his hands against the sides of the man's head, levering his head back to reveal the masked face, no features visible aside from his eyes. With his palms on the side of the face, Greg drove his thumbs into the man's eyes and pressed as hard as he could with all his remaining energy, his own screams of exertion almost drowning out those of his attacker as he bellowed in pain and rage.

The pressure on him eased and Greg released his right hand, closed his fist and drove his elbow down onto his attacker's head. The blow sent a shot of pain through Greg's arm but the hold on him ceased as the man slumped to the floor. Greg was free. Out of breath, he reached for his mobile phone but, in the struggle, it had fallen from the chair and in the dark he couldn't see where it lay. Rummaging around amongst the cushions, he desperately sought to find it, turning his attention to the carpet and falling to his knees.

A hand reached out behind him, grabbing his collar at the base of his neck but Greg lashed out with his arm, making a strong connection. The strangely satisfying thud of fist on flesh and an accompanying groan buoyed him. The urge to flee took over and he gave up on the search, scrabbling across the floor on his hands and knees brushing aside beer cans and the upturned side table and lamp that he couldn't remember being struck. He had to get out as fast as possible.

Murmurs of anger sounded behind him as he reached the door to the hall. The muscles of his right leg burned, his body ached but survival instinct overcame all else and he gripped the door jamb, gritting his teeth and attempting to stand. Leaning against the frame he righted himself, blinking the sweat from his eyes and started into the hall. Someone grasped his ankle with a vice-like grip and yanked at his leg as he tried to shuffle forward using the wall for support. He tried desperately to shake the hand loose but his actions seemed only to have the opposite effect. He screamed both in fear and desperation. His legs gave out beneath him and he fell face first to the floor barely managing to put a hand out to break his fall.

He felt the presence of a second person stepping past the first who held onto Greg's ankle as if their life depended on it. A crushing weight landed on the base of his spine and he yelped, a sound that appeared somehow disembodied despite knowing he'd uttered it. Something smooth brushed past his face and then he felt pain across his throat, a sensation that grew in intensity a second later. He wanted to cry out, to scream louder for someone, anyone to help him but he couldn't, the pressure around his throat grew ever tighter. Greg could feel and smell the breath of his attacker on his face, whiskey and cigarettes, feel the straining of the man's body as he strangled the life from him. He wanted to plead, to beg for his life but couldn't forge a sound.

"No more places to run to, Greg!" The man whispered through gritted teeth. "Nowhere left to hide."

Just as the darkness faded to near blackout, the pressure eased and Greg felt his head drop. He didn't feel the blow as it struck the wooden floor unopposed, his breath coming in ragged gasps. All fight had left him. His fate was now out of his hands.

"Get the car."

The voice was distant, some way off he thought, and commanding. He sensed someone step over him and walk to the front door. He heard the key turn and unlock the door and felt a rush of cold air sweep in over him, smelling the sea air and hearing the wind gusting over the nearby cliff tops.

Greg closed his eyes, all pain forgotten. It was time.

CHAPTER THIRTY-TWO

THE DOOR OPENED CATCHING Cassie by surprise as she reached for the doorbell. There was a moment of hesitation as she eyed the figure standing in front of her, an imposing figure dressed in black with only eyes visible above the scarf tied across his face as a makeshift mask. They stared at each other for what could only have been a second or two, sharing their mutual indecision, before Cassie's eyes drifted to the stricken figure of Greg Beaty lying prostrate on the floor beyond. The man made to slam the door in her face and she reacted, leaning into the door and trying to wedge her foot in the space to stop it. The door was heavy and came at her with force. The pain erupted in both shoulder and foot as they came together and she let out a scream.

"Tom!" she shouted, stumbling back. She need not elaborate further because Tom Janssen was already aware and cannoned past her, throwing himself at the door. The barrier burst inward and Tom and the black-clad figure collided, the latter almost knocked off his feet by Tom's momentum. The two men stumbled against the wall, grappling with one another for advantage. Cassie held back. The hallway was too narrow for her to get past Tom and help to subdue the man. She pulled her radio from her coat pocket and called for urgent assistance, barking the address over the airwaves.

The man wrestling with Tom was smaller in stature but able to hold his own, each man seeking to overpower the other with move and counter move. She thought she saw Beaty try to get up or to at least try to move himself out of harm's way, but he barely moved at all, seemingly giving up. From the adjoining room another figure appeared but didn't look in her direction or seek to come to the aid of the other, turning right and running towards the kitchen.

"Hey! Stop, police!" she called in vain as the man, similarly dressed to the first, took off. At this point, Tom had grasped his opponent's right wrist, pinning his arm against the wall and had his right hand around the man's throat, forcing him down and into submission.

"There's another!" she said.

"GO!" he shouted and Cassie shoved her way past both men carefully sidestepping Beaty, now unconscious on the floor, and hurried after the second man.

Broken glass crunched underfoot as she entered the kitchen, hesitating just in case the man lay in wait for her around the corner, but she realised he'd fled through the back door out into the rear. Ducking her head out, she quickly looked to the left and the right. The side access gate from the driveway was closed, the bolt still locked in place, and the path continued to her right into the garden. It was almost pitch black here, the orange hue in the sky from the town's streetlights barely penetrated the mature trees and shrubbery ringing the garden.

Inching along the path, Cassie drew her extendable ASP from its holster beneath her coat, something she'd decided to carry ever since Eric's stabbing, and flicked it out to full length as she made her way along the side of the house. The garden opened up in front of her just as the clouds parted for the briefest moment to allow a sliver of silver light from the moon to illuminate the area. She couldn't see anyone. Her radio crackled with confirmation of support units coming their way but she instinctively turned the volume down so as not to give herself away. A sound off to her right drew her attention, unmistakably someone attempting to clamber over a fence.

Without hesitation she ran in that direction, bursting through the foliage to see a body almost disappearing over the fence into the garden of the house next door.

"Stop!" she yelled, swinging her ASP at the trailing leg but missing as it disappeared from sight. She backed up and took a run at the fence, easily six feet high, and leaped up, grasping the top and hauling herself over sideways and coming down on her feet setting herself to defend an attack. It didn't come. A silhouette of a tall man was sprinting away from her. She set off. A dog in the house was barking and hurling itself at the patio doors as she passed, lights coming on in the interior but she ignored the occupants, collapsing her ASP, slipping it into its holster, and pulling out her radio and raising it to her lips as she ran.

"DS Knight in pursuit of a male suspect fleeing south-west through the rear of gardens..." she paused to negotiate assailing another fence and dropped to the other side "...on Cliff Parade."

She was gaining ground on her quarry which gave her confidence as he might not be in as good a shape as she was, a plus as she was well aware of her vulnerability being alone in the chase. The garden of each property was a similar width and every obstacle the suspect had to clear slowed him down and brought her that little bit closer. She was already making plans for the inevitable confrontation as he launched himself at the next fence, using a water butt to assist him in getting over. He dropped from sight and was accompanied by a clatter as he hit whatever had been hidden from view on the other side. Cassie drew her ASP again, confident this was the moment. She took a different path over the fence this time, moving to her left and using an outdoor patio table as a step to enable her to leap the fence well clear of where her suspect crossed the boundary.

Cassie landed and brought her ASP to bear. She was vindicated. Her suspect hadn't run. He'd landed on a covered steel barbecue set, toppling it and the associated paraphernalia to the ground around him. He was waiting for her to follow him over, also seemingly resigned to their confrontation, but he seemed surprised she'd chosen a different path. He turned on her, his chest heaving. She slowly advanced, her left hand outstretched in front of her, her right clutching the handle of her ASP and resting it on her shoulder, primed and ready to bring it down if necessary.

"Police! Get on your knees, now!"

He remained where he was, arms at his side as she advanced cautiously.

"I said—"

He leaned to his left, grabbing a steel serving platter and threw it at her as if it was a frisbee followed quickly by several more. Cassie batted them aside but it slowed her advance. Gritting her teeth, she moved forward ready to deploy the ASP only for him to back away from her, reveal a bottle of something from behind his back and squeeze it, sending a stream of liquid at Cassie, who raised her arm to shield her face. The odour was sweet, pungent and unmistakable. It was lighter fuel.

Cassie hesitated, holding her position for a fraction of a second which was when she should have struck. Now she felt a surge of panic seeing her suspect snap open a Zippo lighter and strike the wheel. He stood there holding the lighter in his hand, the flame dancing before her but he didn't speak. She backed away looking around her for somewhere to retreat only to see nothing but open space. He matched her step for step, her eye following the naked flame at every movement.

Nearby shouts carried on the wind. Her colleagues were looking for her. This time the man looked to his left and right, perhaps searching for an escape route of his own. She stood her ground, the overpowering smell of the fuel an ever-present reminder of her predicament.

"Look... no one else needs to get hurt."

He threw the lighter at her and she sought to swat it away with her arm only for the flame to catch the fuel-soaked sleeve of her coat and ignite in a burst of yellow and orange flame. Cassie screamed, holding her arm away from her and turning backwards and hurling herself to the ground. She knew flames travelled up, so the safest place to be was flat on the ground, she'd seen it in riot training when faced with petrol bombs; although a simulation was one thing, this was another. Instinct took over and she rolled on the ground in an attempt to smother the flame whilst trying to remove the coat before the other fuel – notably that on her face and hair – might catch. Feeling her arm come out of the sleeve, she pushed away as fast as she could, rolling out of the coat and continuing on to put distance between herself and her clothing.

A damp, earthy smell was added to the lighter fuel but it couldn't have been better received as she rolled to her front, hands beneath her face, captivated by the scene. The flames were spreading on her coat, looking far larger than she'd imagined. Relief and panic were present in equal measure and then she sensed someone alongside her but she didn't flinch as Tom knelt next to her, putting a supportive hand on her arm. Two uniformed officers clambered over the fence nearby, dropping down alongside them before scanning the garden with their torches.

"Where is he?" she heard Tom ask.

"I don't know," she whispered.

"Where?"

"I don't bloody know, all right!"

Taking the opportunity amidst the confusion of Cassie trying to put herself out, the suspect had fled but she had no idea which way he'd gone.

"I'm sorry," Cassie said, sitting up with Tom's help. She grimaced at the pain in her left forearm and tentatively reached for it but immediately recoiled. As soon as she thought about it, the pain reared up and for a moment she thought her arm was still alight. It wasn't but she'd been burned, how badly she didn't know.

"Are you okay?" Tom asked, casting an eye over her arm. The owners of the house had turned on the exterior garden lights to the patio and for the first time they could see each other properly.

"It can't be too bad," she said, sucking air through her teeth and angling her arm so that she could see in the new-found light. "I can still feel it, so it can't be, right?"

Tom inclined his head. "Come on, we'd better get that seen to." He helped her up. A dog barked signifying the arrival of a dog unit. "We'll find him. He'll not get far."

"The other one?" she asked.

"In custody."

"Who is it?"

"Let's get you checked over first."

"Sod that! Let's go and speak to the other ninja-wannabe and *then* I'll get this looked at." Tom met her eye with a disapproving look but she forced a smile. "Please?"

He nodded. "Okay. Come on."

CASSIE HELD her arm close to her side as they walked but she wasn't going to complain, despite the pain increasing almost with every step. Greg Beaty's house was illuminated by multiple police cars with their blue lights flashing and all observed by neighbours peering from behind curtains. A taxi drove by on the road, the driver slowing to observe them and see what the fuss was about. When Cassie glanced sideways at him, he looked away, increasing his speed a little. Making their way up the drive, DC Eric Collet appeared at the front door to both Tom and Cassie's surprise.

"I heard the call come over the radio," he said to Tom's unasked question then nodded to a car parked on the other side of the road. Cassie looked over to see Becca sitting in the passenger seat, her elbow leaning on the top of the door, her hand supporting her head.

"You brought your seven-months-pregnant fiancée to an emergency shout?" Cassie asked.

Eric looked bashful, his lips parting. "Um... yeah, I guess so."

Cassie smiled. "Nice one, Eric."

He noticed her clutching her arm and immediately a look of concern crossed his face. "Are you all right?"

She waved away his query. "It'll be fine."

"Come in. The paramedics are just giving Greg the once over. I'm sure one of them can check you out too."

Cassie was grateful, feeling her stubbornness wasn't such a bright idea after all. The lights in the hall were on now. Tom noticed and Eric explained.

"Someone pulled the wiring from one of the exterior lights,

crossed the neutral and the earth to short the panel, tripped the whole house off. Beaty is in the dining room, suspect is in the front room."

"Okay," Tom said before looking over his shoulder at Becca waiting patiently in the car. "Maybe you should let Becca go home and one of us can run you back later?"

Eric nodded, trotting out to the car. Tom led Cassie inside, coming to the doorway and peering into the dining room. Greg Beaty was on a chair; a paramedic had completed her assessment and was packing up her things. A uniformed constable hovered in the background watching over proceedings. Until they knew what was going on, everyone was to be kept under close supervision.

Beaty looked up at Tom, smiling sheepishly. "Not quite the evening I had planned."

The paramedic stood up, smiling at Greg and looking sideways at Tom. "He'll be fine. Nothing a bit of rest won't see to."

"Thanks. Would you mind taking a look at my colleague's arm?" Tom indicated Cassie and she didn't protest as the paramedic came closer and frowned at the state of her forearm close to where it met her wrist, the one area of skin uncovered and open to the flames.

"It doesn't look too bad," she said, tentatively rotating Cassie's arm and inspecting. "But you'll need to come back to the hospital and have it seen to."

Cassie nodded. "Ten minutes though, okay?"

The paramedic nodded and set about basic triage which Cassie found almost as painful as leaving it alone but she held her tongue.

"So, Greg," Tom said coming to stand in front of Beaty who appeared nervous all of a sudden, "why were these guys coming for you tonight?"

"I–I have no idea," he said, smiling but it was forced and

looked artificial. "How would I know? I was in bed, asleep... a–and the next thing... these guys are trying to kick my teeth in!"

"Yes, it is a mystery. No idea at all?"

Beaty was indignant, rubbing gently at his throat where a red line was clearly visible. "Like, no! I just said so, didn't I?"

"Well, let's go and have a word with one of them then. Maybe he'll have a better idea," Tom said, beckoning Beaty up and out of his seat with two fingers and nodding towards the front room. "Come on."

Reluctantly, Beaty eased himself out of his chair, now reunited with both his crutches, and Eric and Cassie moved aside to allow him to pass. They all walked into the front room. Beaty's attacker was sitting on a chair beneath the window on the far side of the room, his hands handcuffed behind his back and a constable standing either side of him. He had a cut to the side of his head slightly above his right eye. Someone had applied several Steri-Strips to temporarily hold it together but Tom guessed it might need stitches at some point. Now he was in custody, the man cut a dejected figure, his glare at Tom only deepened when Greg Beaty hobbled into the room behind him.

Tom brought Greg to stand in front of the man who tensed and scowled at both of them.

"Do you know James Cook?" Tom asked.

Beaty looked sideways at Tom and then down at the man in front of him, shaking his head. "N–No, I don't."

Tom nodded. "I'm not surprised. You'll know him better by his father's surname rather than his mother's maiden name, I should imagine. Isn't that right Jimmy?"

The man glared at Tom. Beaty looked at Tom quizzically. "Jimmy?"

"That's right. It's been a few years since you were at school together, he was a year or two below you, weren't you, Jimmy?"

Beaty looked at the man, staring hard at him, his eyes narrowing. "Jimmy? You're... Jimmy Haverson?"

"Yes," Tom said, turning to face Beaty. "I think Ciaran's brother came here to kill you tonight, Greg. Now, why do you think he would want to do something like that?"

CHAPTER THIRTY-THREE

GREG BEATY'S eyes flitted between Tom and the man in custody, finally settling on Jimmy Haverson.

"Jimmy... why... why come here like this?"

"You know damn well why?"

Beaty shook his head, his forehead creasing. "Jimmy, it's been years... I didn't even know you were back in town."

"You killed my brother, you sick bastard!"

"No, no... that's not how it happened, Jimmy," Beaty said averting his eyes from Jimmy's piercing stare, his lower lip trembling as he uttered the denial. "I didn't... no one killed Ciaran!"

"Liar!" Jimmy barked, trying to launch himself at Beaty from his chair only to be restrained by both officers to either side of him and be physically manhandled back into his seat. "You killed him. You, Harry and..." he checked himself, breaking off his glaring look at Beaty.

"And who?" Tom asked but Jimmy wouldn't meet his eye. "There's a lot going on between you lot, isn't there?"

Both Jimmy Haverson and Greg Beaty stared at the floor

rather than see themselves under Tom's watchful eye. Tom hovered in front of Jimmy Haverson.

"You got out of juvenile detention and came home, Jimmy," Tom said. "I gather from speaking to your social worker earlier this evening that it wasn't your choice to return to your home town but it was a condition of your release."

"Why would I want to come back to this place?" Haverson almost spat, lifting his head to face Tom.

"A lot of bad memories... a fractious relationship with your father alongside painful memories of your mother's death and obviously Ciaran's suicide—"

"Suicide!" Haverson scoffed, shaking his head. He glared at Beaty once more. "They killed him." Beaty made to protest but Haverson cut him off. "As near as damn it!"

Tom stepped in between them, breaking their eye contact and looked down at Beaty. His expression was pitiful as the magnitude of the situation seemed to be getting to him.

"What do you say, Greg? Jimmy thinks you killed his big brother—"

"No!" Beaty said, shaking his head, his eyes glazing over. "It wasn't like that, I swear."

"Then what was it like?"

Beaty shook his head, lifting a hand to cover his mouth and nose. "We were just kids, Inspector Janssen." He looked past Tom at Jimmy Haverson, lowering his hand from his face. "Honestly, Jimmy. We were just kids larking around. None of us meant for it to happen, any of it." Tom sat down on a chair, fixing his eye on Greg and gesturing for him to continue. Beaty sighed, looking to the ceiling and exhaling as he bit his lower lip. "We were out for the day – like we always were back then from dawn to dusk – and... we were messing around."

"Define *we* for me, if you wouldn't mind?" Tom asked.

"Me, Harry and Dave... and Ciaran obviously. We were

mucking around in the woods on the common as it got dark, having a couple of beers we'd swiped from your dad." Beaty shot a brief glance in Jimmy Haverson's direction. "We were winding each other up, it was getting dark and we were telling each other ghost stories – putting the frighteners on one another, you know? Just kids' stuff." He hung his head, running his hands through his hair. "Ciaran got scared... took it too seriously."

"Ciaran had Asperger's, Greg," Tom said. "He believed everything he was told, especially when told it by people he trusted."

Greg Beaty's jaw shook, his mouth contorting as he sought not to break down but failed. He exhaled as a deep sob left his mouth. "You d–don't understand... we were just having a laugh."

"My brother died because you lot were *having a laugh*?"

"This didn't just come to you, Greg," Tom said. "Whose idea was the noose?"

Beaty clamped his eyes shut. "I don't remember... all of us probably. It was all of us looking to wind him up." He met Tom's eyes with an expression imploring him to offer some forgiveness. "We were all to blame, all three of us." He returned his gaze to the floor in front of him. "We made up this story about a young boy who'd killed himself centuries ago on that very night, right there on the common. We told him how the boy's soul haunted those woods in an endless search for a body to possess to make him whole again... waiting for the right person, an innocent... a virgin who came there of their own free will..." his eyes flitted to Tom once again and away. "And... once you were there the only way you could avoid his attention was to strip all of your worldly possessions away and run as fast as you could to escape before he claimed you."

"What did you tell him would happen?"

Beaty shook his head. "A lifetime of eternal suffering... torture and misery."

"And Ciaran believed you, didn't he?" Tom said.

Beaty laughed, a dry sound without any genuine humour, and nodded. "Damn... if only he'd known we were all in the same boat, all virgins... each of us as pathetic as one another."

"What was with the noose?" Tom asked. "Because you had it planned well in advance, must have done."

Beaty sighed, pressing thumb and forefinger to his eyes. He sniffed hard, sitting up. "A sign of the spirit's awakening... but how were we supposed to know that... that Ciaran would react like that?" He looked at Tom with pleading eyes. "How? You tell me how?"

Tom raised his eyebrows but didn't comment. Beaty persisted.

"I mean, none of us could know he'd have reacted like that, could we?"

"But you knew he'd hanged himself, right?" Cassie asked.

Beaty looked sideways at her, nodding slowly. "We stayed in the woods, drinking our beer. We were supposed to meet him at the car park on the far side, bring him his clothes and his bike and all that, you know? We meant to give him fifteen minutes or so but, looking back, it must have been more like three quarters of an hour. I even had my camera and was going to take a snap or two, capture the look on his face when he realised it was all a wind up..." he smiled but it faded rapidly. "And then we came out of the woods... and saw him... hanging there." Beaty's expression took on a faraway look, staring blankly straight ahead. "We knew. All of us knew he was gone."

"And what, you just left?" Tom asked.

Beaty's head sank low and he confirmed with a brief nod. "Yes," he all but whispered.

"You left my brother there to die! You evil bastards!"

Beaty's head snapped up. "He was already gone, Jimmy. He was already gone, I swear."

"And you dumped his clothes and his bike as you ran off."

"We were kids, Inspector Janssen," Beaty said, staring at Tom, tears falling. "We were just kids. We panicked... ran... it's what kids do."

"Not the kids I know," Tom said softly. Beaty's head dropped again. "And you never thought to come clean on what happened that night? If only to give the family some closure."

"I'm so, so sorry," Beaty said, lifting his head and looking at Jimmy. "It just got harder and harder... and then what with your mum and everything."

"Don't you dare speak about my mum," Jimmy spat. "You may as well have killed her too. You destroyed my family... all of our lives!"

"I'm sorry."

"Sorry doesn't cut it, Greg!" Jimmy scowled at him, the blood was running from the cut to his face again, reaching as far as his jawline now. "Not at all. You and the others pushed him around, made him the butt of all your jokes... and all he ever wanted was to be accepted."

"I know, I know... and if I could go back, if any of us could go back, we'd have done it differently but it was done, you know? We couldn't change it, none of it. We were just kids."

The last words drifted away, Beaty sounding less convinced of the explanation with every utterance of it. Tom saw Tamara standing in the hallway but she silently indicated for him to ignore her and continue, obviously not wanting to break up the momentum. Tom turned to Jimmy Haverson.

"We had trouble tracking you down, Jimmy," he said.

"What was with taking your mother's maiden name after you came out of detention? A fresh start?"

"Something like that," Jimmy muttered.

"You had no relationship with your father to speak of, but you went to work for David Fysh."

Jimmy shrugged.

"And became close friends with him," Tom said. "I imagine that would have been nigh on impossible if you'd known about all of this." Again, Jimmy said nothing but he was watching Tom warily. "So, I reckon you came upon this information recently?" Tom looked between him and Beaty. "And something changed. What did Gavin Felgate say to you? Did he tip you off as to what he thought might have happened to your brother years ago?"

Jimmy Haverson held Tom's gaze for a moment longer before breaking off and staring at the floor.

"And who else did Felgate speak to who would have as much raw emotion and anger within them to join you in killing Harry Empson and trying to do similar to Greg?"

"You're the policeman, you can figure it out."

"And what about your friend, David Fysh, where is he?"

Jimmy looked directly into Tom's eye. "No comment." There was a gleam in his eye that Tom found unnerving.

Tamara Greave came into the room, immediately crossing to Cassie, noticing her clutching her arm but Cassie mouthed that she was all right brushing off the concern.

"Tom, could I have a word?" Tamara asked. They stepped out into the hall and Tamara made sure no one else could hear them. "I heard back from the local taxi firms. One of them had a pre-arranged booking to pick Harry Empson up from the airport and drive him back to Heacham."

"Great, did the driver see anything?"

"I've not spoken to him but the company confirmed the driver's name... it was Ian Haverson."

Tom ran a hand across his mouth. "He told us he works nights."

"As a taxi driver, yes. I had them check and he was on shift the night of Gavin Felgate's murder too."

"So, he didn't drop him off in Hunstanton as he claimed. More likely he—"

"Ended up on Roydon Common with Felgate... and wound up killing him there."

Tom frowned, piecing it together in his mind. "Then Felgate must have tipped Haverson off about what he thought happened to Ciaran."

"But we still don't know how Felgate found out."

"That was me."

They both turned to see Greg Beaty standing in the doorway, his arrival unnoticed. Tom was a little annoyed no one had seen fit to stop him edging out of the room.

"I'm sorry, I was going to the bathroom," he said, a sheepish-looking Eric standing behind him. Tom waved away both the apology and Eric's awkwardness.

"Go on," Tom said.

"I have a drink problem," Beaty said, glancing around, "which will come as no surprise to anyone I'm quite sure, and I'm trying to get on top of it... although not successfully at the moment, to be honest. I was attending AA for a while... because... well, I'm an alcoholic. The local group were very supportive and although my sponsor didn't live nearby... two of my outreach people do."

"Outreach people?" Tom asked.

He nodded. "People you agree to call every day to provide that support bubble to stop... to stop you falling back into your old habits, you know?"

"Gavin Felgate?" Tamara asked.

Beaty nodded. "Yeah... but I had no idea what he did for a living and in these groups you open up, share what's going on in your life, thoughts and feelings."

"You talked about Ciaran?"

"Not directly, no, but Gavin was... intuitive, chatty. I recall one day I was talking about atonement; about how my use of alcohol numbed me from the world, from my sins. Gavin had his own problems and we kind of helped each other. That's how it works." Beaty looked up at the ceiling, drawing a deep breath. "I had the feeling he was asking too many questions, more than was normal, and I got spooked, dropped out of the programme but..."

"The journalist in him just kept on digging," Tom said.

"Yeah, I guess he did. It's a small town and... maybe he put it together somehow." Beaty supported himself, putting his back against the wall, rubbing at his cheeks with both hands. "What have I done?"

Tamara indicated for Eric to escort Beaty away and turned to Tom once they were alone again.

"So, where is Ian Haverson?"

Tom glanced towards the front room as if he could see Jimmy Haverson through the wall. "Somehow I don't think his son is going to tell us."

"And David Fysh? Do you think he's already dead?"

"Haverson must know we put it together, especially now we have Jimmy," Tom said, thinking hard. "But the fact we haven't found David yet..."

"What is it?"

"I'm just thinking," Tom said, chewing his lower lip. "From what went on here, I'm wondering whether they intended to kill Greg here? Maybe they were looking to take him somewhere else and that's why we haven't found David?"

"But they killed Empson in his home."

"Didn't Eric say Empson put up a fight? Maybe it didn't go down as they expected it to and had to adapt."

"In that case David Fysh might still be alive," Tamara said. Tom nodded. "But where?"

Tom looked her in the eye, inclining his head to one side. "Maybe back where all this started."

CHAPTER THIRTY-FOUR

TOM JANSSEN EMERGED from the woods, opening the gate at the end of the path and stepping out onto the open ground of Roydon Common. The wind had eased now, the clouds parting to bathe the undulating ground in silver light from an almost full moon. From this distance, approximately a hundred yards, he could make out two figures: one stationary, the other circling. Taking a deep breath, he walked towards them. He'd been here before, two Yew trees standing side by side with open grassland in every direction away from them. There was no chance of sneaking up unobserved, perhaps under the cover of total darkness but even then, not with more than a couple of people.

But they had no time to conceive of a better solution. There was no advantage to waiting for a trained negotiator. It was now or never.

As it was, Tom made it to within fifty feet before he was spotted, the darkness of the trees behind him masking his approach. It was David Fysh who saw him first, his startled eyes turning Ian Haverson to face him.

"Stay there!"

Tom did as he was told, stopping where he was and raising both hands in front of him to show he was unarmed and convey a lack of threat. Ian Haverson's eyes flitted around in search of others, disbelieving that someone would venture out against him alone.

"It's just me, Ian. I'm here to talk."

Haverson continued scanning the ground around them, seeing movement in every ripple of the long grass or twitch of a tree in the distance. The nearby car park was empty, aside from the white saloon that he used as his taxi. Tamara and the rest of the team were spread out in the nearby woods, waiting to rush Haverson if they felt the need, although they would still have too much ground to cover to be effective at stopping David Fysh from dying.

Fysh was precariously perched on a stepladder, set upon the uneven ground, a noose around his neck tied to the very same branch as Ciaran was found hanging from. Tom edged closer, figuring he would do so until he was again ordered to stop. Haverson was spinning around, scanning the area in a heightened state of hyper-vigilance. Tom could see David Fysh had his hands tied behind his back making it even harder for him to maintain his balance as the ladder wobbled beneath him, trying to shift his weight to keep it steady. Coming within twenty feet, Haverson finally appeared to notice.

"I *said* stay back!"

He brandished a kitchen knife, waving at Tom, his eyes wild and frantic.

"I won't come any closer, Ian, I promise."

Tom ensured he kept his tone calm and neutral. There was no way he could know how Haverson was going to react to his presence. Gaffer tape covered Fysh's mouth, sweat beaded his brow and even in this light, Tom could see he was terrified. He looked gaunt, although there was extensive swelling around his nose and eyes, undoubtedly the result of a beating, perhaps several. He'd been effectively missing for days now, so where he'd been held and in what conditions, Tom could only guess at. At this point, Tom decided to ignore Fysh. To speak directly to him would likely enrage Haverson and he had to be placated.

"This won't bring Ciaran back, Ian."

"I know!" Haverson hissed in Tom's direction. "That's not what this is about."

"Then what is it about?"

"Justice," he snarled.

Tom pursed his lips. Haverson glared at him.

"This," Tom said, slowly extending his left hand to indicate Fysh, "is not justice. This is revenge, pure and simple."

"Yeah, well so be it."

"Do you mean that, really?" Tom shook his head. "You have another son. What about him? What about Jimmy?"

Haverson's expression momentarily softened, but then the hard steely gaze returned. "He'll understand."

"You think so? He lost the brother he cared about, then his mother and finally the two of you reconcile only for you to destroy everything once again. Is that fair on him? Is that justice?"

Haverson spun on Tom, taking a couple of steps past Fysh and closer to him, still brandishing the knife threateningly with an extended hand.

"They took everything from us! Everything. Why shouldn't we take it back?"

Tom splayed his hands wide. "Because it was an accident, Ian. They were kids fooling around."

"And they deserve what's coming to them."

"What about Gavin Felgate? Did he deserve it too?"

Haverson hesitated, blinking repeatedly. Was he high,

drunk? Tom couldn't tell but there was an internal struggle going on in the man's head, of that he was certain.

"He didn't kill your son, so why did he have to die?"

Haverson took another step, speaking through gritted teeth, snarling. "He wanted to profit from Ciaran's death, to prey on my misery... to make money out of my boy's life, my suffering." Haverson spat in Tom's direction. "He was scum."

"What happened that night, Ian, the night of Gavin's death? What were you doing here?"

"He brought me here... like a lamb to the slaughter. I was doing my job, routine pick-up and he had me drive him out here, told me he could answer my questions... fill in the blanks..."

"And what? He had it set up?"

"Damn right, made me relive it, experience it as if I was here when my boy died... and for what?" He jabbed towards Tom with the blade in his hand. "*For money*... for the story. He thought seeing my reaction firsthand would give him an edge or something. The man was delusional."

"And?"

"And he got the story – he became the story."

Tom shook his head. "But you didn't mean it, did you? You're not a killer."

Haverson visibly shrank before him, his shoulders dropping. "No, of course not. I didn't want any of this... but when he said, when he told me what they'd done to my boy... I–I just lost it... but I *only hit him once*, I swear it was just once and he fell a–and he didn't get up."

Haverson's eyes glazed over. Tom thought he was about to break down but he rallied, steeling himself and blinking away the tears. "It was so easy. He was gone... like I'd switched off a light... just like that." He met Tom's eye. "And then I realised – they all had to pay."

"Not like this, Ian. This isn't the way."

"Then what is the way, Inspector Janssen?"

Haverson stared at Tom. *Did he expect an answer?* Tom wasn't sure. Even if he did, what could he say to the man?

"Your lot investigated it and found nothing, did nothing," Haverson said. "So, what now? How am I supposed to get justice for Ciaran? I wasn't there for him in life but I'm sure as hell going to be there for him in death."

"What does that mean?"

Haverson tilted his head to one side, raising both eyebrows in a knowing look. "It means this." He spun on his heel and marched towards David Fysh. Tom broke into a run but he was too late, Haverson raised a foot and kicked the side of the stepladder with all his might. It toppled and David Fysh's muted scream followed as the support went from beneath him and he swung from the tree, the branch groaning under the man's weight.

"No!" Tom shouted but Haverson turned on him, knife aloft forcing Tom to halt his advance as the two men squared up to one another.

"Too late, Inspector," Haverson said. "It's too late for all of us."

The waiting officers broke cover and ran from the trees, torches lighting up as they hastened across the rough ground. Haverson shot a glance in their direction and back at Tom, still standing between him and the flailing David Fysh, his legs, taped together at the ankles, swinging from side to side like a violently rocking pendulum. Fysh's eyes were wide, protruding and bloodshot, his face turning scarlet with every passing second. Haverson's expression changed from almost manic to calm and serene. Tom's eyes narrowed; he couldn't interpret it. Haverson stiffened himself upright and smiled.

"Too late for all of us," he repeated in a barely audible

whisper and ran the blade across his own throat. Tom stared, unable to believe his eyes as blood fountained from Haverson's neck. The knife tumbled from his grasp and he reached up clutching at the self-inflicted wound with both hands, eyes wide and fearful, before sinking to his knees. Tom rushed past him to the hanging form of David Fysh whose thrashing movements were lessening. Tom wrapped his arms around his dangling legs and used all his strength to take the bodyweight, releasing the strain on Fysh's neck. Fysh repeatedly kicked out in an involuntary motion, instinct taking over in his struggle for life.

Time passed slowly; seconds felt like minutes before support arrived but then police officers were all around them. Tamara and two uniformed constables ran to attend to Ian Haverson and, despite his crude attempt to take his own life, he didn't try to push them away, his own survival instinct no doubt asserting itself. Although Tom didn't rate his chances of survival, judging by the length and depth of the knife wound. Moments later, the stepladder was righted and the rope severed from the branch it was tied to, David Fysh was then lowered to the ground. He'd passed out but at least he was still breathing.

Tom sank onto his knees, looking to the heavens and feeling a sense of relief. Tamara Greave came over and placed a hand on his shoulder. He looked up at her.

"You couldn't have done much more than you did, Tom."

He looked at the team dispensing first aid to both men, an ambulance appearing in the distant car park, lights flashing. Would they be here fast enough? It was over and despite probably saving one man's life, Tom still felt he'd failed.

CHAPTER THIRTY-FIVE

"MUM, can I have some of that cake?"

Tom and Alice broke off their conversation, looking to where Saffy stood on the far side of the kitchen island, a mass of curls, her forehead and piercing blue eyes all that were visible as she eyed a chocolate cake on a cake stand in front of her.

"Not before dinner, darling, no. But you can have it for pudding, okay?"

Saffy let out an exaggerated harrumph but accepted the decision and sauntered over to the breakfast table where the snack buffet was set out. Checking first that neither her mother, Tom, or anyone else for that matter, was paying attention she craftily took a handful of crisps and several biscuits before she scurried away to find a quiet corner to eat them. Tom and Alice noticed but pretended not to, even when Russell, Saffy's pet terrier, followed on with nose in the air and tail erect, Saffy dropping crisps for him to pick up as they went – the duo were forming quite an adolescent criminal pairing these days. Tamara appeared at Alice's side.

"I'm sorry, but could I borrow Tom for a moment," she said. "It's about work but I promise it'll be the last time tonight."

Alice smiled. "I doubt that very much." She wasn't offended. "That'll be like expecting David Attenborough not to talk about nature. I'll see if your mum needs any help."

She touched Tom's forearm affectionately and stepped away to where Francesca Greave was beavering away bringing the main meal together. With the culmination of recent events, Tamara decided the team could do with a relaxing evening together to lighten the mood if not to silence her mother's almost continual demand for them to share Christmas. That was never likely to happen but this was a decent compromise and, if the truth be told, a very good one.

"Thanks for doing this," Tom said, raising his orange juice to Tamara's glass of white wine. She angled her head to one side, noting the re-emergence of Saffy from the adjoining room.

"How could I disappoint the little one?"

Tom smiled. It was true, Saffy had been the most vociferous in her support for Francesca's holiday plans, having not let up since it was first raised.

"I called in at the hospital this afternoon," Tom said, "and it looks like David Fysh will make a full recovery, physically at any rate."

"Good, he'll need all his strength for what he has coming his way," Tamara said. Tom offered her a quizzical look. "I spoke with the CPS today and they've confirmed Fysh will be facing a raft of charges in relation to his business dealings. In their mind there's more than enough evidence to secure a fraud conviction in relation to the dodgy meat he's been supplying through his various businesses. Do you remember a few years back with that scandal surrounding horse meat in ready meals and such?"

"Yes, nasty."

"Well, if they follow that precedent then Fysh will be looking at significant custodial time I should imagine, plus he'll lose his public sector contracts."

"But he'll still be alive, so you have to weigh things up."

Tamara smiled. "Yes, there is that."

"Jimmy Haverson hasn't said a word since we told him his father is dead."

"He'll have to face up to what the two of them have done by himself."

Tom nodded. "I feel for him," Tamara looked at him, surprised, "from a certain point of view. He came out of detention and turned his life around, took a tough job and made something of himself. David Fysh probably took him on out of some personal attempt at redemption for what he did as a teenager, but Jimmy put in the graft."

"Until his estranged father told him what had happened to Ciaran..."

"Yes, exactly. Then the pent-up emotion, the frustration of losing his brother, his mother and the disintegration of his whole childhood, coupled with coercion from his father led him to join in with this vigilante justice."

Tamara shook her head. "He knew right from wrong. He knew what he was getting in to and that's where my sympathy evaporates."

"True. I can empathise but don't condone it. It's just so tragic, such a waste of life. Are the CPS going to look at Ciaran Haverson's suicide again?"

She shrugged to indicate uncertainty. "In light of what we found out this week, I should imagine someone will but I don't see any charges that might be levelled at Fysh or Beaty. It was a horrible prank that went tragically wrong. From what Greg Beaty told us it was what inspired Harry Empson to dedicate his working life to helping those less fortunate. Speaking of which, do we know what brought Empson back the night he died yet?"

Tom frowned. "Not conclusively, no. The day we presume David Fysh was abducted by Ian Haverson, perhaps aided by Jimmy, a phone call was made from Fysh's mobile to a number abroad which I anticipate will come back to be one associated with Harry Empson. My guess, and with Jimmy not cooperating it remains a guess, is that they posed as Fysh and lured Empson back on some grounds relating to Ciaran's death, hence the urgency of the trip and the lies to his employers about his mother's illness."

"That would explain how Haverson knew Empson would be flying in and when." Tamara exhaled deeply. "Even if Ciaran's death isn't reexamined, Fysh and Beaty will have to carry on living with what they did... and it will be even harder now everyone will know. It's tragic that the one man who really tried to make amends by living a selfless life, Harry Empson, is the one who paid the ultimate price. Not that I think the others deserved to trade places with him."

"*A selfless life*? To salve his conscience more like."

"That's a cynical view, Thomas."

"And the optimistic counterpoint is what?"

She smiled. "He wanted to make a better world?"

Tom sighed, lifting his glass and tilting it in her direction. "I prefer yours over mine."

The doorbell sounded. Tamara looked over her shoulder but her mother was already heading to answer it. Passing by the two of them, Francesca tutted at her daughter.

"Don't worry, Tammy, I'll go. The two of you are as thick as thieves as usual. This is supposed to be a night off, you know."

Tamara rolled her eyes, but only once her mother had passed by and wouldn't see.

"Thanks, Mum."

There was a gleam in Tamara's eye and Tom noticed, narrowing his eyes as he looked at her. "What are you up to?" he asked.

"You'll see."

Tamara casually took a couple of steps back so she could see down the hall to the front door, and Tom followed. They both looked on as Francesca pulled the door wide and a man stood waiting, a bouquet of flowers in one hand, a suitcase resting at his feet. He took his cap off with his free hand and smiled, somewhat nervously in Tom's opinion. He looked at Tamara whose smile lit up her face.

"Well," she said quietly, "she can complain about him all she likes but I know she's missing him just as much as he is her."

"Devious," Tom said under his breath.

"Thoughtful."

"Manipulative."

She elbowed him in the ribs. "Caring."

They both hurriedly looked away as Francesca turned to see them watching on. "Well, I suppose seeing as you're here you'd better come in." They both heard Francesca say, stepping to one side so her husband, Tamara's father, could enter.

"Best make a move," Tamara whispered.

"Agreed."

The two of them hurried away from their spot, Tamara going to help Alice while Tom joined Eric and Becca sitting on the sofas next to the hearth with the dancing flames in the wood burner.

"Everyone!" Tamara called as her parents entered the room. "I'd like you to meet my father." Everyone said their hellos and Francesca looked around.

"Who are we waiting on?"

"No one, we're here," Cassie said entering behind

Francesca, a bottle of wine in one hand and her partner, Lauren, at her side. "Sorry we're late. The door was open, so we thought we'd—"

"Honestly, Charles," Francesca said to her husband. "You could have closed the door; you've let all the heat out. It's no wonder you can't cope without me."

"Sorry, love."

"Never mind." There was the faintest hint of a smile threatening to crack Francesca's hard-faced exterior, a clear sign that Tamara had made the right call. Saffy bounded over and clambered onto Tom's lap. He couldn't help but think she wouldn't be able to do that for much longer without crippling him in the process, but he didn't mind because it wouldn't be long before she would no longer want to. He didn't relish that day. If he could keep her at this age forever, then he probably would. Drinks were passed around and Francesca led the toast. Her stance had already softened and she was looking the most relaxed Tom had seen her since she'd arrived. Family and friends could have that effect on people. You never quite know what you are missing until you spend some time apart. They raised their glasses to friends at Christmas... in November.

FREE BOOK GIVEAWAY

Visit the author's website at **www.jmdalgliesh.com** and sign up to the VIP Club and be the first to receive news and previews of forthcoming works.

Here you can download a FREE eBook novella exclusive to club members;

Life & Death - A Hidden Norfolk novella

Never miss a new release.

No spam, ever, guaranteed. You can unsubscribe at any time.

Enjoy this book? You could make a real difference.

Because reviews are critical to the success of an author's career, if you have enjoyed this novel, please do me a massive favour by entering one onto Amazon.

Type the following link into your internet search bar to go to the Amazon page and leave a review;

http://mybook.to/a-dark-sin

If you prefer not to follow the link please visit the sales page where you purchased the title in order to leave a review.

Reviews increase visibility. Your help in leaving one would make a massive difference to this author and I would be very grateful.

TO DIE FOR - PREVIEW
HIDDEN NORFOLK - BOOK 9

THE DOOR CLOSED and the latch clicked as it dropped into place. He looked across the room to the figure standing resolutely at the door, one hand resting on the frame, head bowed. The footsteps on the decking faded as the last guests walked to their cars. The ticking of the clock mounted above the fireplace was the only sound, the same staccato monotonous tone resonating as the hand moved round the face. He watched the movement, sitting bolt upright on the sofa hands on his knees, for almost a full revolution until it hit twelve and the minute hand passed effortlessly to midday.

His brother sighed, drawing his eyes to him as he came to the centre of the room, breaking his concentration. He didn't speak in reply to the gesture which was undoubtedly his brother's intention when making the noise, but he merely followed the younger man with his eyes as he first loosened his tie, unbuttoning his shirt at the collar, and then sank into the armchair to his right shaking his head slowly. His brother looked at the clock.

"It's been a long day."

He nodded briefly but still said nothing.

"And it's only lunchtime."

His brother stared hard at him, his eyes narrowing, their gaze fixed on one another.

"Do you... think we should have done more?"

It was a curious question. Open ended. He shrugged, unsure of what he was expected to say. This was one of the things that regularly irritated him about his sibling, this innate need to analyse every detail, to explore the possibilities of what has happened, could happen or would happen in any given scenario. What did it matter? What was done was done and couldn't be revisited. His brother misinterpreted the movement.

"About holding a wake, I mean?" he said, running the palm of his hand slowly back and forth across his chin. "It's one thing to have a handful of people back here but..."

He cocked his head to one side.

"But what?"

"We could have done more, couldn't we?"

The suggestion irritated him but he didn't know why. His brow furrowed. The expression appeared to please his brother for some reason because a half smile crept onto his face.

"So, you are still in there then."

The irritation grew.

"I wasn't aware that I'd ever left."

His brother sighed again, lowering his head into his hands. He ruffled his hair before sitting up.

"I think it's time we talked, don't you?"

"About what?"

"Well..." he looked around. "This place for starters."

He followed his brother's eye around the room. Everywhere he looked reminded him of their mother. The pictures on the walls were all her choices. She was obsessed with the southern Mediterranean, the mountains of Spain, the vineyards of Bordeaux and the rolling hills of Tuscany, all reflected in her choice of painting or framed photography. They were all prints of course. She'd never been to any of them. In fact, he couldn't remember her ever having left Norfolk let alone ventured abroad. So, what was it? The exotic implication of faraway lands? He didn't know. There was every chance his mother didn't know where any of these places were. It didn't matter. Not to him anyway.

"So, what do you think?"

The tone in his brother's voice suggested this was a repeated question. He met his eye.

"About?"

"Keep or sell? The land is probably worth more if we parcel it up and the house," he looked around again, almost like he could imagine an estate agent appraising the value, "would fetch a tidy sum if we fixed her up a bit."

"It's not for sale."

"Excuse me?"

He licked his lower lip. It felt as dry as his mouth.

"I said it's not for sale. I'm not selling."

"But that's what we need to talk about—"

"No." He shook his head, rising from the sofa and crossing to the sideboard and opening the top drawer. Picking up an envelope, he returned to stand in front of his younger brother and handed it over. His brother took it from him and lifted the flap. He returned to his place on the sofa and sat back down, once again resting his palms on his knees. Looking back at the clock, he watched the second hand begin another pass of the clock face as his brother flipped through the pages nearby.

"B-But… this has to be wrong—"

"It's not wrong," he said, eyes fixed on the clock. "Read it for yourself—"

"I have read it." There was tension in his voice, more than

merely displeasure. Shock, maybe? "I can bloody read! I just can't believe she... why would she do this to me?"

He turned away from the clock to observe his brother who was staring at the pages in his hand, lips parted, eyes wide.

"Like I said. It's not for sale. None of it."

"But she can't do this!"

"And yet she has."

His brother lurched to his feet, scrunching the paper in his grasp and brandishing it before him as he came to stand over him, glaring down at him.

"This wasn't what she said she'd do."

He shook his head. "It doesn't matter what she said. It is what it is."

"And you're happy with this are you?"

It was disbelief. That was what he'd heard in his tone before, disbelief at the decisions their mother had made towards the end of her life. He thought his younger brother a little odd at that moment, but that wasn't for the first time either. They'd always been different as far back as he could remember. Their approach to life, friendships – parents – were vastly at odds with one another and noticeably so to the point that if they didn't look so alike one might conclude they were of different parentage.

He shrugged. "Like I said. It is what it is."

"You did this!" His brother shook the paper in front of him and then, having not elicited the expected response, threw the papers in his face. The disbelief was gone now, replaced first by indignation and now by fury. "I'll not take it lying down."

He angled his head to one side, pursed his lips and looked up at his brother. The skin of his face was blotchy, turning that pinky-red colour it does when frustration gets the better of you resulting in a flash of anger that must be kept in check no matter what. The alternative was to lose control. That was something else his brother was good at, losing control. He was one of the most undisciplined people he'd ever known. Most people would feel vulnerable at this point faced with such a combustible individual as this, but he remained calm, unfazed by the explosion of anger and bitter resentment threatening to spill over in front of him. His brother was many things, many of them bad, but violence had never been a thing up to this point in his life at any rate.

"There are things I can do… people I can go to… solicitors and stuff."

He shrugged. "Do what you feel you have to—"

"I'm entitled to what's mine, damn you."

"That's not what mum thought."

"You did this to me, didn't you? Staying here, working on her day after day? You did this."

He shook his head. "We didn't talk about it, not until near the end. It is what she wanted, not me."

His brother was furious, his hands by his side, fists balled and hands shaking.

"So, what are you going to do? How will you manage?"

"I will… somehow."

His anger seemed to dissipate then and he threw back his head and laughed. A dismissive sound, hollow and artificial.

"*You'll manage!* Have you seen all these?" he said, marching over to the kitchen table and returning with a stack of envelopes, many unopened and stamped on the exterior with red ink, and hurling them at him. The envelopes bounced off him harmlessly and he ignored the confrontational gesture, turning his gaze back to the clock. "If mum and dad, with your help, couldn't make this place work how the hell are you going to go it alone?"

"I'll manage," he said slowly, a smile crossing his face.

He didn't watch his brother leave nor did he hear the

cursing of his parents' names or the door slamming shut. The sound of footsteps on the decking receded and he looked around the family home, picturing the memories in his mind's eye, children, fun and family occasions. His eye drifted to an old grainy photograph taken on the beach barely a quarter of a mile from where he was sitting, the two boys in dungarees, smiling, each holding a mother's hand as they paddled in the gentle surf. They couldn't have been more than five or six years old that day. Days like those would return.

He would find a way. What else did he have to do?

To Die For
Hidden Norfolk - Book 9

BOOKS BY J M DALGLIESH

Audiobooks

In the Hidden Norfolk Series

One Lost Soul
Bury Your Past
Kill Our Sins
Tell No Tales
Hear No Evil

In the Dark Yorkshire Series

Divided House
Blacklight
The Dogs in the Street
Blood Money
Fear the Past
The Sixth Precept

Audiobook Box Sets

Dark Yorkshire Books 1-3
Dark Yorkshire Books 4-6

9 781800 809987